PENGUIN CLASSICS

QUICKSAND

NELLA LARSEN, one of the most acclaimed and influential writers of the Harlem Renaissance, was born Nellie Walker on April 13, 1891, in Chicago. In the 1910s she moved to New York, where she trained and worked as a nurse, and in 1919 she married a research physicist. She began publishing stories in the mid-1920s and published her first novel, *Quicksand*, in 1928. Her next novel, *Passing*, came out the following year. Larsen was awarded a William E. Harmon Bronze Award for Distinguished Achievement Among Negroes and a Guggenheim fellowship. Encountering personal and professional struggles, she was unable to have her third novel accepted for publication, and by the end of the 1930s had stopped writing altogether. She worked full time as a nurse until her death in 1964.

THADIOUS M. DAVIS is G. C. Vanderbilt Professor of English at Vanderbilt University and the author of *Nella Larsen: Novelist of the Harlem Renaissance*. She previously taught at Brown University and the University of North Carolina, Chapel Hill. She has been a fellow at the Huntington Library, San Marino, California, and the Center for Scholars and Writers, the New York Public Library. She is the editor of the Penguin Classics edition of Nella Larsen's *Passing*.

NELLA LARSEN

Quicksand

Edited with an Introduction and Notes by
THADIOUS M. DAVIS

PENGUIN BOOKS

PENGUIN BOOKS
Published by the Penguin Group
Penguin Group (USA) Inc., 375 Hudson Street, New York, New York 10014, U.S.A.
Penguin Group (Canada), 90 Eglinton Avenue East, Suite 700, Toronto, Ontario,
Canada M4P 2Y3 (a division of Pearson Penguin Canada Inc.)
Penguin Books Ltd, 80 Strand, London WC2R 0RL, England
Penguin Ireland, 25 St Stephen's Green, Dublin 2, Ireland (a division of Penguin Books Ltd)
Penguin Group (Australia), 250 Camberwell Road, Camberwell, Victoria 3124,
Australia (a division of Pearson Australia Group Pty Ltd)
Penguin Books India Pvt Ltd, 11 Community Centre, Panchsheel Park,
New Delhi – 110 017, India
Penguin Group (NZ), 67 Apollo Drive, Rosedale, North Shore 0745,
Auckland, New Zealand (a division of Pearson New Zealand Ltd)
Penguin Books (South Africa) (Pty) Ltd, 24 Sturdee Avenue, Rosebank,
Johannesburg 2196, South Africa

Penguin Books Ltd, Registered Offices: 80 Strand, London WC2R 0RL, England

First published in the United States of America by Alfred A. Knopf, Inc. 1928
Published in Penguin Books 1987
This edition with an introduction and notes by Thadious M. Davis published in
Penguin Books 2002

15   17   19   20   18   16

Introduction and notes copyright © Thadious M. Davis, 2002
All rights reserved

LIBRARY OF CONGRESS CATALOGING IN PUBLICATION DATA
Larsen, Nella.
Quicksand / Nella Larsen; edited with an introduction and notes by Thadious M. Davis.
p. cm.—(Penguin twentieth-century classics)
Includes bibliographical references.
ISBN 978-0-14-118127-1 (pbk. : alk. paper)
1. Harlem (New York, N.Y.)—Fiction.   2. African American women—Fiction.
3. Racially mixed people—Fiction.   4. Danish American women—Fiction.
5. Copenhagen (Denmark)—Fiction.   6. Young women—Fiction.   I. Davis,
Thadious M., 1944–   II. Title.   III. Series.
PS3523.A7225 Q55 2002
813'.52—dc21   2001054863

Printed in the United States of America
Set in Stemple Garamond

CONTENTS

INTRODUCTION

During the first half of the twentieth century, African Americans were traveling and residing far beyond the borders of the United States, and African-American culture increasingly took on an international dimension. In the 1920s, performers routinely made their way to Europe and England: Florence Mills, Valaida Snow, and Paul Robeson all had lengthy engagements overseas. A number of those associated with the Harlem Renaissance went abroad to work, study, or just travel. Langston Hughes and Claude McKay were in France and Africa during the early 1920s, when Bricktop (Ada Smith) managed her Paris nightclubs, and Josephine Baker went from New York chorus girl to headlining star in Paris. In 1924, after her first novel appeared, Jessie Fauset went to France and North Africa to study and relax; Jean Toomer spent the summer of that year at the Institute for the Harmonious Development of Man, near Fountainebleau, studying with the Russian mystic Gurdjieff. Walter White brought his entire family to France during 1927–1928 while there on a Guggenheim Foundation Creative Writing Fellowship, followed in 1929 by Countee Cullen, who also went to France on a Guggenheim. The internationalization of African Americans, particularly in the aftermath of World War I, coincided with Nella Larsen's rise to prominence as a novelist during the Harlem Renaissance.

A part Scandinavian, part West Indian citizen of the United States with traces of German and African ancestry, Larsen embodied the American "melting pot." But that term, frequently used in connection with European immigrants at the end of the nineteenth century, was rarely applied to people of color during that period, because unless a person's "race" was configured as "white," assimilation was not an option. On April 13, 1891, Larsen was born "Nellie Walker," the daughter of a Danish immigrant mother and a father whose nationality or place of birth was not listed, but whose racial designation appeared on the birth certificate as "Colored." The infant Nellie Walker was also designated "Colored," and her mixed-race status and non-white appearance would complicate her relationship not only to the diverse but primarily white immigrant communities on Chicago's State Street where she spent much of her childhood, but also to her own family, who would become increasingly a part of the city's economically mobile population.

As a native of Chicago in the era of the Columbian New World Exhibition (1893) and its fabled White City, Nella Larsen grew up in an urban environment where ethnic identity, like its racial counterpart, was not necessarily a badge of honor. "Greenhorns" and newly arrived immigrants tried as quickly as possible to adopt "the American way," because telltale signs of their difference could delay, and quite possibly deny, their attaining the American dream. As part of an upwardly mobile, working-class immigrant family self-identified as white, Larsen knew firsthand the complexity of race within immigrant groups accustomed to identifying themselves by nationality and language rather than by skin color. She often pointed to her father's origins in the Danish Virgin Islands and her mother's in Denmark as markers of her cultural internationality rather than of racial nationalism. Given both her ethnic and racial heritage and her formative years in turn-of-the-century Chicago, it is not surprising that in her fiction she employed multiple frames of reference.

Double-visioned, and at least triple-voiced, Nella Larsen was one of several major novelists to emerge during the Harlem Renaissance and the heyday of the "New Negro" in New York during the 1920s. Like Jean Toomer, Larsen explored the impact of race and gender markers on identity; she explored the instability of race within a mobile, transient, and transforming society by showing mixed-race individuals who consciously accepted the fluidity of race. Like both Rudolph Fisher and Walter White, Larsen was fascinated by the spatial and cultural differences between life in the rural American South and in the urban North for modern African Americans. Like Claude McKay, the Jamaican-born radical writer who encoded an islander's political voice and migration ideology into his poetry and fiction, Larsen understood the politics of global movement and dispersal of black people and often claimed the Virgin Islands as her actual birthplace. Like Jessie Fauset, to whom she is frequently compared, Larsen placed the travels of a new woman free from conventional restrictions at the center of her fiction, and after receiving a Guggenheim Fellowship in 1930, she herself traveled extensively and often alone in Spain and France.

Larsen's transnational concerns and international themes represent areas of the cultural movement often unnoticed in the literary production but remarked in political discourses largely due to the consciousness-raising presence of two race leaders, Marcus Garvey and W. E. B. Du Bois. Both addressed the worldwide problem of racism and its negative impact on the lives of black people represented, even in Africa. Although different in ideology, their public discourses on race, along with the international meetings of the Pan-African Congress in 1919 and 1921, gave a wider geographic face to issues related to African Americans by foregrounding Africa and the dispersal of black people throughout the African diaspora. Larsen turned to writing fiction in a cosmopolitan New York, with Harlem as a racialized culture capital, at a time when Africa, the Caribbean, and the South provided a triangulated locus within the diasporic heritage of black people. Europe, nevertheless, was not absent from the expansive landscape blacks utilized to address their concerns, but often functioned as a space associated with relative freedom from the overt racism that had characterized the experience of black World War I soldiers overseas. France, and Paris especially, represented the European place most socially receptive to African Americans.

A major part of Nella Larsen's transnational identity, however, was invested not in France but in her Danish heritage. Her first novel, *Quicksand* (1928), explores the possibilities inherent in her identification with dual racial and ethnic heritages. Both her American and her European background inform her depiction of Helga Crane, a restless modern protagonist who is determined to escape the traps of marriage and motherhood, which she links to the proscriptions of race as much as of gender in the United States and to the repressions of proper middle-class black life. Helga embodies the tensions stratifying the places, psychological and material, occupied by African-descended people. The dispersal of people of color throughout the western hemisphere and their treatment because of their color difference became one of Larsen's dominant themes: she approached racism through a lens not simply of nationalism but also of sexism and gender oppression.

Helga is represented in terms of her difference. Echoing Larsen's own background, Helga's mother was white and Danish, and her father black but his ethnicity unspecified. Racially Helga is mixed, but she is identified as black, as she declares, "I'm a Negro too." Ethnically Danish and Northern-born but dark-skinned and Southern-educated, Helga is a modern amalgamation of new-world subjectivities for people of color. She has suffered multiple dislocations because her biological father abandoned the family, her white stepfather and her stepbrothers and stepsisters treated her badly, and her emotionally distant mother did not come to her defense. Her conflicting emotions about her identity are linked to her conception of the United States as racially diverse yet racially restrictive, and of Scandinavia, though largely white, as somehow accommodating racial difference. Denmark, according to Helga's thinking, is "an older, more polished civilization," yet she knows also that "the continuously gorgeous panorama of Harlem fascinated her, thrilled her." In New York, however, she is warned: "I wouldn't mention that my people are white. . . . Colored people won't understand it. . . . What others don't know can't hurt you." In Copenhagen, her Danish aunt tells her: "You're young and a foreigner and—and different." Equally out of place in the United States and in Denmark, as it turns out, she comprehends her difference as a cultural hybridity for which there is no name beyond the race-inflected term "mulatto," and no solution beyond a partial self-negation required by the fixity of identity: black or white, American or Danish.

Harlem and Copenhagen come to symbolize the yin and yang, the push and pull, the attraction and repulsion of Helga's racial and cultural existence. She contrasts "the miraculous joyousness" and "heedless abandon" of Harlem's "gorgeous care-free revel" with the "pretentious stately life" and "heavy solemnity of a church service" that is Copenhagen. Despite the joy that appeases her loneliness in Harlem, Helga understands all too well the costs blacks have paid to escape the reality of racism: "In spite of its glamour, existence in America, even in Harlem, was for Negroes too cramped, too uncertain, too cruel; something not to be endured for a lifetime if one could escape; something demanding a courage greater than was in her. No. She couldn't stay. Nor, she saw now, could she remain away. Leaving, she would have to come back." Realizing the dichotomy will always pervade her life, Helga faces a future split into two parts—"into two parts in two lands, into physical freedom in Europe and spiritual freedom in America"—each one equally unsatisfactory without the other.

Most noticeable in Larsen's portrayal of the contrasting cultures is her technical facility in embedding the story or narrative in a tableau vivant scene. The tableau as a representational device was one of the hallmarks of Copenhagen's Dansk Folkenmuseum, to which Larsen refers in her novel when she has Helga pose for her portrait in an artist's studio located across from the museum. Founded in 1885, the folk museum depicted the traditional culture of Danish people in dioramas featuring life-sized figures in authentic folk dress. A precursor to modern living-history and open-air museums, the Dansk Folkenmuseum preserved the clothing, manners, occupations, customs, and daily activities of the nation, especially in rural areas. Not just innovative, these dioramas or tableaux were instantly popular with museumgoers. Modern in their acceptance of and dependence on the interactive spectator, tableaux anticipated photoplays and silent film by establishing a visual narrative in a succession of frames.

Larsen is aware of the power of spectatorship particularly within the Copenhagen context of her novel. When Helga attends a performance at the Circus, a Danish entertainment palace with a variety of shows, Larsen presents it as the site of spectacle and desire. Helga's self-conscious gaze ignites her longing for the sight and sound of black Americans and precipitates her dissatisfaction with the all-white environment in Denmark. Returning again and again to view the performances by black entertainers, Helga is "always alone, gazing intently and solemnly at the gesticulating black figures, an ironical and silent speculative spectator." The notion of a "speculative spectator" corresponds to the expectations about the audience at the Dansk Folkenmuseum, and it suggests one way of approaching the richly textured, finely constructed tableaux featuring Helga Crane that Larsen emphasizes throughout *Quicksand*.

The very opening description of Helga Crane's physical body positions her not only in the world of mulattoes but also within a three-dimensional tableau set in Naxos, a Southern college with a name borrowed from the Cycladic Island where in Greek mythology Theseus abandoned Ariadne:

An observer would have thought her well fitted to that framing of light and shade. A slight girl of twenty-two years, with narrow, sloping shoulders and delicate, but well-turned, arms and legs, she had, none the less, an air of radiant, careless health. In vivid green and gold negligee and glistening brocaded mules, deep sunk in the big high-backed chair, against whose dark tapestry her sharply cut face, with skin like yellow satin, was distinctly outlined, she was— to use a hackneyed word—attractive. Black, very broad brows over soft, yet penetrating, dark eyes, and a pretty mouth, whose sensitive and sensuous lips had a slight questioning petulance and a tiny dissatisfied droop, were the features on which the observer's attention would fasten; though her nose was good, her ears delicately chiseled, and her curly blue-black hair plentiful and always straying in a little wayward, delightful way. Just then it tumbled, falling unrestrained about her face and on to her shoulders.

Framed within a pictorial scene vividly rendered for "an observer," or "a speculative spectator," to use both of Larsen's terms for the viewer, Helga is objectified, but she is also made "real," an actual human being captured in a characteristic and revelatory moment of everyday life. Extending the idea of a decorative Helga situated within a tableau, one of her fellow teachers in Naxos remarks: "It's nice having you here, Helga. We all think so. . . . We need a few decorations to brighten our sad lives." Helga's conduct, including her way of dressing in heavy silks of rich jewel-toned colors, becomes part of a framed scene, a moving slice of life, in which one woman's struggle for subjectivity can be observed as spectacle and appreciated as art.

Roland Barthes's interpretation of description in "Model of Painting" seems applicable to Larsen's stylized framing and descriptive technique. According to Barthes: "Every literary description is a view. . . . To describe is . . . to place the empty frame . . . in front of a collection or continuum of objects inaccessible to language. . . . in order to speak about it, the writer . . . must transform the 'real' into a painted object." Larsen, however, both utilizes and goes beyond description as a painting. Throughout the text, she replicates the pattern of a self-conscious Helga within a multi-dimensional tableau, both inviting the discerning gaze of the observer-spectator and momentarily fixing Helga's otherwise in-expressible identity against change or conflict, disparateness or instability. Each successive tableau—each speech act—contextual-izes Helga's identity. But just as the narrative can accommodate a succession only of single scenes, so the conventional construction of social, racial, sexual, or political identities can be made only in singular terms. There is no place, spatially or culturally, for a mul-tiplicity of identities.

Helga's two heredities, made visible by her appearance, signify her multiple cultural allegiances and her contradictory impulses. Her biraciality is both constrictive, because of the rigid division of the races in the United States, and expansive, because of the in-creased possibilities for cultural connections outside of national boundaries. Critics such as Mary V. Dearborn, Hortense E. Thorn-ton, Amritjit Singh, and Hazel Carby have noted the difference between Larsen's portrait of Helga and the cultural construct termed the "tragic mulatto," stereotypically the passive victim of two different and oppositional bloods. This familiar motif precon-ditions some readers into oversimplifying Helga into a tragically divided self, but Larsen complicates any figure of division by rais-ing not merely the timeless issues of nature versus nurture, of heredity versus environment, but also the new scientific theories of human behavior in her representation and exploration of Helga's problems. Alain Locke, one of the promoters of the New Negro movement, recognized as much when he praised the novel precisely for its failure to adhere to the conventional and tired no-tions of mulattoes trapped within a racial binary. Though he made no reference to the gender-related issues so central to Larsen's text, Locke applauded the new directions charted in the novel: "Indeed this whole side of the problem which was once handled exclusively as a grim tragedy of blood and fateful heredity now shows a tendency to shift to another plane of discussion, as the problem of divided social loyalties and the issues of the conflict of cultures." Helga's mixed-race status does not determine the out-come of her story; cultural conflicts and social divisions, including class, play significant roles. In fact, Helga as mulatto is perhaps more properly one of the ways Larsen places pressure on any uncomplicated reading of the text. Carby, for instance, in her interpretive reading places the mulatto figure into a position of mediation, as a device to both express and explore the relationship between the races.

In addition to establishing Helga as a racialized object in a tableau at the novel's beginning, the decorative framing of the female body initiates a major discourse on gender. Larsen poses a self-conscious young woman of elegant yet exotic beauty according to white standards. Framed in light, her yellow skin and her green and gold negligee emphasize the material value of her body and dramatize her sexuality. The focus on Helga's femaleness, combined with her race, in the privacy of the sexually charged atmosphere of her bedroom sets the stage for her seeking to define a space for self-actualization and to redefine herself as subject in all aspects of her being.

The tableau initially invites viewing as an appropriate response, but almost immediately viewing becomes intertwined with interpretation. In one of his critical statements about viewing scenes, Henry James pointed out that objects become interesting by means of "the relations of a human figure or a social occurrence" but these same relations make objects "difficult to isolate, to surround with the sharp black line, to frame in the square, the circle, the charming oval, that helps any arrangement of objects to become a picture." Larsen solves the problem of framing three-dimensional objects by surrounding them with books, including the active process of reading. Incorporating and presuming interpretation, the acts of reading that open and close *Quicksand* frame the text, so that the objects arranged between the covers of the book become a picture. At the beginning and at the end, two specific acts of reading expand the textual boundaries by encapsulating visually "exotic" foreign tales of spiritualism and historical consciousness into Helga Crane's modern story. Books as pictures—featuring "bright covers" and geographically diverse locales—expand the notion of pictorial and personal location; they simultaneously signify Helga's aesthetic sense and make legible her psychological state and intellectual disposition.

In the opening scene, Helga is reading Marmaduke Pickthall's *Saïd the Fisherman* (1903; republished in 1925). Although she has selected it because she "wanted forgetfulness, complete mental relaxation," the entertaining book is not "light" reading. Set in Palestine, Syria, England, and Egypt of the second half of the nineteenth century, the novel follows the adventures of a simple but roguish fisherman who is a devout Muslim. It presents a visual focus on the eastern, ancient lands associated with several major world religions, and by the time *Quicksand* was published in 1928, Pickthall's books were well known among readers in the United States. The use of Pickthall's novel accentuates Helga's fashionable, wide-ranging tastes that distinguish her from her Naxos colleagues, who are stoutly Christian.

Noticeably, then, Larsen chooses to represent Helga's cosmopolitanism, not simply to portray an antagonism to Christianity. This aspect of her narrative construction becomes even more apparent when at the end of *Quicksand* she interjects "The Procurator of Judea," a sobering story about memory and forgetfulness by the French writer Anatole France, as the reading Helga selects to soothe her recovery from the complications of childbirth. "The Procurator of Judea" offers an ironic and international perspective on the transience of human experience and the resiliency of individuals. While Helga requests that the story be read to her as a diversion from "the sounds of joyous religious abandon," she also intends it as an antidote to her own condition.

Like *Saïd the Fisherman*, "The Procurator of Judea" evokes distant lands and the travels of a profligate whose adventures in Syria, Palestine, Cappadocia, Armenia, Antioch, and Jerusalem also involve issues of religion and nation: the rise of the Samaritans and Jews against pax romana. In France's story the protagonist chances upon Pontius Pilate in the coastal town Baiae. Pilate is the former Procurator of Judea, and his failure to remember Jesus Christ's infamous trial, his most historically significant case, extends the critique of numbing forgetfulness associated both with the quasireligious environment of Naxos, the southern boarding school where Helga initially teaches, and with the fundamentalist church in the southern community where she is finally trapped in her marriage to a preacher. If she could forget her former life, her claims of autonomy, agency, and self-fulfillment, then she would be satisfied being confined to a life as the wife of a southern pastor to a "primitive flock." *Said the Fisherman* at the beginning of *Quicksand* and "The Procurator of Judea" at the end frame Larsen's novel, complementing its picaresque narrative and its underlying theme of spiritual quest in a world of expanding borders for African Americans.

Larsen found a fresh expansiveness in her own life when she entered the New York Public Library's Library School in 1923. Training as a librarian enabled her to pursue a career built upon the love she had for books and reading from her childhood. Circumstances had never allowed her to receive a college degree, but in both her studies at the Library School and her first career as a trained, licensed nurse, she took advantage of the many opportunities for reading and exploring the world of books beyond the assigned course work. After her marriage in 1919 to Elmer Imes, a Michigan-educated physicist, she redoubled her efforts to broaden her education through reading as self-improvement. When she left work as a librarian in 1926 to concentrate on writing and publishing, she found a supportive husband in Imes, who shared her love of books and to whom she would dedicate *Quicksand*.

By deploying historical fiction produced by "foreign" or international writers as bookends for her narrative, Larsen effectively links *Quicksand* to world literature and insinuates its connection with texts by writers such as the Danish Jens Peter Jacobsen, the Italian Grazia Deledda (who in 1926 won the Nobel Prize, only the second woman to do so), the Norwegian Henrik Ibsen, and the American expatriate Gertrude Stein. Before the official publication of *Quicksand* on March 30, 1928, Larsen sent an advance copy to Stein in Paris with a note: "Carl [Van Vechten, a mutual friend and supporter] asked me to send you my poor first book, and I am doing so. Please don't think me too presumptuous. I hope some day to have that great good fortune of seeing and talking with you." Through labeling *Quicksand* her "poor first book," Larsen linked it by implication to Stein's *Three Lives*, and to "Melanctha" in particular, which, she revealed, she had "read many times. And always I get from it some new thing—a truly great story." Inscribed within the letter to Stein is Larsen's hope for the greatness of *Quicksand* in capturing, as she believed

"Melanctha" had, the interior spirit of an African-American woman: "I never cease to wonder how you came to write it ["Melanctha"] and just why you and not one of us should so accurately have caught the spirit of this race of mine." Larsen clearly felt her own novel and its protagonist captured the emotional, psychological, and sexual internality and spirit of the race. Instinctively, she moves beyond the North-South binary common to most African-American fiction of the period, and boldly locates her subject within an international landscape with the inference of a worldwide scale of literary significance.

As a *bildungsroman* interrelating psychological and social forces in Helga Crane's search for definition, *Quicksand* relies on each phase of a spatial journey—Naxos, Chicago, Harlem, Denmark, Alabama—to represent a stage in Helga's developing consciousness. The distinct places allow for a succession of tableaux: Helga's movement is encased in scenes that exemplify the terms and objectives of her search. Following the seasons of the year, the episodic narrative structure depends upon the physical transformation of scene to converge action and meaning in Helga's spiritual quest for growth, emergence, and identity. Throughout Larsen shows an integral relationship between environmental landscapes and mental processes, between physical shapes and boundaries and human manners and styles, between racial structures and economic ones. For example, the home in New York where Helga lives as a guest is "in complete accord with what she designated as her 'aesthetic sense' " because the large, cream-colored rooms are tastefully and richly appointed with "historic things mingl[ing] harmoniously and comfortably with brass-bound Chinese tea-chests, luxurious deep chairs and davenports, tiny tables of gay colors, a lacquered jade-green settee with gleaming black satin cushions, lustrous Eastern rugs, ancient copper, Japanese prints, some fine etchings, profusion of precious bric-a-brac, and endless shelves filled with books." Such detailed descriptions evoke the exotic opulence of distant cultures associated with the Orientalism in vogue during the 1920s and with the cosmopolitanism of early twentieth-century American tastes, while also suggesting the leisurely attention to the setting of a nineteenth-century British novel or the fiction of the American internationalists Edith Wharton and Henry James, particularly *The House of Mirth* (1905) and *Portrait of a Lady* (1881).

In *Quicksand*, the exotic and the foreign also mask Helga's private dissatisfactions. Her signature throughout the narrative stages remains her ability to surround herself with rare, expensive, and, typically, foreign things not only as an attempt to forestall what she describes as her "formidable antagonist," the unnamed but "ruthless force, a quality within herself . . . frustrating her," but also as markers of her otherwise suppressed relationship to a larger, more multifaceted world than most communities allow. All around Helga are singleminded, repressed individuals such as Robert Anderson, who is described in "his ascetic protest against the sensuous, the physical," and Anne Grey, who is imprisoned in the hegemony of hierarchical, paternalistic attitudes toward race ("She hated white people with a deep and burning hatred . . . But she aped their clothes, their manners, and their gracious way of living. While proclaiming loudly the undiluted good of all things Negro, she yet disliked the songs, the dances, and the soft blurred speech of the race.").

At every stage in the narrative, Larsen emphasizes the conception of space, private and public, occupied by her protagonist in her journey-quest. The epigraph ("My old man died in a fine big house,/ My ma died in a shack./ I wonder where I'm going to die,/ Being neither white nor black?") from the poem "Cross" by Langston Hughes, raises the notion of movement and space—of place reference and mobility or lack thereof for biracial people of color. Larsen seizes the cross-cultural and interracial tropes, along with the notions of conflict with heritage and quest for place or identity, in depicting Helga Crane. While the external spatial movement of the journey provides a structural device, the internal psychological space offers a fresh, modern take on interiority as a vast uncharted territory to be explored, particularly in relation to women's desires and ambitions. Introduced by her physicist husband to the new sciences, along with the concept of relativity and its relationship to motion as well as behavior, Larsen was more than a little interested in space, in random motion, and in psychological explanations. She attends in detail to interior rooms and their decorative furnishings, to the landscapes of the rural southern campus and the church community, and to the exterior cityscapes of Chicago, New York, and Copenhagen. She mines all of these as manifestations and extensions of Helga Crane's mental, emotional, and psychological states, juxtaposing an urban and a rural, a European/Scandinavian and an American/United States aesthetic.

At the time Larsen was writing, the prototypical expatriate text by an American black author was James Weldon Johnson's *Autobiography of an Ex-Colored Man* (1912). In 1927, when Johnson's novel was reissued, its episodic, migratory mode not only defined one way of handling the multidimensional spaces occupied by people of African descent in the United States, but it also charted relations among migratory African Americans in Europe and between interracial, inter-ethnic couples. Initially published pseudonymously, *Autobiography of an Ex-Colored Man* gave voice to the modern choices facing African Americans in the twentieth century. Johnson's mixed-race but visually white narrator decides to leave Europe, a place of both success and of freedom from issues of racial heritage, and return to his people in the United States to perform the work of racial uplift through his musical talent. By doing so, he must confront the legacy of enslavement and bondage, but he also faces new horizons and the potential for black creativity and achievement. Movement and travel are the motifs representing his search for racial selfhood and cultural identity. Although diaspora was not then in use as a term applied to the displacement of Africans into the Americas, Britain, and Europe, it is an appropriate designation for the territorial patterns of spatial movement and racial consciousness experienced by Johnson's nameless protagonist. Moreover, the disaporic travel traced in Johnson's text becomes not merely a model for Larsen in her first novel but an endorsement of her more pronounced emphasis on the connection between race and geography in her fiction.

Jean Toomer's *Cane* (1923), which became one of the more influential and innovative books by an African-American writer in the decade following World War I, explores sexuality within the geographies of gender and race in the United States in ways that moved beyond what Johnson achieved in *Autobiography of an*

Ex-Colored Man. Johnson confronts sexuality only obliquely, depicting it as muting gender identity and overlapping with a white racial hierarchy. For Toomer, however, sexuality is central to cultural, regional, and personal epistemologies of identity. He focuses on women and their relation to a dying culture, their struggle with entering a modern world, with issues of sexuality, expression or repression, and fulfillment.

Interpretations of *Cane* usually depend upon recognizing the unnamed narrator's identification with the spirituality even more than the physicality of the women characters. Indeed, Toomer disassociates vigorous masculinity from his text. His sexually ambivalent and socially effacing narrator collapses his subjectivity with that of the women: he poses them as subjects but, in effect, manipulates them as objects by constructing them as dependent and by articulating their desires. In choosing the African-American woman to represent societal and cultural tensions figured in terms of race, Toomer goes against the grain of the post–World War I white American authors, such as Hemingway and Faulkner, who position their male protagonists as struggling with or against the prevailing notions of masculine strength, male prerogative, and patriarchal power. In effect, he opened the way for Jessie Fauset, Walter White, Wallace Thurman, and Nella Larsen to move African-American female protagonists and issues of gender to the center of modernist fiction concerned with race and geography, and especially with place and identity.

The tripartite scheme of *Cane* (South, North, South), with its emphasis on movement, location, and dislocation, figures in the background of Larsen's text. The Southern section, in particular, with its critique of the social and political landscape and of religious culture in the South, is one prototype for the integral connection Larsen makes between physical environment and psychological state in *Quicksand*. But Larsen adds another angle, Europe, in working out the migratory patterns of Helga Crane's search for identity and subjectivity. Moreover, Larsen may well have intended *Quicksand* as a novel that would speak back to *Cane*, to allow the women characters, especially her protagonist, to achieve agency, subjectivity, and mobility in their own lives and in public spaces.

In both her novels, *Quicksand* and *Passing* (1929), Larsen follows and displaces Toomer and Johnson by redefining the black urban novel as a woman's genre, reclaiming urban geography, and exploring all of the possibilities inherent in cityscapes as the public domain as much of women as of men. While Johnson's *Autobiography of an Ex-Colored Man* plays against a masculinized response of fighting back—resistance to race violence, segregation, and subjugation—compared with emotion, feeling, and dependency ascribed to females, and especially to the narrator's mother, Larsen's *Quicksand* is a woman's version of a similar response. Mapping the body within the spaces though which it moves, Larsen confronts cultural phenomena such as the oppression of women under the institutions of patriarchy, in particular the organized church, the commodification of women within modern consumer culture in northern cities, the colonialization of blacks in the South of racial uplift schools, and more. There is a veritable catalogue of space and gender intersectional themes infusing the text with politically savvy ideologies rarely in evidence in the novels produced during the New Negro movement.

The narrative follows Helga's search for changes in and control over her emotional and psychological states by moving to different geographic locations: "She began to make plans to dream delightful dreams of changes, of life somewhere else. Some place where at last she would be permanently satisfied . . . where she would be appreciated, and understood." No single place measures up to her expectations and needs. Even Harlem occasions secretive excursions outside its boundaries, defiant responses to the injunction against revealing the miscegenation that produced her; Mrs. Hayes-Rore, an advocate for racial justice who hires Helga, "felt that [Helga's story] dealing as it did with race intermingling and possible adultery, was beyond definite discussion. For among black people, as among white people, it is tacitly understood that these things are not mentioned—and therefore they do not exist." Helga's very existence, then, is at stake in her residence in Harlem; the substance of that existence can only be affirmed by her excursions into white New York. Resolutely independent, she resists marriage and concubinage as forms of entrapment and subservience, which she reads both in her mother's life and in the social relations of all sexually active women.

In rendering Helga's active quest for agency and empowerment, Larsen handles realistically the complexities of cultural experiences for a woman of color in a modern world. She raises issues of privilege, otherness, marginality, and identity to provide a substantive conceptual core to the life of a woman who is socially constructed as black in a world in which the majority culture is white and in which the dominant representations of blacks come from whites. But she also uses those same issues to challenge the social roles available to women in a patriarchal culture.

Larsen shows how the environmental and material trappings of a mainly middle-class commodity culture in small southern communities, large northern cities, and a foreign capitol intersect with and inform Helga's individuality. The Harlem segments contain a richly detailed portrait of place within a specific cultural context, the emergence of modern black New York. Copenhagen provides the foreign backdrop for Helga's quest within a white foreign world. The interlude in Denmark embodies old world wealth, class privilege, and ethnic certainty. The texture and diversity of the physical settings combine with the intensity and necessity of Helga's gendered and racial search to mark one of Larsen's major achievements in *Quicksand*.

Setting a segment of the novel in Denmark, Larsen departs from the expected terrain of African-American women writers. Although Jessie Fauset had attended the International Congress and studied in Paris, as had the artist and writer Gwendolyn Bennett, fewer African-American women writers than men were part of the internationalization occurring in the 1920s. Larsen draws upon her heritage as a Danish person of color, and upon her own interest in a broader geography than that defined conventionally by black Americans. Attracted to the social world of blacks as it was expanding after World War I and yet reminded of the discomforts of racism and color prejudice, Larsen wrote her first novel to reflect both the familiar and the foreign spaces in which African Americans found themselves.

One of the characteristic devices she deploys stems in part from a particular sense of spatial well being central to the ideology of Danes. The Danish term *hyggelig* is implicit in Helga Crane's search for identity and subjectivity. It suggests closeness and comfort, particularly as related to family life. *Hygge* connotes both a spatial configuration and an emotional state. For Helga Crane, whose very name evokes the disjuncture between her Danish heritage and her American origins, *hyggelig* will be unattainable within any space, and her inability to secure it will lead to her unhappiness, insecurity, and restlessness.

In each place she attempts to construct a cozy environment to support and sustain herself. In Naxos, she surrounds herself with beautiful, comfortable objects; in New York she finds a place that exudes warmth and security (including financial security); and everywhere she goes, she attempts to find people who will complete the comfortable family life associated with *hyggelig*. In Naxos, for example, Helga's room is carefully appointed to provide "tranquility" and "quiet," an "intentional" retreat from classroom and campus: "Only a single reading lamp, dimmed by a great black and red shade, made a pool of light on the blue Chinese carpet, on the bright covers of the books which she had taken down from their long shelves, on the white pages of the opened one selected, on the shining brass bowl covered with many-colored nasturtiums beside her on the low table, and on the oriental silk which covered the stool at the slim feet." As a personalized comfort zone within a context of cold conformity, "the room which held her" both reflects and extends Helga's interiority and her Danish heritage. Distinctive furnishings and fabrics define her alienated personality as well as her values: "All her life Helga Crane had loved and longed for nice things. Indeed, it was this craving, this urge for beauty which had helped to bring her into disfavor" in Naxos. Jewel colors, exotic patterns, rare fabrics, and antique objects, all constitute her preference for beauty and comfort over utility and austerity and are markers not only of her participation in a commodity culture but also of her difference from the black community in which she finds herself a misfit. When she travels to Copenhagen, her aunt, Katrina Dahl, and her uncle, Poul Dahl, satisfy her longing for beauty and comfort, but they do so in order to prepare her—and themselves—for social mobility.

In Copenhagen she quickly discovers that she is deemed an exotic foreigner, attractive to Danes because of her "primitive" African heritage. Although her aunt and uncle love her and are not racists, they emphasize her difference and her dependency by carefully dressing her in brilliant colors, décolleté gowns, and outlandish finery. Helga becomes an object, her body is commodified, and she is placed on the marriage market. Her relative's great ambition is to marry her off to one of Denmark's most famous artists, and thereby increase their own social standing. Ibsen's character Nora is figured in Helga's plight, and the Dahls' name evokes *A Doll's House,* his play in which Nora appears. The measures the Dahls use to establish their niece in Danish society force Helga to acknowledge the complexity of her situation and the manipulation of her body. She understands that her relatives are transforming her into both a pampered doll and a sexual commodity. While she yearns to move backward in time and reclaim her youth, she desires to do so as an adult and as an agent. She realizes that she cannot accomplish her purpose in Denmark among Scandinavians who have no understanding of what it means to be a woman of color and specifically an African American. Helga's desire for the enclosed safe traditional Danish *hygge* is at odds with her modern and mixed racial, ethnic, and national heritages. Her discomfort is both public and private.

The power of *Quicksand* emanates from the core of Helga's existence and from the interpolation of an interracial family saga into Helga's own. Her Danish mother, Karen Nilssen, long dead when the narrative opens, and her black father, a gambler whom she has never known, both intrude upon Helga's present. Her father's legacy to his daughter is entanglement in a male, racialized story. Because Helga inherits her father's race, and with it the culture's racial restrictions, her restless quest conforms superficially to the race-defined and gender-specific story of a black male's search for recognition and place. Certainly, early in life Helga has been scarred by the desertion of her father, a "gay suave scoundrel." At the same time, she is implicated in her mother's self-conscious quest for love and happiness. Throughout her adult life, Helga carries the pain caused by the remoteness of her "sad, cold" mother, who had been "flung into poverty, sordidness, and dissipation." Not only had Helga's mother risked all in violating racial taboos and marrying Helga's father, but later, motivated by need rather than desire, she had also sacrificed her child for the sake of another man and her own happiness: "Her thoughts lingered with her mother . . . A fair Scandinavian girl in love with life, with love, passion, dreaming, and risking all in one blind surrender. A cruel sacrifice. In forgetting all but love she had forgotten, or had perhaps never known, that some things the world never forgives. But as Helga knew, she had remembered, or had learned in suffering and longing all the rest of her life."

Her mother's sacrifice in marrying a second time is not lost on Helga, who suffers nonetheless because of her racial difference from her mother and stepfather: "That second marriage, to a man of her own race, but not of her own kind—so passionately, so instinctively resented by Helga even at the trivial age of six—she now understood as a grievous necessity. Even foolish, despised women must have food and clothing; even unloved little Negro girls must be somehow provided for." Although Helga claims to understand her mother's action, she has never forgiven her mother for choosing a man over her. Because of her mother's choices, Helga's childhood, already marked by her father's abandonment, was "one long, changeless stretch of aching misery of soul," punctuated by "ugly scarifying quarrels," "her own childish self-effacement," and "her mother's careful management," their mutual attempt to mediate the "spiritual wounds" of their daily lives. As an adult, Helga has suppressed her anger toward her mother, particularly for her complicity in Helga's childhood suffering; she has even further repressed her anger toward her father not merely for leaving her but for marking her racially.

It is Helga's anger, nonetheless, that both pervades her inner life and fuels much of the narrative tension. In Naxos, for instance, she labels her furious decision to leave a "new revolt . . . a lack of Acquiescence." Anger, often diffused and misdirected, erupts suddenly. In reflecting upon her revelations about her mother, however, she questions her own motives: "Why, if she had said so much, hadn't she said more about herself and her mother? . . . Why had she lost her temper and given way to angry half-truths?—Angry half-truths—Angry half—." In leaving unfinished and unexplored these questions that she raises early in the narrative, Helga gestures toward locating her story within the parameters of her relationship to her mother.

The adult Helga recognizes that her "inherent aloneness," an essential "part of her very being," stems from her childhood isolation within a destructive family. Nevertheless, because consciously she can neither come to terms with her mother's role in her "aloneness," nor recover from her sense of maternal deprivation, Helga is unable to reconstitute a supportive family or relinquish her desire for one. She cannot adequately break the cultural proscription against anger in the female or the social proscription against a child's anger toward a mother. Thus forbidden healthy expressions of anger, she is unable to resolve her ambivalences regarding her desire for control over her life. Deflecting her anger away from her mother and toward her white relatives or the black bourgeoisie, Helga assumes various guises for spiritual, psychical, and racial acceptance. Culturally disinherited by her mother's white husband and his children during her youth and economically marginalized by her father's desertion, however, she cannot articulate the severity of her deprivations, her sense of herself as an illegitimate child and a social orphan. Therefore, Helga is silenced; she can neither voice her innermost reality to others nor express that reality in her own story. She re-enacts her mother's story, but without the maturity to interpret its meaning.

While she suffers from absent parents, her missing father and her remote mother, she also endures the incompleteness associated with the being both similar to and different from her father. Although within the given gender narrative of the man's mobility and the father's power, Helga would be excluded, she shapes her existence around the supposedly "racial" traits of her father. She configures herself as a composite image of him with a difference that is primarily gendered. She takes her father's place within the world even while subsuming his burden of a black racial identity. Thus, importantly, Helga duplicates her father's subject-constituting action: flight as movement away from the difficult or problematic aspects of individual existence, and into a spatial location of communal identity connected to race, as well as the constructions and perceptions of race.

It is in Denmark during her "courting" by Axel Olsen, a prominent Danish painter, that Helga has an epiphany involving both herself and her father. When Olsen unveils his portrait of her as a sexualized "jungle" creature ("some disgusting sensual creature with her features," as Helga sees it), and then propositions her rather than proposes, he prompts a two-fold discovery on Helga's part. She is a sensual being with deep feelings, not merely an embodiment of a sort of primitive sexuality underpinning her controlled exterior, and she misses the companionship of blacks in her all-white environment. Although Olsen cares enough for her to propose marriage after recognizing his mistake, he is unshaken in his judgment of her: " 'You know, Helga, you are a contradiction. . . . You have the warm impulsive nature of the women of Africa, but, my lovely, you have, I fear, the soul of a prostitute. You sell yourself to the highest buyer.' " Helga's response surprises Olsen and herself: " 'I'm not for sale. Not to you. Not to any white man. I don't care at all to be owned. Even by you.' " Although her words stress female autonomy and independence, they underscore racial memory and acceptance. She recognizes her salability in the marriage marketplace, but Helga insists on defining that market as an African-American one: " 'I couldn't marry a white man. . . . It isn't just you, not just personal. . . . It's deeper, broader than that. It's racial. . . . if we were married you might come to be ashamed of me, to hate me, to hate all dark people. My mother did that.' " Helga focuses not on her own potential response to an interracial marriage, but on Olsen's, because the painful model available to her is her mother's reaction both to her father and to Helga herself.

Yet there in Denmark, surrounded by whites and far from the community of blacks in the United States, she puts aside the responses of white people, such as her mother or Olsen, and in the central apotheosis, has a vision of her father and his motives:

> For the first time, Helga Crane felt sympathy rather than contempt and hatred for that father, who so often and so angrily she had blamed for his desertion of her mother. She understood, now, his rejection, his repudiation, of the formal claim her mother had represented. She understood his yearning, his intolerable need for the inexhaustible humor and the incessant hope of his own kind, his need for those things, not material, indigenous to all Negro environments. She understood and could sympathize with his facile surrender to the irresistible ties of race, now that they dragged at her own heart.

Helga's recognition of her father's need for "the inexhaustible humor and the incessant hope of his own kind" precipitates her acknowledgment of her own desire for "things, not material," as had been the case with most of her previous yearnings, but for things "indigenous to all Negro environments," as she puts it. Larsen situates this new awareness within the foreign, transnational, and "white" space of Denmark, and uses it to catapult Helga into rejecting Olsen's proposal and its unstated sinecure: a secure, contained "white" life as an exceptional, exotic woman in Copenhagen.

Satisfied in a black cultural identity that includes an awareness of her physicality separate from an object-state, Helga resolves to return to New York, meaning Harlem and a black community. She becomes less passive and reactive, particularly in recognizing her own desires and fulfilling her own sexual drives within a "black" racial context. At peace with her father and comfortable with her identification with him beyond the matter of color, she also consciously enters a different spatial relation to her mother. In the final sequence of *Quicksand*, it is her mother and not her father who has a prominent place in her mind and emotions: "There was her mother, whom she had loved from a distance and finally so scornfully blamed, who appeared as she always remembered her, unbelievably beautiful, young, and remote." An emotional, maternal bond, this appearance is a final testament to Helga's attraction to the Danish, foreign, and white side of her being and to its inseparability from her core existence, just as is her connection to the racial and cultural legacies of her father.

Back in New York, Helga's religious experience in a storefront church moves her not only spiritually but also physically. During the church service's "Bacchic vehemence," her old self is shattered, and out of the destruction comes her new, black-defined existence: "Maddened, she grasped at the railing, and with no previous intention began to yell like one insane . . . while torrents of tears streamed down her face. She was unconscious of the words she uttered, or their meaning." The incoherent testifying by the once controlled, articulate Helga lays bare her desire for succor. In separating words from meaning, Larsen allows the sound of voice to be overpowered by the image of tears, so that this visualization, another of *Quicksand*'s tableaux, becomes the signifying trope of her rebirth experience.

Against the logic of her former subjectivity and self-consciousness, Helga marries the Reverend Pleasant Green, the country preacher conducting the revival, and returns with him to his native Alabama. Helga's emotional conversation frees her of any inhibitions and anxieties retarding self-expression, but it also ends her self-development, in favor of her new racially and communally derived subjectivity. With her surrender to religious and sexual ecstasy, she no longer attempts to bridge the division between her emotions, arrested in childhood, and her intellect, matured and analytical.

The marriage satisfies Helga's search for a father and for a place to provide comfort. In the now familiar geography of the South, she accepts Reverend Green as a reconfiguration of her father—as a combination of Pastor/Husband/Father/God—and associates him with the emotional freedom and joy of black existence within community. Her rush into marriage fulfills the convoluted logic both of her search for family and of her repression of sexuality, because her emotional freedom, recovered in a religious frenzy akin to a sexual climax, quickly translates into the traditional female roles that she now inhabits as wife and mother. Green offers Helga an uncomplicated life as a minister's wife and as a member of a religion that subordinates human responsibility to God's will: "Actually and metaphorically she bowed her head before God, trusting in Him to see her through. Secretly she was glad that she had not to worry about herself or anything. It was a relief . . . to put the entire responsibility on someone else."

On an emotional level, the marriage satisfies Helga's longing to return to childhood and to correct its unhappy state. It allows her to conceal and repress her adult female self. She idealizes the simplicity of existing in a childlike state while being sexually satisfied as an adult woman. Initially pleased with her new husband, ultimately Helga is unfulfilled in her union with the pompous, unkempt Green, who becomes synonymous with the triple threat Helga had feared would engulf and destroy her: southernness (as seen in rural unglorified black folk); submission (in particular to paternal and spiritual authority); and sexuality (in primitive abandon to desire).

Life with Green in the poor Alabama community allows Helga little expression for her particular aesthetic values, for her sensibility asserting beauty and comfort over utility, or for her mixed-race identity and transnational perspective. She intends to transform the women in the congregation by instructing them "according to her ideas of beauty," but despite their agreeable smiles and promises she detects disinterest. The women appreciate much more her fashion-conscious double in the community, Clementine Richards, "a strapping black beauty of magnificent Amazon proportions and bold shining eyes of jet-like hardness. A person of awesome appearance. All chains, strings of beads, jingling bracelets, flying ribbons, feathery neckpieces, and flowery hats." Clementine is presented as a folk counterpart to bourgeois Helga, who in Denmark was described in similar finery that paid tribute to her African heritage and exoticized her appearance. Even more than the other women, "Clementine was inclined to treat Helga with only partially concealed contempt, considering her a poor thing without style. . . ." For Helga, whose notions of aesthetics and beauty are Eurocentric and white, Clementine is an expression of her own repressed otherness, though in acknowledging Clementine's dazzling appearance, Helga does not modify her sense of mission or of herself. In the narrative, however, Clementine becomes a powerful corrective to the othering of African people in Denmark.

Once the reality of her own household work—gardening, "cooking, dish-washing, sweeping, dusting, mending, and darning," and conjugal duties—sets in, Helga sadly admits, "there was no time for the pursuit of beauty, or for the uplifting of other harassed and teeming women, or for the instruction of their neglected children." Her roles as helpmeet and mother channel her creativity into narrow outlets unsuited to her temperament and sensibilities. Southern "folk" culture and rural subsistence do not empower Helga or liberate her from anxiety; instead they lead to a more pronounced psychic rage. The poverty of the community and her own deprivation are so alien that she can neither be happy nor "subdue the cleanly scrubbed ugliness of her own surroundings into soft inoffensive beauty."

Two pregnancies within twenty months deplete her energy and leave her virtually incapable of caring for her twin boys, her daughter, or herself. With the birth of her fourth child, she becomes too weak to fulfill her social roles as wife and mother. She retreats into herself, surrendering to the care and authority of others. Although Helga thinks she will leave her husband and return to the material comforts of the smart set in New York, she cannot abandon her children: "she wanted to leave them. . . . The recollection of her own childhood, lonely, unloved rose too poignantly before her for her to consider calmly such a solution. . . . to leave them would be a tearing agony, a rending of deepest fibers." The emancipatory strategies of Helga's past are no longer viable, because she will not replicate the desertion by her black father and the indifference of her white mother. These tangled realities combine with all her lost opportunities for happiness to create an oppressive sense of powerlessness and emptiness, a condition even her children cannot displace.

Helga ends, much as she begins in Naxos, in a tableau and isolated within a small room and in bed where she "could think, would have a certain amount of quiet. Of aloneness." The bed, however, has become tomb-like and dangerous. *Quicksand* concludes with Helga's becoming pregnant with a fifth child before she has recovered from the birth of the fourth. Her loss of autonomy and self-determination is signaled by her inability to control her body and by the debilitating effects of reproduction and motherhood. The Helga Crane who has dominated the narrative is symbolically dead.

Lacking the means to repair her life, she slips into fantasy, a "serene haven" in which she envisions the figures from her past— her mother, Robert Anderson (the Naxos Principal and object of her desire), James Vayle (her former fiancé), Axel Olsen, Audrey Denny, Mrs. Hayes-Rore (her one-time employer), and the Dahls—all of whom symbolize her lost opportunities for connection and expression. Of these, Audrey Denny, the only character with whom Helga never directly interacts, represents an element of Helga's own self that she has not allowed herself to become.

First seen at a Harlem cabaret in the company of Robert Anderson, Audrey resembles Helga in appearance and taste, but she expresses her personality differently. Helga views her as a "beautiful, calm cool girl who had the assurance, the courage, so placidly to ignore racial barriers and give her attention to people" and regards her with "envious admiration," because Audrey is bound neither by conventional models for African-American women nor by traditional roles for women. Recognizing what she wants, Audrey has the courage to define her own life in keeping with her objectives and her knowledge of herself and lives not only fully but also creatively.

That Helga cannot act upon the intersectional aspects of her identity that Audrey Denny represents signals that healthy survival in racial and sexual contexts is impossible. The dramatic ending with Helga Crane ironically aware of her disintegrating self may seem too drastic a shift of fortune from the search for self-affirmation she has undertaken, but it is thematically and symbolically in keeping with her downward spiral into despair and destruction. Even in her weakened state, she sees the "terrible reality" of her position:

> At first she had felt only an astonished anger at the quagmire in which she had engulfed herself. She had ruined her life. Made it impossible ever again to do the things that she wanted, have the things that she loved, mingle with the people she liked. She had, to put it as brutally as anyone could, been a fool. The damnedest kind of a fool. And she had paid for it. Enough. More than enough.

In assessing her responsibility for her life, Helga settles on the word "fool," echoing the label she had formerly applied to her mother. She does not have the personal resources and strength necessary to extricate herself from her situation or to formulate a positive definition of herself within her roles as wife and mother. Ultimately, there is in her position "a quality of passivity, of resignation, of suppressed anger that results," Mary Helen Washington says, "from the stifling of desire and energy."

Although for a time in the mid-twentieth century, Larsen was rendered largely invisible by lack of attention to her fiction, she was by no means overlooked when her novels were first published. *Quicksand*, for example, not only won the Harmon Foundation's Bronze Award for Distinguished Achievement Among Negroes in Literature, but it also received more than twenty-five reviews and numerous announcements between April 8, 1928, when *The New York Times Book Review* first featured the book in "Latest Works of Fiction," and January 1929, when *Opportunity* carried Alain Locke's "1928: A Retrospective," which featured Larsen prominently. From newspapers, such as the *Amsterdam News*, New

York *Herald Tribune,* and *The New York Times,* to magazines, including *Saturday Review of Literature, The Crisis, Opportunity,* the major New York publications, black and white, all took notice of *Quicksand,* and in turn newspapers and periodicals around the nation and in England recognized it as the work of an important new novelist. W. E. B. Du Bois, writing in *The Crisis,* hailed Larsen's novel as "fine, thoughtful and courageous. It is, on the whole, the best piece of fiction that Negro America has produced since the heyday of [Charles] Chesnutt, and stands easily with Jessie Fauset's *There Is Confusion,* in its subtle comprehension of the curious cross currents that swirl about the black American" ("Two Novels," *The Crisis,* XXXV, June 1928). Du Bois painted an admiring portrait of Helga as "master of her whimsical, unsatisfied soul," and as one "typical of the new, honest, young fighting Negro woman," who "beaten down even to death . . . never will utterly surrender to hypocrisy and convention." Like Du Bois, Alain Locke, who by the end of the 1920s had become the most important spokesperson for the Harlem Renaissance, was impressed by Larsen's ability to render contemporary issues with a fresh perspective. He termed *Quicksand* "a social document of importance, and as well, a living, moving picture of a type not often in the foreground of Negro fiction, and here treated for the first time with adequacy" ("1928: A Retrospective Review," *Opportunity,* VII, January 1929).

Larsen's second novel, *Passing,* was published in April 1929. With its sweep into the stylistics of high modernism, it displayed Larsen's maturation as a storyteller and novelist. Not surprisingly, like *Quicksand, Passing,* too, enjoyed widespread coverage in the United States and abroad; it also was nominated for, but did not win, the 1929 Harmon Foundation award in literature.

Larsen received a 1930 Guggenheim Foundation Fellowship in Creative Writing to further develop her international themes around racial difference in her third novel with research in France and Spain, but she subsequently failed to gain a publisher for the book. Thus began her long, slow decline into obscurity as a novelist. Although charges of plagiarism of a short story clouded her reputation as she left the United States in 1930, she spent nearly two productive years working on several novels in France and Spain. Upon her return to the United States in 1932, she confronted the end of her marriage, the collapse of the American economy, and the demise of the Harlem Renaissance. After the death of her former husband in 1941 and the end of the alimony that sustained her during the Depression, and with the inability to publish her third novel as an added impetus, Larsen returned to nursing. At the time of her death in 1964, she was remembered by friends and associates as a dedicated nurse-supervisor—but not as a novelist.

By the end of the twentieth century, however, Larsen was restored to visibility as a major writer of the Harlem Renaissance. In the aftermath of the Civil Rights and Women's Movements, renewed interest in the writings of minorities and women inspired a resurgence of attention to Larsen and her two novels. But it is the skill and vision she employs in portraying race and gender issues in black women's lives that have created a prominent place for her in the pantheon of Harlem Renaissance artists, and make her a major American novelist of the first half of the twentieth century.

—Thadious M. Davis

SUGGESTIONS FOR FURTHER READING

Anderson, Jervis. *This Was Harlem, 1900–1950.* New York: Farrar Straus Giroux, 1982.

Bell, Bernard. *The Afro-American Novel and Its Tradition.* Amherst: University of Massachusetts Press, 1989.

Carby, Hazel V. *Reconstructing Womanhood: The Emergence of the Afro-American Woman Novelist.* New York: Oxford University Press, 1987.

Christian, Barbara. *Black Feminist Criticism: Perspectives on Black Women Writers.* New York: Pergamon Press, 1985.

Collins, Patricia Hill. *Black Feminist Thought: Knowledge, Consciousness, and the Politics of Empowerment.* New York: Routledge, 1990.

Davis, Thadious M. *Nella Larsen, Novelist of the Harlem Renaissance: A Woman's Life Unveiled.* Baton Rouge: Louisiana State University Press, 1994.

duCille, Ann. *The Coupling Convention: Sex, Text, and Tradition in Black Women's Fiction.* New York: Oxford University Press, 1993.

Felski, Rita. *The Gender of Modernity.* Cambridge: Harvard University Press, 1995.

Huggins, Nathan Irvin. *Harlem Renaissance.* New York: Oxford University Press, 1971.

Kellner, Bruce, ed. *The Harlem Renaissance: A Historical Dictionary for the Era.* New York: Methuen, 1987.

Lewis, David Levering. *When Harlem Was in Vogue.* New York: Vintage Books, 1982.

McAlpine, Carole Watson *Prologue: The Novels of Black American Women, 1891–1965.* Westport, CT: Greenwood, 1985.

McDowell, Deborah E. *"The Changing Same": Black Women's Literature, Criticism, and Theory.* Bloomington: Indiana University Press, 1995.

McLendon, Jacquelyn. *The Politics of Color in the Fiction of Jessie Fauset and Nella Larsen*. Charlottesville: University Press of Virginia, 1995.

Singh, Amritjit. *The Novels of the Harlem Renaissance*. University Park: Pennsylvania State University Press, 1976.

Tate, Claudia. *Psychoanalysis and Black Novels: Desire and the Protocols of Race*. New York: Oxford University Press, 1998.

Wall, Cheryl A. *Women of the Harlem Renaissance*. Bloomington: Indiana University Press, 1995.

Washington, Mary Helen. *Invented Lives: Narratives of Black Women, 1860–1960*. Garden City, NY: Anchor, 1987.

Wintz, Cary D. *Black Culture and the Harlem Renaissance*. Houston: Rice University Press, 1988.

Young, Robert J. C. *Colonial Desire: Hybridity in Theory Culture and Race*. London and New York: Routledge, 1995.

A NOTE ON THE TEXT

The text of this edition is based on the first edition of *Quicksand*, which was published by Alfred A. Knopf in 1928. Chapter 25 in the original was misnumbered "Chapter 23." With the exception of minor typographical errors, which have been silently corrected, the original punctuation, spelling, and division of words have been retained throughout this text. In several cases, the spelling of Danish place names has been amended when a typographical error, rather than an error in transcription from Danish to English, is apparent; for example, *"Amielenborg"* has been changed to *"Amalienborg,"* and *"Konigens"* to *"Kongens,"* and two different spellings of the street, *"Kirkplads* and *"Kirkeplads,"* have been regularized.

QUICKSAND

FOR E. S. I.[1]

My old man died in a fine big house.
My ma died in a shack.
I wonder where I'm gonna die,
Being neither white nor black?[1]

LANGSTON HUGHES[2]

ONE

HELGA CRANE sat alone in her room, which at that hour, eight in the evening, was in soft gloom. Only a single reading lamp, dimmed by a great black and red shade, made a pool of light on the blue Chinese carpet, on the bright covers of the books which she had taken down from their long shelves, on the white pages of the opened one selected, on the shining brass bowl crowded with many-colored nasturtiums beside her on the low table, and on the oriental silk which covered the stool[1] at her slim feet. It was a comfortable room, furnished with rare and intensely personal taste, flooded with Southern sun in the day, but shadowy just then with the drawn curtains and single shaded light. Large, too. So large that the spot where Helga sat was a small oasis in a desert of darkness. And eerily quiet. But that was what she liked after her taxing day's work, after the hard classes, in which she gave willingly and unsparingly of herself with no apparent return. She loved this tranquillity, this quiet, following the fret and strain of the long hours spent among fellow members of a carelessly unkind and gossiping faculty, following the strenuous rigidity of conduct required in this huge educational community of which she was an insignificant part. This was her rest, this intentional isolation for a short while in the evening, this little time in her own attractive room with her own books. To the rapping of other teachers, bearing fresh scandals, or seeking information, or other more concrete favors, or merely talk, at that hour Helga Crane never opened her door.

An observer would have thought her well fitted to that framing of light and shade. A slight girl of twenty-two years, with narrow, sloping shoulders and delicate, but well-turned, arms and legs, she had, none the less, an air of radiant, careless health. In vivid green and gold negligee and glistening brocaded mules, deep sunk in the big high-backed chair, against whose dark tapestry her sharply cut face, with skin like yellow satin, was distinctly outlined, she was—to use a hackneyed word—attractive. Black, very broad brows over soft, yet penetrating, dark eyes, and a pretty mouth, whose sensitive and sensuous lips had a slight questioning petulance and a tiny dissatisfied droop, were the features on which the observer's attention would fasten; though her nose was good, her ears delicately chiseled, and her curly blue-black hair plentiful and always straying in a little wayward, delightful way. Just then it was tumbled, falling unrestrained about her face and on to her shoulders.

Helga Crane tried not to think of her work and the school as she sat there. Ever since her arrival in Naxos² she had striven to keep these ends of the days from the intrusion of irritating thoughts and worries. Usually she was successful. But not this evening. Of the books which she had taken from their places she had decided on Marmaduke Pickthall's *Saïd the Fisherman*.³ She wanted forgetfulness, complete mental relaxation, rest from thought of any kind. For the day had been more than usually crowded with distasteful encounters and stupid perversities. The sultry hot Southern spring had left her strangely tired, and a little unnerved. And annoying beyond all other happenings had been that affair of the noon period, now again thrusting itself on her already irritated mind.

She had counted on a few spare minutes in which to indulge in the sweet pleasure of a bath and a fresh, cool change of clothing. And instead her luncheon time had been shortened, as had that of everyone else, and immediately after the hurried gulping down of a heavy hot meal the hundreds of students and teachers had been herded into the sun-baked chapel to listen to the banal, the patronizing, and even the insulting remarks of one of the renowned white preachers of the state.

Helga shuddered a little as she recalled some of the statements made by that holy white man of God to the black folk sitting so respectfully before him.

This was, he had told them with obvious sectional pride, the finest school for Negroes anywhere in the country, north or south; in fact, it was better even than a great many schools for white children. And he had dared any Northerner to come south and after looking upon this great institution to say that the Southerner mistreated the Negro. And he had said that if all Negroes would only take a leaf out of the book of Naxos and conduct themselves in the manner of the Naxos products, there would be no race problem, because Naxos Negroes knew what was expected of them. They had good sense and they had good taste. They knew enough to stay in their places, and that, said the preacher, showed good taste. He spoke of his great admiration for the Negro race, no other race in so short a time had made so much progress, but he had urgently besought them to know when and where to stop. He hoped, he sincerely hoped, that they wouldn't become avaricious and grasping, thinking only of adding to their earthly goods, for that would be a sin in the sight of Almighty God. And then he had spoken of contentment, embellishing his words with scriptural quotations and pointing out to them that it was their duty to be satisfied in the estate to which they had been called, hewers of wood and drawers of water.[4] And then he had prayed.

Sitting there in her room, long hours after, Helga again felt a surge of hot anger and seething resentment. And again it subsided in amazement at the memory of the considerable applause which had greeted the speaker just before he had asked his God's blessing upon them.

The South. Naxos. Negro education. Suddenly she hated them all. Strange, too, for this was the thing which she had ardently desired to share in, to be a part of this monument to one man's genius and vision.[5] She pinned a scrap of paper about the bulb under the lamp's shade, for, having discarded her book in the certainty that in such a mood even *Saïd* and his audacious villainy could not charm her, she wanted an even more soothing darkness. She wished it were vacation, so that she might get away for a time.

"No, forever!" she said aloud.

The minutes gathered into hours, but still she sat motionless, a disdainful smile or an angry frown passing now and then across her face. Somewhere in the room a little clock ticked time away. Somewhere outside, a whippoorwill wailed. Evening died. A sweet smell of early Southern flowers rushed in on a newly-risen breeze which suddenly parted the thin silk curtains at the opened windows. A slender, frail glass vase fell from the sill with a tingling crash, but Helga Crane did not shift her position. And the night grew cooler, and older.

At last she stirred, uncertainly, but with an overpowering desire
for action of some sort. A second she hesitated, then rose abruptly
and pressed the electric switch with determined firmness, flooding
suddenly the shadowy room with a white glare of light. Next she
made a quick nervous tour to the end of the long room, paused a
moment before the old bow-legged secretary that held with almost articulate protest her school-teacher paraphernalia of drab
books and papers. Frantically Helga Crane clutched at the lot and
then flung them violently, scornfully toward the wastebasket. It
received a part, allowing the rest to spill untidily over the floor.
The girl smiled ironically, seeing in the mess a simile of her own
earnest endeavor to inculcate knowledge into her indifferent
classes.

Yes, it was like that; a few of the ideas which she tried to put
into the minds behind those baffling ebony, bronze, and gold faces
reached their destination. The others were left scattered about.
And, like the gay, indifferent wastebasket, it wasn't their fault. No,
it wasn't the fault of those minds back of the diverse colored faces.
It was, rather, the fault of the method, the general idea behind the
system. Like her own hurried shot at the basket, the aim was bad,
the material drab and badly prepared for its purpose.

This great community, she thought, was no longer a school. It
had grown into a machine. It was now a show place in the black
belt,[6] exemplification of the white man's magnanimity, refutation
of the black man's inefficiency. Life had died out of it. It was,
Helga decided, now only a big knife with cruelly sharp edges
ruthlessly cutting all to a pattern, the white man's pattern. Teachers as well as students were subjected to the paring process, for it
tolerated no innovations, no individualisms. Ideas it rejected, and
looked with open hostility on one and all who had the temerity to
offer a suggestion or ever so mildly express a disapproval. Enthusiasm, spontaneity, if not actually suppressed, were at least openly
regretted as unladylike or ungentlemanly qualities. The place was
smug and fat with self-satisfaction.

A peculiar characteristic trait, cold, slowly accumulated unrea-
son in which all values were distorted or else ceased to exist, had
with surprising ferociousness shaken the bulwarks of that self-
restraint which was also, curiously, a part of her nature. And now
that it had waned as quickly as it had risen, she smiled again, and

this time the smile held a faint amusement, which wiped away the little hardness which had congealed her lovely face. Nevertheless she was soothed by the impetuous discharge of violence, and a sigh of relief came from her.

She said aloud, quietly, dispassionately: "Well, I'm through with that," and, shutting off the hard, bright blaze of the overhead lights, went back to her chair and settled down with an odd gesture of sudden soft collapse, like a person who had been for months fighting the devil and then unexpectedly had turned round and agreed to do his bidding.

Helga Crane had taught in Naxos for almost two years, at first with the keen joy and zest of those immature people who have dreamed dreams of doing good to their fellow men. But gradually this zest was blotted out, giving place to a deep hatred for the trivial hypocrisies and careless cruelties which were, unintentionally perhaps, a part of the Naxos policy of uplift.[7] Yet she had continued to try not only to teach, but to befriend those happy singing children, whose charm and distinctiveness the school was so surely ready to destroy. Instinctively Helga was aware that their smiling submissiveness covered many poignant heartaches and perhaps much secret contempt for their instructors. But she was powerless. In Naxos between teacher and student, between condescending authority and smoldering resentment, the gulf was too great, and too few had tried to cross it. It couldn't be spanned by one sympathetic teacher. It was useless to offer her atom of friendship, which under the existing conditions was neither wanted nor understood.

Nor was the general atmosphere of Naxos, its air of self-rightness and intolerant dislike of difference, the best of mediums for a pretty, solitary girl with no family connections. Helga's essentially likable and charming personality was smudged out. She had felt this for a long time. Now she faced with determination that other truth which she had refused to formulate in her thoughts, the fact that she was utterly unfitted for teaching, even for mere existence, in Naxos. She was a failure here. She had, she conceded now, been silly, obstinate, to persist for so long. A failure. Therefore, no need, no use, to stay longer. Suddenly she longed for immediate departure. How good, she thought, to go now, tonight!—and frowned to remember how impossible that would be. "The dignitaries," she said, "are not in their offices, and there will be yards and yards of red tape to unwind, gigantic, impressive spools of it."

And there was James Vayle to be told, and much-needed money to be got. James, she decided, had better be told at once. She looked at the clock racing indifferently on. No, too late. It would have to be tomorrow.

She hated to admit that money was the most serious difficulty. Knowing full well that it was important, she nevertheless rebelled at the unalterable truth that it could influence her actions, block her desires. A sordid necessity to be grappled with. With Helga it was almost a superstition that to concede to money its importance magnified its power. Still, in spite of her reluctance and distaste, her financial situation would have to be faced, and plans made, if she were to get away from Naxos with anything like the haste which she now so ardently desired.

Most of her earnings had gone into clothes, into books, into the furnishings of the room which held her. All her life Helga Crane had loved and longed for nice things. Indeed, it was this craving, this urge for beauty which had helped to bring her into disfavor in Naxos—"pride" and "vanity" her detractors called it.

The sum owing to her by the school would just a little more than buy her ticket back to Chicago. It was too near the end of the school term to hope to get teaching-work anywhere. If she couldn't find something else, she would have to ask Uncle Peter for a loan. Uncle Peter was, she knew, the one relative who thought kindly, or even calmly, of her. Her stepfather, her stepbrothers and sisters, and the numerous cousins, aunts, and other uncles could not be even remotely considered. She laughed a little, scornfully, reflecting that the antagonism was mutual, or, perhaps, just a trifle keener on her side than on theirs. They feared and hated her. She pitied and despised them. Uncle Peter was different. In his contemptuous way he was fond of her. Her beautiful, unhappy mother had been his favorite sister. Even so, Helga Crane knew that he would be more likely to help her because her need would strengthen his oft-repeated conviction that because of her Negro blood she would never amount to anything, than from motives of affection or loving memory. This knowledge, in its present aspect of truth, irritated her to an astonishing degree. She regarded

Uncle Peter almost vindictively, although always he had been extraordinarily generous with her and she fully intended to ask his assistance. "A beggar," she thought ruefully, "cannot expect to choose."

Returning to James Vayle, her thoughts took on the frigidity of complete determination. Her resolution to end her stay in Naxos would of course inevitably end her engagement to James. She had been engaged to him since her first semester there, when both had been new workers, and both were lonely. Together they had discussed their work and problems in adjustment, and had drifted into a closer relationship. Bitterly she reflected that James had speedily and with entire ease fitted into his niche. He was now completely "naturalized," as they used laughingly to call it. Helga, on the other hand, had never quite achieved the unmistakable Naxos mold, would never achieve it, in spite of much trying. She could neither conform, nor be happy in her unconformity. This she saw clearly now, and with cold anger at all the past futile effort. What a waste! How pathetically she had struggled in those first months and with what small success. A lack somewhere. Always she had considered it a lack of understanding on the part of the community, but in her present new revolt she realized that the fault had been partly hers. A lack of acquiescence. She hadn't really wanted to be made over. This thought bred a sense of shame, a feeling of ironical disillusion. Evidently there were parts of her she couldn't be proud of. The revealing picture of her past striving was too humiliating. It was as if she had deliberately planned to steal an ugly thing, for which she had no desire, and had been found out.

Ironically she visualized the discomfort of James Vayle. How her maladjustment had bothered him! She had a faint notion that it was behind his ready assent to her suggestion anent a longer engagement than, originally, they had planned. He was liked and approved of in Naxos and loathed the idea that the girl he was to marry couldn't manage to win liking and approval also. Instinctively Helga had known that secretly he had placed the blame upon her. How right he had been! Certainly his attitude had gradually changed, though he still gave her his attention. Naxos pleased him and he had become content with life as it was lived there. No longer lonely, he was now one of the community and so beyond the need or the desire to discuss its affairs and its failings with an outsider. She was, she knew, in a queer indefinite way, a disturbing factor. She knew too that a something held him, a something against which he was powerless. The idea that she was in but one nameless way necessary to him filled her with a sensation amounting almost to shame. And yet his mute helplessness against that ancient appeal by which she held him pleased her and fed her vanity—gave her a feeling of power. At the same time she shrank away from it, subtly aware of possibilities she herself couldn't predict.

Helga's own feelings defeated inquiry, but honestly confronted, all pretense brushed aside, the dominant one, she suspected, was relief. At least, she felt no regret that tomorrow would mark the end of any claim she had upon him. The surety that the meeting would be a clash annoyed her, for she had no talent for quarreling—when possible she preferred to flee. That was all.

The family of James Vayle, in near-by Atlanta, would be glad. They had never liked the engagement, had never liked Helga Crane. Her own lack of family disconcerted them. No family. That was the crux of the whole matter. For Helga, it accounted for everything, her failure here in Naxos, her former loneliness in Nashville.[8] It even accounted for her engagement to James. Negro society, she had learned, was as complicated and as rigid in its ramifications as the highest strata of white society. If you couldn't prove your ancestry and connections, you were tolerated, but you didn't "belong." You could be queer, or even attractive, or bad, or brilliant, or even love beauty and such nonsense if you were a Rankin, or a Leslie, or a Scoville; in other words, if you had a family.[9] But if you were just plain Helga Crane, of whom nobody had ever heard, it was presumptuous of you to be anything but inconspicuous and conformable.

To relinquish James Vayle would most certainly be social suicide, for the Vayles were people of consequence. The fact that they were a "first family" had been one of James's attractions for the obscure Helga. She had wanted social background, but—she had not imagined that it could be so stuffy.

She made a quick movement of impatience and stood up. As she did so, the room whirled about her in an impish, hateful way. Familiar objects seemed suddenly unhappily distant. Faintness closed about her like a vise. She swayed, her small, slender hands gripping the chair arms for support. In a moment the faintness receded, leaving in its wake a sharp resentment at the trick which her strained nerves had played upon her. And after a moment's rest she got hurriedly into bed, leaving her room disorderly for the first time.

Books and papers scattered about the floor, fragile stockings and underthings and the startling green and gold negligee dripping about on chairs and stool, met the encounter of the amazed eyes of the girl who came in the morning to awaken Helga Crane.

TWO

SHE WOKE IN THE MORNING unrefreshed and with that feeling of half-terrified apprehension peculiar to Christmas and birthday mornings. A long moment she lay puzzling under the sun streaming in a golden flow through the yellow curtains. Then her mind returned to the night before. She had decided to leave Naxos. That was it.

Sharply she began to probe her decision. Reviewing the situation carefully, frankly, she felt no wish to change her resolution. Except—that it would be inconvenient. Much as she wanted to shake the dust of the place from her feet forever, she realized that there would be difficulties. Red tape. James Vayle. Money. Other work. Regretfully she was forced to acknowledge that it would be vastly better to wait until June, the close of the school year. Not so long, really. Half of March, April, May, some of June. Surely she could endure for that much longer conditions which she had borne for nearly two years. By an effort of will, her will, it could be done. *&as women told to just put up w/ things often*

But this reflection, sensible, expedient, though it was, did not reconcile her. To remain seemed too hard. Could she do it? Was it possible in the present rebellious state of her feelings? The uneasy sense of being engaged with some formidable antagonist, nameless and ununderstood, startled her. It wasn't, she was suddenly aware, merely the school and its ways and its decorous stupid people that oppressed her. There was something else, some other more ruthless force, a quality within herself, which was frustrating her, had always frustrated her, kept her from getting the things she had wanted. Still wanted. *—→the world telling her she can't*

But just what did she want? Barring a desire for material security, gracious ways of living, a profusion of lovely clothes, and a goodly share of envious admiration, Helga Crane didn't know, couldn't tell. But there was, she knew, something else. Happiness,

talking about happiness/ emotion

she supposed. Whatever that might be. What, exactly, she wondered, was happiness. Very positively she wanted it. Yet her conception of it had no tangibility. She couldn't define it, isolate it, and contemplate it as she could some other abstract things. Hatred, for instance. Or kindness.

The strident ringing of a bell somewhere in the building brought back the fierce resentment of the night. It crystallized her wavering determination.

From long habit her biscuit-coloured feet had slipped mechanically out from under the covers at the bell's first unkind jangle. Leisurely she drew them back and her cold anger vanished as she decided that, now, it didn't at all matter if she failed to appear at the monotonous distasteful breakfast which was provided for her by the school as part of her wages.

In the corridor beyond her door was a medley of noises incident to the rising and preparing for the day at the same hour of many schoolgirls—foolish giggling, indistinguishable snatches of merry conversation, distant gurgle of running water, patter of slippered feet, low-pitched singing, good-natured admonitions to hurry, slamming of doors, clatter of various unnamable articles, and—suddenly—calamitous silence.

Helga ducked her head under the covers in the vain attempt to shut out what she knew would fill the pregnant silence—the sharp sarcastic voice of the dormitory matron. It came.

"Well! Even if every last one of you did come from homes where you weren't taught any manners, you might at least try to pretend that you're capable of learning some here, now that you have the opportunity. Who slammed the shower-baths door?"

Silence.

"Well, you needn't trouble to answer. It's rude, as all of you know. But it's just as well, because none of you can tell the truth. Now hurry up. Don't let me hear of a single one of you being late for breakfast. If I do there'll be extra work for everybody on Saturday. And *please* at least try to act like ladies and not like savages from the backwoods."

On her side of the door, Helga was wondering if it had ever occurred to the lean and desiccated Miss MacGooden that most of her charges had actually come from the backwoods. Quite recently too. Miss MacGooden, humorless, prim, ugly, with a face like dried leather, prided herself on being a "lady" from one of the best families—an uncle had been a congressman in the period of the Reconstruction. She was therefore, Helga Crane reflected, perhaps unable to perceive that the inducement to act like a lady, her own acrimonious example, was slight, if not altogether negative. And thinking on Miss MacGooden's "ladyness," Helga grinned a little as she remembered that one's expressed reason for never having married, or intending to marry. There were, so she had been given to understand, things in the matrimonial state that were of necessity entirely too repulsive for a lady of delicate and sensitive nature to submit to.

Soon the forcibly shut-off noises began to be heard again, as the evidently vanishing image of Miss MacGooden evaporated from the short memories of the ladies-in-making. Preparations for the intake of the day's quota of learning went on again. Almost naturally.

"So much for that!" said Helga, getting herself out of bed.

She walked to the window and stood looking down into the great quadrangle below, at the multitude of students streaming from the six big dormitories which, two each, flanked three of its sides, and assembling into neat phalanxes preparatory to marching in military order to the sorry breakfast in Jones Hall on the fourth side. Here and there a male member of the faculty, important and resplendent in the regalia of an army officer, would pause in his prancing or strutting, to jerk a negligent or offending student into the proper attitude or place. The massed phalanxes increased in size and number, blotting out pavements, bare earth, and grass. And about it all was a depressing silence, a sullenness almost, until with a horrible abruptness the waiting band blared into "The Star Spangled Banner." The goose-step began.[1] Left, right. Left, right. Forward! March! The automatons moved. The squares disintegrated into fours. Into twos. Disappeared into the gaping doors of Jones Hall. After the last pair of marchers had entered, the huge doors were closed. A few unlucky late-comers, apparently already discouraged, tugged half-heartedly at the knobs, and finding, as they had evidently expected, that they were indeed barred out, turned resignedly away.

Helga Crane turned away from the window, a shadow dimming the pale amber loveliness of her face. Seven o'clock it was now. At twelve those children who by some accident had been a little minute or two late would have their first meal after five hours of work and so-called education. Discipline, it was called.

There came a light knocking on her door.

"Come in," invited Helga unenthusiastically. The door opened to admit Margaret Creighton, another teacher in the English department and to Helga the most congenial member of the whole Naxos faculty. Margaret, she felt, appreciated her.

Seeing Helga still in night robe seated on the bedside in a mass of cushions, idly dangling a mule across bare toes like one with all the time in the world before her, she exclaimed in dismay: "Helga Crane, do you know what time it is? Why, it's long after half past seven. The students—"

"Yes, I know," said Helga defiantly, "the students are coming out from breakfast. Well, let them. I, for one, wish that there was some way that they could forever stay out from the poisonous stuff thrown at them, literally thrown at them, Margaret Creighton, for food. Poor things."

Margaret laughed. "That's just ridiculous sentiment, Helga, and you know it. But you haven't had any breakfast, yourself. Jim Vayle asked if you were sick. Of course nobody knew. You never tell anybody anything about yourself. I said I'd look in on you."

"Thanks awfully," Helga responded, indifferently. She was watching the sunlight dissolve from thick orange into pale yellow. Slowly it crept across the room, wiping out in its path the morning shadows. She wasn't interested in what the other was saying.

"If you don't hurry, you'll be late to your first class. Can I help you?" Margaret offered uncertainly. She was a little afraid of Helga. Nearly everyone was.

"No. Thanks all the same." Then quickly in another, warmer tone: "I do mean it. Thanks, a thousand times, Margaret. I'm really awfully grateful, but—you see, it's like this, I'm not going to be late to my class. I'm not going to be there at all."

The visiting girl, standing in relief, like old walnut against the buff-colored wall, darted a quick glance at Helga. Plainly she was curious. But she only said formally: "Oh, then you *are* sick." For something there was about Helga which discouraged questionings.

No, Helga wasn't sick. Not physically. She was merely disgusted. Fed up with Naxos. If that could be called sickness. The truth was that she had made up her mind to leave. That very day. She could no longer abide being connected with a place of shame, lies, hypocrisy, cruelty, servility, and snobbishness. "It ought," she concluded, "to be shut down by law."

"But, Helga, you can't go now. Not in the middle of the term." The kindly Margaret was distressed.

"But I can. And I am. Today."

"They'll never let you," prophesied Margaret.

"*They* can't stop me. Trains leave here for civilization every day. All that's needed is money," Helga pointed out.

"Yes, of course. Everybody knows that. What I mean is that you'll only hurt yourself in your profession. They won't give you a reference if you jump up and leave like this now. At this time of the year. You'll be put on the black list.[2] And you'll find it hard to get another teaching-job. Naxos has enormous influence in the South. Better wait till school closes."

"Heaven forbid," answered Helga fervently, "that I should ever again want work anywhere in the South! I hate it." And fell silent, wondering for the hundredth time just what form of vanity it was that had induced an intelligent girl like Margaret Creighton to turn what was probably nice live crinkly hair, perfectly suited to her smooth dark skin and agreeable round features, into a dead straight, greasy, ugly mass.

Looking up from her watch, Margaret said: "Well, I've really got to run, or I'll be late myself. And since I'm staying— Better think it over, Helga. There's no place like Naxos, you know. Pretty good salaries, decent rooms, plenty of men, and all that. Ta-ta." The door slid to behind her.

But in another moment it opened. She was back. "I do wish you'd stay. It's nice having you here, Helga. We all think so. Even the dead ones. We need a few decorations to brighten our sad lives." And again she was gone.

Helga was unmoved. She was no longer concerned with what anyone in Naxos might think of her, for she was now in love with the piquancy of leaving. Automatically her fingers adjusted the Chinese-looking pillows on the low couch that served for her bed. Her mind was busy with plans for departure. Packing, money, trains, and—could she get a berth?

THREE

ON ONE SIDE of the long, white, hot sand road that split the flat green, there was a little shade, for it was bordered with trees. Helga Crane walked there so that the sun could not so easily get at her. As she went slowly across the empty campus she was conscious of a vague tenderness for the scene spread out before her. It was so incredibly lovely, so appealing, and so facile. The trees in their spring beauty sent through her restive mind a sharp thrill of pleasure. Seductive, charming, and beckoning as cities were, they had not this easy unhuman loveliness. The trees, she thought, on city avenues and boulevards, in city parks and gardens, were tamed, held prisoners in a surrounding maze of human beings. Here they were free. It was human beings who were prisoners. It was too bad. In the midst of all this radiant life. They weren't, she knew, even conscious of its presence. Perhaps there was too much of it, and therefore it was less than nothing.

In response to her insistent demand she had been told that Dr. Anderson[1] could give her twenty minutes at eleven o'clock. Well, she supposed that she could say all that she had to say in twenty minutes, though she resented being limited. Twenty minutes. In Naxos, she was as unimportant as that.

He was a new man, this principal, for whom Helga remembered feeling unaccountably sorry, when last September he had first been appointed to Naxos as its head. For some reason she had liked him, although she had seen little of him; he was so frequently away on publicity and money-raising tours. And as yet he had made but few and slight changes in the running of the school. Now she was a little irritated at finding herself wondering just how she was going to tell him of her decision. What did it matter to him? Why should she mind if it did? But there returned to her that indistinct sense of sympathy for the remote silent man with the tired gray eyes, and she wondered again by what fluke of fate such a man, apparently a humane and understanding person, had chanced into the command of this cruel educational machine. Suddenly, her own resolve loomed as an almost direct unkindness. This increased her annoyance and discomfort. A sense of defeat, of being cheated of justification, closed down on her. Absurd!

She arrived at the administration building in a mild rage, as unreasonable as it was futile, but once inside she had a sudden attack of nerves[2] at the prospect of traversing that great outer room which was the workplace of some twenty odd people. This was a disease from which Helga had suffered at intervals all her life, and it was a point of honor, almost, with her never to give way to it. So, instead of turning away, as she felt inclined, she walked on, outwardly indifferent. Half-way down the long aisle which divided the room, the principal's secretary, a huge black man, surged toward her.

"Good-morning, Miss Crane, Dr. Anderson will see you in a few moments. Sit down right here."

She felt the inquiry in the shuttered eyes. For some reason this dissipated her self-consciousness and restored her poise. Thanking him, she seated herself, really careless now of the glances of the stenographers, book-keepers, clerks. Their curiosity and slightly veiled hostility no longer touched her. Her coming departure had released her from the need for conciliation which had irked her for so long. It was pleasant to Helga Crane to be able to sit calmly looking out of the window on to the smooth lawn, where a few leaves quite prematurely fallen dotted the grass, for once uncaring whether the frock which she wore roused disapproval or envy.

Turning from the window, her gaze wandered contemptuously over the dull attire of the women workers. Drab colors, mostly navy blue, black, brown, unrelieved, save for a scrap of white or tan about the hands and necks. Fragments of a speech made by the dean of women floated through her thoughts—"Bright colors are vulgar"—"Black, gray, brown, and navy blue are the most becoming colors for colored people"—"Dark-complected people shouldn't wear yellow, or green or red."—The dean was a woman from one of the "first families"—a great "race" woman; she, Helga Crane, a despised mulatto, but something intuitive, some unanalyzed driving spirit of loyalty to the inherent racial need for gorgeousness told her that bright colours *were* fitting and that dark-complexioned people *should* wear yellow, green, and red. Black, brown, and gray were ruinous to them, actually destroyed the luminous tones lurking in their dusky skins. One of the loveliest sights Helga had ever seen had been a sooty black girl decked out in a flaming orange dress, which a horrified matron had next day consigned to the dyer. Why, she wondered, didn't someone write *A Plea for Color*?

These people yapped loudly of race, of race consciousness, of race pride, and yet suppressed its most delightful manifestations, love of color, joy of rhythmic motion, naïve, spontaneous laughter. Harmony, radiance, and simplicity, all the essentials of spiritual beauty in the race they had marked for destruction.

She came back to her own problems. Clothes had been one of her difficulties in Naxos. Helga Crane loved clothes, elaborate ones. Nevertheless, she had tried not to offend. But with small success, for, although she had affected the deceptively simple variety, the hawk eyes of dean and matrons had detected the subtle difference from their own irreproachably conventional garments. Too, they felt that the colors were queer; dark purples, royal blues, rich greens, deep reds, in soft, luxurious woolens, or heavy, clinging silks. And the trimmings—when Helga used them at all— seemed to them odd. Old laces, strange embroideries, dim brocades. Her faultless, slim shoes made them uncomfortable and her small plain hats seemed to them positively indecent. Helga smiled inwardly at the thought that whenever there was an evening affair for the faculty, the dear ladies probably held their breaths until she had made her appearance. They existed in constant fear that she might turn out in an evening dress. The proper evening wear in Naxos was afternoon attire. And one could, if one wished, garnish the hair with flowers.

Quick, muted footfalls sounded. The secretary had returned.

"Dr. Anderson will see you now, Miss Crane."

She rose, followed, and was ushered into the guarded sanctum, without having decided just what she was to say. For a moment she felt behind her the open doorway and then the gentle impact of its closing. Before her at a great desk her eyes picked out the figure of a man, at first blurred slightly in outline in that dimmer light. At his "Miss Crane?" her lips formed for speech, but no sound came. She was aware of inward confusion. For her the situ-

ation seemed charged, unaccountably, with strangeness and something very like hysteria. An almost overpowering desire to laugh
seized her. Then, miraculously, a complete ease, such as she had
never known in Naxos, possessed her. She smiled, nodded in answer to his questioning salutation, and with a gracious "Thank
you" dropped into the chair which he indicated. She looked at him
frankly now, this man still young, thirty-five perhaps, and found it
easy to go on in the vein of a simple statement.

"Dr. Anderson, I'm sorry to have to confess that I've failed in
my job here. I've made up my mind to leave. Today."

A short, almost imperceptible silence, then a deep voice of peculiarly pleasing resonance, asking gently: "You don't like Naxos,
Miss Crane?"

She evaded. "Naxos, the place? Yes, I like it. Who wouldn't like
it? It's so beautiful. But I—well—I don't seem to fit here."

The man smiled, just a little. "The school? You don't like the
school?"

The words burst from her. "No, I don't like it. I hate it!"

"Why?" The question was detached, too detached.

In the girl blazed a desire to wound. There he sat, staring
dreamily out of the window, blatantly unconcerned with her or
her answer. Well, she'd tell him. She pronounced each word with
deliberate slowness.

"Well, for one thing, I hate hypocrisy. I hate cruelty to students, and to teachers who can't fight back. I hate backbiting, and
sneaking, and petty jealousy. Naxos? It's hardly a place at all. It's
more like some loathsome, venomous disease. Ugh! Everybody
spending his time in a malicious hunting for the weaknesses of
others, spying, grudging, scratching."

"I see. And you don't think it might help to cure us, to have
someone who doesn't approve of these things stay with us? Even
just one person, Miss Crane?"

She wondered if this last was irony. She suspected it was humor
and so ignored the half-pleading note in his voice.

"No, I don't! It doesn't do the disease any good. Only irritates
it. And it makes me unhappy, dissatisfied. It isn't pleasant to be always made to appear in the wrong, even when I know I'm right."

His gaze was on her now, searching. "Queer," she thought,

"how some brown people have gray eyes. Gives them a strange, unexpected appearance. A little frightening."

The man said, kindly: "Ah, you're unhappy. And for the reasons you've stated?"

"Yes, partly. Then, too, the people here don't like me. They don't think I'm in the spirit of the work. And I'm not, not if it means suppression of individuality and beauty."

"And does it?"

"Well, it seems to work out that way."

"How old are you, Miss Crane?"

She resented this, but she told him, speaking with what curtness she could command only the bare figure: "Twenty-three."

"Twenty-three. I see. Some day you'll learn that lies, injustice, and hypocrisy are a part of every ordinary community. Most people achieve a sort of protective immunity, a kind of callousness, toward them. If they didn't, they couldn't endure. I think there's less of these evils here than in most places, but because we're trying to do such a big thing, to aim so high, the ugly things show more, they irk some of us more. Service is like clean white linen, even the tiniest speck shows." He went on, explaining, amplifying, pleading.

Helga Crane was silent, feeling a mystifying yearning which sang and throbbed in her. She felt again that urge for service, not now for her people, but for this man who was talking so earnestly of his work, his plans, his hopes. An insistent need to be a part of them sprang in her. With compunction tweaking at her heart for even having entertained the notion of deserting him, she resolved not only to remain until June, but to return next year. She was shamed, yet stirred. It was not sacrifice she felt now, but actual desire to stay, and to come back next year.

He came, at last, to the end of the long speech, only part of which she had heard. "You see, you understand?" he urged.

"Yes, oh yes, I do."

"What we need is more people like you, people with a sense of values, and proportion, an appreciation of the rarer things of life. You have something to give which we badly need here in Naxos. You mustn't desert us, Miss Crane."

She nodded, silent. He had won her. She knew that she would

stay. "It's an elusive something," he went on. "Perhaps I can best explain it by the use of that trite phrase, 'You're a lady.' You have dignity and breeding."

At these words turmoil rose again in Helga Crane. The intricate pattern of the rug which she had been studying escaped her. The shamed feeling which had been her penance evaporated. Only a lacerated pride remained. She took firm hold of the chair arms to still the trembling of her fingers.

"If you're speaking of family, Dr. Anderson, why, I haven't any. I was born in a Chicago slum."

The man chose his words, carefully he thought. "That doesn't at all matter, Miss Crane. Financial, economic circumstances can't destroy tendencies inherited from good stock. You yourself prove that!"

Concerned with her own angry thoughts, which scurried here and there like trapped rats, Helga missed the import of his words. Her own words, her answer, fell like drops of hail.

"The joke is on you, Dr. Anderson. My father was a gambler who deserted my mother, a white immigrant. It is even uncertain that they were married. As I said at first, I don't belong here. I shall be leaving at once. This afternoon. Good-morning."

FOUR

LONG, SOFT WHITE CLOUDS, clouds like shreds of incredibly fine cotton, streaked the blue of the early evening sky. Over the flying landscape hung a very faint mist, disturbed now and then by a languid breeze. But no coolness invaded the heat of the train rushing north. The open windows of the stuffy day coach, where Helga Crane sat with others of her race, seemed only to intensify her discomfort. Her head ached with a steady pounding pain. This, added to her wounds of the spirit, made traveling something little short of a medieval torture. Desperately she was trying to right the confusion in her mind. The temper of the morning's interview rose before her like an ugly mutilated creature crawling horribly over the flying landscape of her thoughts. It was no use. The ugly thing pressed down on her, held her. Leaning back, she tried to doze as others were doing. The futility of her effort exasperated her.

Just what had happened to her there in that cool dim room under the quizzical gaze of those piercing gray eyes? Whatever it was had been so powerful, so compelling, that but for a few chance words she would still be in Naxos. And why had she permitted herself to be jolted into a rage so fierce, so illogical, so disastrous, that now after it was spent she sat despondent, sunk in shameful contrition? As she reviewed the manner of her departure from his presence, it seemed increasingly rude. be women arent allowed to be reactionary

She didn't, she told herself, after all, like this Dr. Anderson. He was too controlled, too sure of himself and others. She detested cool, perfectly controlled people. Well, it didn't matter. He didn't matter. But she could not put him from her mind. She set it down to annoyance because of the cold discourtesy of her abrupt action. She disliked rudeness in anyone.

She had outraged her own pride, and she had terribly wronged her mother by her insidious implication. Why? Her thoughts lingered with her mother, long dead. A fair Scandinavian girl in love with life, with love, with passion, dreaming, and risking all in one blind surrender. A cruel sacrifice. In forgetting all but love she had forgotten, or had perhaps never known, that some things the world never forgives. But as Helga knew, she had remembered, or had learned in suffering and longing all the rest of her life. Her daughter hoped she had been happy, happy beyond most human creatures, in the little time it had lasted, the little time before that gay suave scoundrel, Helga's father, had left her. But Helga Crane doubted it. How could she have been? A girl gently bred, fresh from an older, more polished civilization, flung into poverty, sordidness, and dissipation. She visualized her now, sad, cold, and—yes, remote. The tragic cruelties of the years had left her a little pathetic, a little hard, and a little unapproachable.

That second marriage, to a man of her own race, but not of her own kind—so passionately, so instinctively resented by Helga even at the trivial age of six—she now understood as a grievous necessity. Even foolish, despised women must have food and clothing; even unloved little Negro girls must be somehow provided for. Memory, flown back to those years following the marriage, dealt her torturing stabs. Before her rose the pictures of her mother's careful management to avoid those ugly scarifying quarrels which even at this far-off time caused an uncontrollable shudder, her own childish self-effacement, the savage unkindness of her stepbrothers and sisters, and the jealous, malicious hatred of her mother's husband. Summers, winters, years, passing in one long, changeless stretch of aching misery of soul. Her mother's death, when Helga was fifteen. Her rescue by Uncle Peter, who had sent her to school, a school for Negroes,[1] where for the first time she could breathe freely, where she discovered that because one was dark, one was not necessarily loathsome, and could, therefore, consider oneself without repulsion.

Six years. She had been happy there, as happy as a child unused to happiness dared be. There had been always a feeling of strangeness, of outsideness, and one of holding her breath for fear that it wouldn't last. It hadn't. It had dwindled gradually into eclipse of painful isolation. As she grew older, she became gradually aware of a difference between herself and the girls about her. They had mothers, fathers, brothers, and sisters of whom they spoke frequently, and who sometimes visited them. They went home for the vacations which Helga spent in the city where the school was located. They visited each other and knew many of the same people. Discontent for which there was no remedy crept upon her, and she was glad almost when these most peaceful years which she had yet known came to their end. She had been happier, but still horribly lonely.

She had looked forward with pleasant expectancy to working in Naxos when the chance came. And now this! What was it that stood in her way? Helga Crane couldn't explain it, put a name to it. She had tried in the early afternoon in her gentle but staccato talk with James Vayle. Even to herself her explanation had sounded inane and insufficient; no wonder James had been impatient and unbelieving. During their brief and unsatisfactory conversation she had had an odd feeling that he felt somehow cheated. And more than once she had been aware of a suggestion of suspicion in his attitude, a feeling that he was being duped, that he suspected her of some hidden purpose which he was attempting to discover.

Well, that was over. She would never be married to James Vayle now. It flashed upon her that, even had she remained in Naxos, she would never have been married to him. She couldn't have married him. Gradually, too, there stole into her thoughts of him a curious sensation of repugnance, for which she was at a loss to account. It was new, something unfelt before. Certainly she had never loved him overwhelmingly, not, for example, as her mother must have loved her father, but she *had* liked him, and she had expected to love him, after their marriage. People generally did love then, she imagined. No, she had not loved James, but she had wanted to. Acute nausea rose in her as she recalled the slight quivering of his lips sometimes when her hands had unexpectedly touched his; the throbbing vein in his forehead on a gay day when they had wandered off alone across the low hills and she had allowed him frequent kisses under the shelter of some low-hanging willows. Now she shivered a little, even in the hot train, as if she had suddenly come out from a warm scented place into cool, clear air. She must have been mad, she thought; but she couldn't tell why she thought so. This, too, bothered her.

Laughing conversation buzzed about her. Across the aisle a bronze baby, with bright staring eyes, began a fretful whining, which its young mother essayed to silence by a low droning croon. In the seat just beyond, a black and tan young pair were absorbed in the eating of a cold fried chicken, audibly crunching the ends of the crisp, browned bones. A little distance away a tired laborer slept noisily. Near him two children dropped the peelings of oranges and bananas on the already soiled floor. The smell of stale food and ancient tobacco irritated Helga like a physical pain. A man, a white man, strode through the packed car and spat twice, once in the exact centre of the dingy door panel, and once into the receptacle which held the drinking-water. Instantly Helga became aware of stinging thirst. Her eyes sought the small watch at her wrist. Ten hours to Chicago. Would she be lucky enough to prevail upon the conductor to let her occupy a berth,[2] or would she have to remain here all night, without sleep, without food, without drink, and with that disgusting door panel to which her purposely averted eyes were constantly, involuntarily straying?

Her first effort was unsuccessful. An ill-natured "No, you know you can't," was the answer to her inquiry. But farther on along the road, there was a change of men. Her rebuff had made her reluctant to try again, but the entry of a farmer carrying a basket containing live chickens, which he deposited on the seat (the only vacant one) beside her, strengthened her weakened courage. Timidly, she approached the new conductor, an elderly gray-mustached man of pleasant appearance, who subjected her to a keen, appraising look, and then promised to see what could be done. She thanked him, gratefully, and went back to her shared seat, to wait anxiously. After half an hour he returned, saying he could "fix her up," there was a section she could have, adding: "It'll cost you ten dollars." She murmured: "All right. Thank you." It was twice the price, and she needed every penny, but she knew she was fortunate to get it even at that, and so was very thankful, as she followed his tall, loping figure out of that car and through seemingly endless others, and at last into one where she could rest a little.

She undressed and lay down, her thoughts still busy with the morning's encounter. Why hadn't she grasped his meaning? Why, if she had said so much, hadn't she said more about herself and her mother? He would, she was sure, have understood, even sympathized. Why had she lost her temper and given way to angry half-truths?— Angry half-truths— Angry half—

GRAY CHICAGO SEETHED, surged, and scurried about her. Helga shivered a little, drawing her light coat closer. She had forgotten how cold March could be under the pale skies of the North. But she liked it, this blustering wind. She would even have welcomed snow, for it would more clearly have marked the contrast between this freedom and the cage which Naxos had been to her. Not but what it was marked plainly enough by the noise, the dash, the crowds.

Helga Crane, who had been born in this dirty, mad, hurrying city, had no home here. She had not even any friends here. It would have to be, she decided, the Young Women's Christian Association.[1] "Oh dear! The uplift. Poor, poor colored people. Well, no use stewing about it. I'll get a taxi to take me out, bag and baggage, then I'll have a hot bath and a really good meal, peep into the shops—mustn't buy anything—and then for Uncle Peter. Guess I won't phone. More effective if I surprise him."

It was late, very late, almost evening, when finally Helga turned her steps northward, in the direction of Uncle Peter's home. She had put it off as long as she could, for she detested her errand. The fact that that one day had shown her its acute necessity did not decrease her distaste. As she approached the North Side,[2] the distaste grew. Arrived at last at the familiar door of the old stone house, her confidence in Uncle Peter's welcome deserted her. She gave the bell a timid push and then decided to turn away, to go back to her room and phone, or, better yet, to write. But before she could retreat, the door was opened by a strange red-faced maid, dressed primly in black and white. This increased Helga's mistrust. Where, she wondered, was the ancient Rose, who had, ever since she could remember, served her uncle.

The hostile "Well?" of this new servant forcibly recalled the reason for her presence there. She said firmly: "Mr. Nilssen, please."

"Mr. Nilssen's not in," was the pert retort. "Will you see Mrs. Nilssen?"

Helga was startled. "Mrs. Nilssen! I beg your pardon, did you say Mrs. Nilssen?"

"I did," answered the maid shortly, beginning to close the door.

"What is it, Ida?" A woman's soft voice sounded from within.

"Someone for Mr. Nilssen, m'am." The girl looked embarrassed.

In Helga's face the blood rose in a deep-red stain. She explained: "Helga Crane, his niece."

"She says she's his niece, m'am."

"Well, have her come in."

There was no escape. She stood in the large reception hall, and was annoyed to find herself actually trembling. A woman, tall, exquisitely gowned, with shining gray hair piled high, came forward murmuring in a puzzled voice: "His niece, did you say?"

"Yes, Helga Crane. My mother was his sister, Karen Nilssen. I've been away. I didn't know Uncle Peter had married." Sensitive to atmosphere, Helga had felt at once the latent antagonism in the woman's manner.

"Oh, yes! I remember about you now. I'd forgotten for a moment. *Well,* he isn't exactly your uncle, is he? Your mother wasn't married, was she? I mean, to your father?"

"I—I don't know," stammered the girl, feeling pushed down to the uttermost depths of ignominy.

"Of course she wasn't." The clear, low voice held a positive note. "Mr. Nilssen has been very kind to you, supported you, sent you to school. But you mustn't expect anything else. And you mustn't come here any more. It—well, frankly, it isn't convenient. I'm sure an intelligent girl like yourself can understand that."

"Of course," Helga agreed, coldly, freezingly, but her lips quivered. She wanted to get away as quickly as possible. She reached the door. There was a second of complete silence, then Mrs. Nilssen's voice, a little agitated: "And please remember that my husband is not your uncle. No indeed! Why, that, that would make me your aunt! He's not—"

But at last the knob had turned in Helga's fumbling hand. She gave a little unpremeditated laugh and slipped out. When she was in the street, she ran. Her only impulse was to get as far away from her uncle's house, and this woman, his wife, who so plainly wished to dissociate herself from the outrage of her very existence. She was torn with mad fright, an emotion against which she knew but two weapons: to kick and scream, or to flee.

The day had lengthened. It was evening and much colder, but Helga Crane was unconscious of any change, so shaken she was and burning. The wind cut her like a knife, but she did not feel it. She ceased her frantic running, aware at last of the curious glances of passersby. At one spot, for a moment less frequented than others, she stopped to give heed to her disordered appearance. Here a man, well groomed and pleasant-spoken, accosted her. On such occasions she was wont to reply scathingly, but, tonight, his pale Caucasian face struck her breaking faculties as too droll. Laughing harshly, she threw at him the words: "You're not my uncle."

He retired in haste, probably thinking her drunk, or possibly a little mad.

Night fell, while Helga Crane in the rushing swiftness of a roaring elevated train sat numb. It was as if all the bogies and goblins that had beset her unloved, unloving, and unhappy childhood had come to life with tenfold power to hurt and frighten. For the wound was deeper in that her long freedom from their presence had rendered her the more vulnerable. Worst of all was the fact that under the stinging hurt she understood and sympathized with Mrs. Nilssen's point of view, as always she had been able to understand her mother's, her stepfather's, and his children's points of view. She saw herself for an obscene sore in all their lives, at all costs to be hidden. She understood, even while she resented. It would have been easier if she had not.

Later in the bare silence of her tiny room she remembered the unaccomplished object of her visit. Money. Characteristically, while admitting its necessity, and even its undeniable desirability, she dismissed its importance. Its elusive quality she had as yet never known. She would find work of some kind. Perhaps the library. The idea clung. Yes, certainly the library. She knew books and loved them.

She stood intently looking down into the glimmering street, far below, swarming with people, merging into little eddies and disengaging themselves to pursue their own individual ways. A few minutes later she stood in the doorway, drawn by an uncontrollable desire to mingle with the crowd. The purple sky showed tremulous clouds piled up, drifting here and there with a sort of endless lack of purpose. Very like the myriad human beings pressing hurriedly on. Looking at these, Helga caught herself wondering who they were, what they did, and of what they thought. What was passing behind those dark molds of flesh? Did they really think at all? Yet, as she stepped out into the moving multi-colored crowd, there came to her a queer feeling of enthusiasm, as if she were tasting some agreeable, exotic food—sweetbreads, smothered with truffles and mushrooms—perhaps. And, oddly enough, she felt, too, that she had come home. She, Helga Crane, who had no home.

SIX

HELGA WOKE TO THE SOUND OF RAIN. The day was leaden gray, and misty black, and dullish white. She was not surprised, the night had promised it. She made a little frown, remembering that it was today that she was to search for work.

She dressed herself carefully, in the plainest garments she possessed, a suit of fine blue twill faultlessly tailored, from whose left pocket peeped a gay kerchief, an unadorned, heavy silk blouse, a small, smart, fawn-colored hat, and slim, brown oxfords, and chose a brown umbrella. In a near-by street she sought out an appealing little restaurant, which she had noted in her last night's ramble through the neighborhood, for the thick cups and the queer dark silver of the Young Women's Christian Association distressed her.

After a slight breakfast she made her way to the library, that ugly gray building, where was housed much knowledge and a little wisdom, on interminable shelves. The friendly person at the desk in the hall bestowed on her a kindly smile when Helga stated her business and asked for directions.

"The corridor to your left, then the second door to your right," she was told.

Outside the indicated door, for half a second she hesitated, then braced herself and went in. In less than a quarter of an hour she came out, in surprised disappointment. "Library training"— "civil service"—"library school"—"classification"—"cataloguing" —"training class"—"examination"—"probation period"—flitted through her mind.

"How erudite they must be!" she remarked sarcastically to herself, and ignored the smiling curiosity of the desk person as she went through the hall to the street. For a long moment she stood on the high stone steps above the avenue, then shrugged her shoulders and stepped down. It *was* a disappointment, but of course there were other things. She would find something else. But what? Teaching, even substitute teaching, was hopeless now, in March. She had no business training, and the shops didn't employ colored clerks or sales-people, not even the smaller ones. She couldn't sew, she couldn't cook. Well, she *could* do housework, or wait on tables, for a short time at least. Until she got a little money together. With this thought she remembered that the Young Women's Christian Association maintained an employment agency.[1]

"Of course, the very thing!" She exclaimed, aloud. "I'll go straight back."

But, though the day was still drear, rain had ceased to fall, and Helga, instead of returning, spent hours in aimless strolling about the hustling streets of the Loop district.[2] When at last she did retrace her steps, the business day had ended, and the employment office was closed. This frightened her a little, this and the fact that she had spent money, too much money, for a book and a tapestry purse, things which she wanted, but did not need and certainly could not afford. Regretful and dismayed, she resolved to go without her dinner, as a self-inflicted penance, a well as an economy— and she would be at the employment office the first thing tomorrow morning.

But it was not until three days more had passed that Helga Crane sought the Association, or any other employment office. And then it was sheer necessity that drove her there, for her money had dwindled to a ridiculous sum. She had put off the hated moment, had assured herself that she was tired, needed a bit of vacation, was due one. It had been pleasant, the leisure, the walks, the lake, the shops and streets with their gay colors, their movement, after the great quiet of Naxos. Now she was panicky.

In the office a few nondescript women sat scattered about on the long rows of chairs. Some were plainly uninterested, others wore an air of acute expectancy, which disturbed Helga. Behind a desk two alert young women, both wearing a superior air, were busy writing upon and filing countless white cards. Now and then one stopped to answer the telephone.

"Y. W. C. A. employment. . . . Yes. . . . Spell it, please. . . . Sleep in or out? Thirty dollars? . . . Thank you, I'll send one right over."

Or, "I'm awfully sorry, we haven't anybody right now, but I'll send you the first one that comes in."

Their manners were obtrusively business-like, but they ignored the already embarrassed Helga. Diffidently she approached the desk. The darker of the two looked up and turned on a little smile.

"Yes?" she inquired.

"I wonder if you can help me? I want work," Helga stated simply.

"Maybe. What kind? Have you references?"

Helga explained. She was a teacher. A graduate of Devon.[3] Had been teaching in Naxos.

The girl was not interested. "Our kind of work wouldn't do for you," she kept repeating at the end of each of Helga's statements. "Domestic mostly."

When Helga said that she was willing to accept work of any kind, a slight, almost imperceptible change crept into her manner and her perfunctory smile disappeared. She repeated her question about the reference. On learning that Helga had none, she said sharply, finally: "I'm sorry, but we never send out help without references."

With a feeling that she had been slapped, Helga Crane hurried out. After some lunch she sought out an employment agency on State Street.[4] An hour passed in patient sitting. Then came her turn to be interviewed. She said, simply, that she wanted work, work of any kind. A competent young woman, whose eyes stared frog-like from great tortoise-shell-rimmed glasses, regarded her with an appraising look and asked for her history, past and present, not forgetting the "references." Helga told her that she was a graduate of Devon, had taught in Naxos. But even before she arrived at the explanation of the lack of references, the other's interest in her had faded.

"I'm sorry, but we have nothing that you would be interested in," she said and motioned to the next seeker, who immediately came forward, proffering several much worn papers.

"References," thought Helga, resentfully, bitterly, as she went out the door into the crowded garish street in search of another agency, where her visit was equally vain.

Days of this sort of thing. Weeks of it. And of the futile scan-

ning and answering of newspaper advertisements. She traversed
acres of streets, but it seemed that in that whole energetic place
nobody wanted her services. At least not the kind that she offered.
A few men, both white and black, offered her money, but the price
of the money was too dear. Helga Crane did not feel inclined to
pay it.

She began to feel terrified and lost. And she was a little hungry
too, for her small money was dwindling and she felt the need to
economize somehow. Food was the easiest.

In the midst of her search for work she felt horribly lonely too.
This sense of loneliness increased, it grew to appalling proportions, encompassing her, shutting her off from all of life around
her. Devastated she was, and always on the verge of weeping. It
made her feel small and insignificant that in all the climbing
massed city no one cared one whit about her.

Helga Crane was not religious. She took nothing on trust. Nevertheless on Sundays she attended the very fashionable, very high
services in the Negro Episcopal church on Michigan Avenue.[5] She
hoped that some good Christian would speak to her, invite her to
return, or inquire kindly if she was a stranger in the city. None
did, and she became bitter, distrusting religion more than ever. She
was herself unconscious of that faint hint of offishness which
hung about her and repelled advances, an arrogance that stirred
in people a peculiar irritation. They noticed her, admired her
clothes, but that was all, for the self-sufficient uninterested manner adopted instinctively as a protective measure for her acute sensitiveness, in her child days, still clung to her.

An agitated feeling of disaster closed in on her, tightened. Then,
one afternoon, coming in from the discouraging round of agencies
and the vain answering of newspaper wants to the stark neatness
of her room, she found between door and sill a small folded note.
Spreading it open, she read:

Miss Crane:
   Please come into the employment office as soon as you return.
                                                    Ida Ross

Helga spent some time in the contemplation of this note. She
was afraid to hope. Its possibilities made her feel a little hysterical.

Finally, after removing the dirt of the dusty streets, she went down, down to that room where she had first felt the smallness of her commercial value. Subsequent failures had augmented her feeling of incompetence, but she resented the fact that these clerks were evidently aware of her unsuccess. It required all the pride and indifferent hauteur she could summon to support her in their presence. Her additional arrogance passed unnoticed by those for whom it was assumed. They were interested only in the business for which they had summoned her, that of procuring a traveling-companion for a lecturing female on her way to a convention.

"She wants," Miss Ross told Helga, "someone intelligent, someone who can help her get her speeches in order on the train. We thought of you right away. Of course, it isn't permanent. She'll pay your expenses and there'll be twenty-five dollars besides. She leaves tomorrow. Here's her address. You're to go to see her at five o'clock. It's after four now. I'll phone that you're on your way."

The presumptuousness of their certainty that she would snatch at the opportunity galled Helga. She became aware of a desire to be disagreeable. The inclination to fling the address of the lecturing female in their face stirred in her, but she remembered the lone five-dollar bill in the rare old tapestry purse swinging from her arm. She couldn't afford anger. So she thanked them very politely and set out for the home of Mrs. Hayes-Rore on Grand Boulevard,⁶ knowing full well that she intended to take the job, if the lecturing one would take her. Twenty-five dollars was not to be looked at with nose in air when one was the owner of but five. And meals—meals for four days at least.

Mrs. Hayes-Rore proved to be a plump lemon-colored woman with badly straightened hair and dirty finger-nails. Her direct, penetrating gaze was somewhat formidable. Notebook in hand, she gave Helga the impression of having risen early for consultation with other harassed authorities on the race problem, and having been in conference on the subject all day. Evidently, she had had little time or thought for the careful donning of the five-years-behind-the-mode garments which covered her, and which even in their youth could hardly have fitted or suited her. She had a tart personality, and prying. She approved of Helga, after asking her endless questions about her education and her opinions on the race problem, none of which she was permitted to answer, for

Mrs. Hayes-Rore either went on to the next or answered the question herself by remarking: "Not that it matters, if you can only do what I want done, and the girls at the 'Y' said that you could. I'm on the Board of Managers,[7] and I know they wouldn't send me anybody who wasn't all right." After this had been repeated twice in a booming, oratorical voice, Helga felt that the Association secretaries had taken an awful chance in sending a person about whom they knew as little as they did about her.

"Yes, I'm sure you'll do. I don't really need ideas, I've plenty of my own. It's just a matter of getting someone to help me get my speeches in order, correct and condense them, you know. I leave at eleven in the morning. Can you be ready by then? . . . That's good. Better be here at nine. Now, don't disappoint me. I'm depending on you."

As she stepped into the street and made her way skillfully through the impassioned human traffic, Helga reviewed the plan which she had formed, while in the lecturing one's presence, to remain in New York. There would be twenty-five dollars, and perhaps the amount of her return ticket. Enough for a start. Surely she could get work there. Everybody did. Anyway, she would have a reference.

With her decision she felt reborn. She began happily to paint the future in vivid colors. The world had changed to silver, and life ceased to be a struggle and became a gay adventure. Even the advertisements in the shop windows seemed to shine with radiance.

Curious about Mrs. Hayes-Rore, on her return to the "Y" she went into the employment office, ostensibly to thank the girls and to report that that important woman would take her. Was there, she inquired, anything that she needed to know? Mrs. Hayes-Rore had appeared to put such faith in their recommendation of her that she felt almost obliged to give satisfaction. And she added: "I didn't get much chance to ask questions. She seemed so—er—busy."

Both the girls laughed. Helga laughed with them, surprised that she hadn't perceived before how really likable they were.

"We'll be through here in ten minutes. If you're not busy, come in and have your supper with us and we'll tell you about her," promised Miss Ross.

SEVEN

HAVING FINALLY TURNED her attention to Helga Crane, Fortune now seemed determined to smile, to make amends for her shameful neglect. One had, Helga decided, only to touch the right button, to press the right spring, in order to attract the jade's notice.[1]

For Helga that spring had been Mrs. Hayes-Rore. Ever afterwards on recalling that day on which with wellnigh empty purse and apprehensive heart she had made her way from the Young Women's Christian Association to the Grand Boulevard home of Mrs. Hayes-Rore, always she wondered at her own lack of astuteness in not seeing in the woman someone who by a few words was to have a part in the shaping of her life.

The husband of Mrs. Hayes-Rore had at one time been a dark thread in the soiled fabric of Chicago's South Side politics,[2] who, departing this life hurriedly and unexpectedly and a little mysteriously, and somewhat before the whole of his suddenly acquired wealth had had time to vanish, had left his widow comfortably established with money and some of that prestige which in Negro circles had been his. All this Helga had learned from the secretaries at the "Y." And from numerous remarks dropped by Mrs. Hayes-Rore herself she was able to fill in the details more or less adequately.

On the train that carried them to New York, Helga had made short work of correcting and condensing the speeches, which Mrs. Hayes-Rore as a prominent "race" woman and an authority on the problem was to deliver before several meetings of the annual convention of the Negro Women's League of Clubs,[3] convening the next week in New York. These speeches proved to be merely patchworks of others' speeches and opinions. Helga had heard other lecturers say the same things in Devon and again in Naxos. Ideas, phrases, and even whole sentences and paragraphs were lifted bodily from previous orations and published works of Wendell Phillips, Frederick Douglass, Booker T. Washington,[4] and other doctors of the race's ills. For variety Mrs. Hayes-Rore had seasoned hers with a peppery dash of Du Bois[5] and a few vinegary statements of her own. Aside from these it was, Helga reflected, the same old thing.

But Mrs. Hayes-Rore was to her, after the first short, awkward period, interesting. Her dark eyes, bright and investigating, had, Helga noted, a humorous gleam, and something in the way she held her untidy head gave the impression of a cat watching its prey so that when she struck, if she so decided, the blow would be unerringly effective. Helga, looking up from a last reading of the speeches, was aware that she was being studied. Her employer sat leaning back, the tips of her fingers pressed together, her head a bit on one side, her small inquisitive eyes boring into the girl before her. And as the train hurled itself frantically toward smoke-infested Newark, she decided to strike.

"Now tell me," she commanded, "how is it that a nice girl like you can rush off on a wildgoose chase like this at a moment's notice. I should think your people'd object, or'd make inquiries, or something."

At that command Helga Crane could not help sliding down her eyes to hide the anger that had risen in them. Was she to be forever explaining her people—or lack of them? But she said courteously enough, even managing a hard little smile: "Well you see, Mrs. Hayes-Rore, I haven't any people. There's only me, so I can do as I please."

"Ha!" said Mrs. Hayes-Rore.

Terrific, thought Helga Crane, the power of that sound from the lips of this woman. How, she wondered, had she succeeded in investing it with so much incredulity.

"If you didn't have people, you wouldn't be living. Everybody has people, Miss Crane. Everybody."

"*I* haven't, Mrs. Hayes-Rore."

Mrs. Hayes-Rore screwed up her eyes. "Well, that's mighty mysterious, and I detest mysteries." She shrugged, and into those eyes there now came with alarming quickness an accusing criticism.

"It isn't," Helga said defensively, "a mystery. It's a fact and a mighty unpleasant one. Inconvenient too," and she laughed a little, not wishing to cry.

Her tormentor, in sudden embarrassment, turned her sharp eyes to the window. She seemed intent on the miles of red clay sliding past. After a moment, however, she asked gently: "You wouldn't like to tell me about it, would you? It seems to bother you. And I'm interested in girls."

Annoyed, but still hanging, for the sake of the twenty-five dollars, to her self-control, Helga gave her head a little toss and flung out her hands in a helpless, beaten way. Then she shrugged. What did it matter? "Oh, well, if you really want to know. I assure you, it's nothing interesting. Or nasty," she added maliciously. "It's just plain horrid. For me." And she began mockingly to relate her story.

But as she went on, again she had that sore sensation of revolt, and again the torment which she had gone through loomed before her as something brutal and undeserved. Passionately, tearfully, incoherently, the final words tumbled from her quivering petulant lips.

The other woman still looked out of the window, apparently so interested in the outer aspect of the drab sections of the Jersey manufacturing city through which they were passing that, the better to see, she had now so turned her head that only an ear and a small portion of cheek were visible.

During the little pause that followed Helga's recital, the faces of the two women, which had been bare, seemed to harden. It was almost as if they had slipped on masks. The girl wished to hide her turbulent feeling and to appear indifferent to Mrs. Hayes-Rore's opinion of her story. The woman felt that the story, dealing as it did with race intermingling and possibly adultery, was beyond definite discussion. For among black people, as among white people, it is tacitly understood that these things are not mentioned—and therefore they do not exist.

Sliding adroitly out from under the precarious subject to a safer, more decent one, Mrs. Hayes-Rore asked Helga what she was thinking of doing when she got back to Chicago. Had she anything in mind?

Helga, it appeared, hadn't. The truth was she had been thinking of staying in New York. Maybe she could find something there. Everybody seemed to. At least she could make the attempt.

Mrs. Hayes-Rore sighed, for no obvious reason. "Um, maybe I can help you. I know people in New York. Do you?"

"No."

"New York's the lonesomest place in the world if you don't know anybody."

"It couldn't possibly be worse than Chicago," said Helga savagely, giving the table support a violent kick.

They were running into the shadow of the tunnel.[6] Mrs. Hayes-Rore murmured thoughtfully: "You'd better come uptown and stay[7] with me a few days. I may need you. Something may turn up."

It was one of those vicious mornings, windy and bright. There seemed to Helga, as they emerged from the depths of the vast station, to be a whirling malice in the sharp air of this shining city. Mrs. Hayes-Rore's words about its terrible loneliness shot through her mind. She felt its aggressive unfriendliness. Even the great buildings, the flying cabs, and the swirling crowds seemed manifestations of purposed malevolence. And for that first short minute she was awed and frightened and inclined to turn back to that other city, which, though not kind, was yet not strange. This New York seemed somehow more appalling, more scornful, in some inexplicable way even more terrible and uncaring than Chicago. Threatening almost. Ugly. Yes, perhaps she'd better turn back.

The feeling passed, escaped in the surprise of what Mrs. Hayes-Rore was saying. Her oratorical voice boomed above the city's roar. "I suppose I ought really to have phoned Anne from the station. About you, I mean. Well, it doesn't matter. She's got plenty of room. Lives alone in a big house, which is something Negroes in New York don't do. They fill 'em up with lodgers usually. But Anne's funny. Nice, though. You'll like her, and it will be good for you to know her if you're going to stay in New York. She's a widow, my husband's sister's son's wife. The war, you know."[8]

"Oh," protested Helga Crane, with a feeling of acute misgiving, "but won't she be annoyed and inconvenienced by having me brought in on her like this? I supposed we were going to the 'Y' or a hotel or something like that. Oughtn't we really to stop and phone?"

The woman at her side in the swaying cab smiled, a peculiar invincible, self-reliant smile, but gave Helga Crane's suggestion no other attention. Plainly she was a person accustomed to having things her way. She merely went on talking of other plans. "I think maybe I can get you some work. With a new Negro insurance company. They're after me to put quite a tidy sum into it. Well, I'll just tell them that they may as well take you with the money," and she laughed.

"Thanks awfully," Helga said, "but will they like it? I mean being made to take me because of the money."

"They're not being made," contradicted Mrs. Hayes-Rore. "I intended to let them have the money anyway, and I'll tell Mr. Darling so—after he takes you. They ought to be glad to get you. Colored organizations always need more brains as well as more money. Don't worry. And don't thank me again. You haven't got the job yet, you know."

There was a little silence, during which Helga gave herself up to the distraction of watching the strange city and the strange crowds, trying hard to put out of her mind the vision of an easier future which her companion's words had conjured up; for, as had been pointed out, it was, as yet, only a possibility.

Turning out of the park into the broad thoroughfare of Lenox Avenue,[9] Mrs. Hayes-Rore said in a too carefully casual manner: "And, by the way, I wouldn't mention that my people are white, if I were you. Colored people won't understand it, and after all it's your own business. When you've lived as long as I have, you'll know that what others don't know can't hurt you. I'll just tell Anne that you're a friend of mine whose mother's dead. That'll place you well enough and it's all true. I never tell lies. She can fill in the gaps to suit herself and any one else curious enough to ask."

"Thanks," Helga said again. And so great was her gratitude that she reached out and took her new friend's slightly soiled hand in one of her own fastidious ones, and retained it until their cab turned into a pleasant tree-lined street and came to a halt before one of the dignified houses in the center of the block. Here they got out.

In after years Helga Crane had only to close her eyes to see herself standing apprehensively in the small cream-colored hall, the floor of which was covered with deep silver-hued carpet; to see Mrs. Hayes-Rore pecking the cheek of the tall slim creature beautifully dressed in a cool green tailored frock; to hear herself being introduced to "my niece, Mrs. Grey" as "Miss Crane, a little friend of mine whose mother's died, and I think perhaps a while in New York will be good for her"; to feel her hand grasped in quick sympathy, and to hear Anne Grey's pleasant voice, with its faint note of wistfulness, saying: "I'm so sorry, and I'm glad Aunt Jeanette brought you here. Did you have a good trip? I'm sure you must be worn out. I'll have Lillie take you right up." And to feel like a criminal.

EIGHT

A YEAR THICK with various adventures had sped by since that spring day on which Helga Crane had set out away from Chicago's indifferent unkindness for New York in the company of Mrs. Hayes-Rore. New York she had found not so unkind, not so unfriendly, not so indifferent. There she had been happy, and secured work, had made acquaintances and another friend. Again she had had that strange transforming experience, this time not so fleetingly, that magic sense of having come home. Harlem, teeming black Harlem, had welcomed her and lulled her into something that was, she was certain, peace and contentment.

The request and recommendation of Mrs. Hayes-Rore had been sufficient for her to obtain work with the insurance company in which that energetic woman was interested. And through Anne it had been possible for her to meet and to know people with tastes and ideas similar to her own. Their sophisticated cynical talk, their elaborate parties, the unobtrusive correctness of their clothes and homes, all appealed to her craving for smartness, for enjoyment. Soon she was able to reflect with a flicker of amusement on that constant feeling of humiliation and inferiority which had encompassed her in Naxos. Her New York friends looked with contempt and scorn on Naxos and all its works. This gave Helga a pleasant sense of avengement. Any shreds of self-consciousness or apprehension which at first she may have felt vanished quickly, escaped in the keenness of her joy at seeming at last to belong somewhere. For she considered that she had, as she put it, "found herself."

Between Anne Grey and Helga Crane there had sprung one of those immediate and peculiarly sympathetic friendships. Uneasy at first, Helga had been relieved that Anne had never returned to the uncomfortable subject of her mother's death so intentionally mentioned on their first meeting by Mrs. Hayes-Rore, beyond a tremulous brief: "You won't talk to me about it, will you? I can't bear the thought of death. Nobody ever talks to me about it. My husband, you know." This Helga discovered to be true. Later, when she knew Anne better, she suspected that it was a bit of a pose assumed for the purpose of doing away with the necessity of speaking regretfully of a husband who had been perhaps not too greatly loved.

After the first pleasant weeks, feeling that her obligation to Anne was already too great, Helga began to look about for a permanent place to live. It was, she found, difficult. She eschewed the "Y" as too bare, impersonal, and restrictive. Nor did furnished rooms or the idea of a solitary or a shared apartment appeal to her. So she rejoiced when one day Anne, looking up from her book, said lightly: "Helga, since you're going to be in New York, why don't you stay here with me? I don't usually take people. It's too disrupting. Still, it *is* sort of pleasant having somebody in the house and I don't seem to mind you. You don't bore me, or bother me. If you'd like to stay— Think it over."

Helga didn't, of course, require to think it over, because lodgment in Anne's home was in complete accord with what she designated as her "æsthetic sense." Even Helga Crane approved of Anne's house and the furnishings which so admirably graced the big cream-colored rooms. Beds with long, tapering posts to which tremendous age lent dignity and interest, bonneted old highboys, tables that might be by Duncan Phyfe,[1] rare spindle-legged chairs, and others whose ladder backs gracefully climbed the delicate wall panels. These historic things mingled harmoniously and comfortably with brass-bound Chinese tea-chests, luxurious deep chairs and davenports,[2] tiny tables of gay color, a lacquered jade-green settee with gleaming black satin cushions, lustrous Eastern rugs, ancient copper, Japanese prints,[3] some fine etchings, a profusion of precious bric-a-brac, and endless shelves filled with books.

Anne Grey herself was, as Helga expressed it, "almost too good to be true." Thirty, maybe, brownly beautiful, she had the face of a golden Madonna, grave and calm and sweet, with shining black hair and eyes. She carried herself as queens are reputed to bear themselves, and probably do not. Her manners were as agreeably gentle as her own soft name. She possessed an impeccably fastidious taste in clothes, knowing what suited her and wearing it with

an air of unconscious assurance. The unusual thing, a native New
Yorker, she was also a person of distinction, financially independent, well connected and much sought after. And she was interesting, an odd confusion of wit and intense earnestness; a vivid and
remarkable person. Yes, undoubtedly, Anne was almost too good
to be true. She was almost perfect.

Thus established, secure, comfortable, Helga soon became
thoroughly absorbed in the distracting interests of life in New
York. Her secretarial work with the Negro insurance company
filled her day. Books, the theater, parties, used up the nights.
Gradually in the charm of this new and delightful pattern of her
life she lost that tantalizing oppression of loneliness and isolation
which always, it seemed, had been a part of her existence.

But, while the continuously gorgeous panorama of Harlem
fascinated her, thrilled her, the sober mad rush of white New
York failed entirely to stir her. Like thousands of other Harlem
dwellers, she patronized its shops, its theaters, its art galleries, and
its restaurants, and read its papers, without considering herself a
part of the monster. And she was satisfied, unenvious. For her this
Harlem was enough. Of that white world, so distant, so near, she
asked only indifference. No, not at all did she crave, from those
pale and powerful people, awareness. Sinister folk, she considered
them, who had stolen her birthright. Their past contribution to
her life, which had been but shame and grief, she had hidden away
from brown folk in a locked closet, "never," she told herself, "to
be reopened."

Some day she intended to marry one of those alluring brown or
yellow men who danced attendance on her. Already financially
successful, any one of them could give to her the things which she
had now come to desire, a home like Anne's, cars of expensive
makes such as lined the avenue, clothes and furs from Bendel's and
Revillon Frères',[4] servants, and leisure.

Always her forehead wrinkled in distaste whenever, involuntarily, which was somehow frequently, her mind turned on the speculative gray eyes and visionary uplifting plans of Dr. Anderson.
That other, James Vayle, had slipped absolutely from her consciousness. Of him she never thought. Helga Crane meant, now,
to have a home and perhaps laughing, appealing dark-eyed children in Harlem. Her existence was bounded by Central Park,

Fifth Avenue, St. Nicholas Park, and One Hundred and Forty-fifth Street.[5] Not at all a narrow life, as Negroes live it, as Helga Crane knew it. Everything was there, vice and goodness, sadness and gayety, ignorance and wisdom, ugliness and beauty, poverty and richness. And it seemed to her that somehow of goodness, gayety, wisdom, and beauty always there was a little more than of vice, sadness, ignorance, and ugliness. It was only riches that did not quite transcend poverty.

"But," said Helga Crane, "what of that? Money isn't everything. It isn't even the half of everything. And here we have so much else—and by ourselves. It's only outside of Harlem among those others that money really counts for everything."

In the actuality of the pleasant present and the delightful vision of an agreeable future she was contended, and happy. She did not analyze this contentment, this happiness, but vaguely, without putting it into words or even so tangible a thing as a thought, she knew it sprang from a sense of freedom, a release from the feeling of smallness which had hedged her in, first during her sorry, unchildlike childhood among hostile white folk in Chicago, and later during her uncomfortable sojourn among snobbish black folk in Naxos.

NINE

BUT IT DIDN'T LAST, this happiness of Helga Crane's.

Little by little the signs of spring appeared, but strangely the enchantment of the season, so enthusiastically, so lavishly greeted by the gay dwellers of Harlem, filled her only with restlessness. Somewhere, within her, in a deep recess, crouched discontent. She began to lose confidence in the fullness of her life, the glow began to fade from her conception of it. As the days multiplied, her need of something, something vaguely familiar, but which she could not put a name to and hold for definite examination, became almost intolerable. She went through moments of overwhelming anguish. She felt shut in, trapped. "Perhaps I'm tired, need a tonic, or something," she reflected. So she consulted a physician, who, after a long, solemn examination, said that there was nothing wrong, nothing at all. "A change of scene, perhaps for a week or so, or a few days away from work," would put her straight most likely. Helga tried this, tried them both, but it was no good. All interest had gone out of living. Nothing seemed any good. She became a little frightened, and then shocked to discover that, for some unknown reason, it was of herself she was afraid.

Spring grew into summer, languidly at first, then flauntingly. Without awareness on her part, Helga Crane began to draw away from those contacts which had so delighted her. More and more she made lonely excursions to places outside of Harlem. A sensation of estrangement and isolation encompassed her. As the days became hotter and the streets more swarming, a kind of repulsion came upon her. She recoiled in aversion from the sight of the grinning faces and from the sound of the easy laughter of all these people who strolled, aimlessly now, it seemed, up and down the avenues. Not only did the crowds of nameless folk on the street annoy her, she began also actually to dislike her friends.

Even the gentle Anne distressed her. Perhaps because Anne was obsessed by the race problem and fed her obsession. She frequented all the meetings of protest, subscribed to all the complaining magazines, and read all the lurid newspapers spewed out by the Negro yellow press.[1] She talked, wept, and ground her teeth dramatically about the wrongs and shames of her race. At times she lashed her fury to surprising heights for one by nature so placid and gentle. And, though she would not, even to herself, have admitted it, she reveled in this orgy of protest.

"Social equality," "Equal opportunity for all," were her slogans, often and emphatically repeated. Anne preached these things and honestly thought that she believed them, but she considered it an affront to the race, and to all the vari-colored peoples that made Lenox and Seventh Avenues the rich spectacles which they were,[2] for any Negro to receive on terms of equality any white person.

"To me," asserted Anne Grey, "the most wretched Negro prostitute that walks One Hundred and Thirty-fifth Street[3] is more than any president of these United States, not excepting Abraham Lincoln."[4] But she turned up her finely carved nose at their lusty churches, their picturesque parades, their naïve clowning on the streets. She would not have desired or even have been willing to live in any section outside the black belt, and she would have refused scornfully, had they been tendered, any invitation from white folk. She hated white people with a deep and burning hatred, with the kind of hatred which, finding itself held in sufficiently numerous groups, was capable some day, on some great provocation, of bursting into dangerously malignant flames.

But she aped their clothes, their manners, and their gracious ways of living. While proclaiming loudly the undiluted good of all things Negro, she yet disliked the songs, the dances, and the softly blurred speech of the race. Toward these things she showed only a disdainful contempt, tinged sometimes with a faint amusement. Like the despised people of the white race, she preferred Pavlova to Florence Mills, John McCormack to Taylor Gordon, Walter Hampden to Paul Robeson.[5] Theoretically, however, she stood for the immediate advancement of all things Negroid, and was in revolt against social inequality.

Helga had been entertained by this racial ardor in one so little affected by racial prejudice as Anne, and by her inconsistencies. But suddenly these things irked her with a great irksomeness and

she wanted to be free of this constant prattling of the incon-
gruities, the injustices, the stupidities, the viciousness of white
people. It stirred memories, probed hidden wounds, whose poignant ache bred in her surprising oppression and corroded the
fabric of her quietism. Sometimes it took all her self-control to
keep from tossing sarcastically at Anne Ibsen's remark about there
being assuredly something very wrong with the drains, but after
all there were other parts of the edifice.[6]

It was at this period of restiveness that Helga met again Dr. Anderson. She was gone, unwillingly, to a meeting, a health meeting,
held in a large church[7]—as were most of Harlem's uplift activities—as a substitute for her employer, Mr. Darling. Making her
tardy arrival during a tedious discourse by a pompous saffron-
hued physician, she was led by the irritated usher, whom she had
roused from a nap in which he had been pleasantly freed from the
intricacies of Negro health statistics, to a very front seat. Complete
silence ensued while she subsided into her chair. The offended
doctor looked at the ceiling, at the floor, and accusingly at Helga,
and finally continued his lengthy discourse. When at last he had
ended and Helga had dared to remove her eyes from his sweating
face and look about, she saw with a sudden thrill that Robert Anderson was among her nearest neighbors. A peculiar, not wholly
disagreeable, quiver ran down her spine. She felt an odd little
faintness. The blood rushed to her face. She tried to jeer at herself
for being so moved by the encounter.

He, meanwhile, she observed, watched her gravely. And having
caught her attention, he smiled a little and nodded.

When all who so desired had spouted to their hearts' content—
if to little purpose—and the meeting was finally over, Anderson
detached himself from the circle of admiring friends and acquaintances that had gathered around him and caught up with Helga
half-way down the long aisle leading out to fresher air.

"I wondered if you were really going to cut me. I see you
were," he began, with that half-quizzical smile which she remembered so well.

She laughed. "Oh, I didn't think you'd remember me." Then
she added: "Pleasantly, I mean."

The man laughed too. But they couldn't talk yet. People kept
breaking in on them. At last, however, they were at the door, and

then he suggested that they share a taxi "for the sake of a little breeze." Helga assented.

Constraint fell upon them when they emerged into the hot street, made seemingly hotter by a low-hanging golden moon and the hundreds of blazing electric lights. For a moment, before hailing a taxi, they stood together looking at the slow moving mass of perspiring human beings. Neither spoke, but Helga was conscious of the man's steady gaze. The prominent gray eyes were fixed upon her, studying her, appraising her. Many times since turning her back on Naxos she had in fancy rehearsed this scene, this re-encounter. Now she found that rehearsal helped not at all. It was so absolutely different from anything that she had imagined.

In the open taxi they talked of impersonal things, books, places, the fascination of New York, of Harlem. But underneath the exchange of small talk lay another conversation of which Helga Crane was sharply aware. She was aware, too, of a strange ill-defined emotion, a vague yearning rising within her. And she experienced a sensation of consternation and keen regret when with a lurching jerk the cab pulled up before the house in One Hundred and Thirty-ninth Street.[8] So soon, she thought.

But she held out her hand calmly, coolly. Cordially she asked him to call some time. "It is," she said, "a pleasure to renew our acquaintance." Was it, she was wondering, merely an acquaintance?

He responded seriously that he too thought it a pleasure, and added: "You haven't changed. You're still seeking for something, I think."

At his speech there dropped from her that vague feeling of yearning, that longing for sympathy and understanding which his presence evoked. She felt a sharp stinging sensation and a recurrence of that anger and defiant desire to hurt which had so seared her on that past morning in Naxos. She searched for a biting remark, but, finding none venomous enough, she merely laughed a little rude and scornful laugh and, throwing up her small head, bade him an impatient good-night and ran quickly up the steps.

Afterwards she lay for long hours without undressing, thinking angry self-accusing thoughts, recalling and reconstructing that other explosive contact. That memory filled her with a sort of aching delirium. A thousand indefinite longings beset her. Eagerly she desired to see him again to right herself in his thoughts. Far into the night she lay planning speeches for their next meeting, so that it was long before drowsiness advanced upon her.

When he did call, Sunday, three days later, she put him off on Anne and went out, pleading an engagement, which until then she had not meant to keep. Until the very moment of his entrance she had had no intention of running away, but something, some imp of contumacy, drove her from his presence, though she longed to stay. Again abruptly had come the uncontrollable wish to wound. Later, with a sense of helplessness and inevitability, she realized that the weapon which she had chosen had been a boomerang, for she herself had felt the keen disappointment of the denial. Better to have stayed and hurled polite sarcasms at him. She might then at least have had the joy of seeing him wince.

In this spirit she made her way to the corner and turned into Seventh Avenue. The warmth of the sun, though gentle on that afternoon, had nevertheless kissed the street into marvelous light and color. Now and then, greeting an acquaintance, or stopping to chat with a friend, Helga was all the time seeing its soft shining brightness on the buildings along its sides or on the gleaming bronze, gold, and copper faces of its promenaders. And another vision, too, came haunting Helga Crane; level gray eyes set down in a brown face which stared out at her, coolly, quizzically, disturbingly. And she was not happy.

The tea to which she had so suddenly made up her mind to go she found boring beyond endurance, insipid drinks, dull conversation, stupid men. The aimless talk glanced from John Wellinger's lawsuit for discrimination because of race against a downtown restaurant[9] and the advantages of living in Europe, especially in France,[10] to the significance, if any, of the Garvey movement.[11] Then it sped to a favorite Negro dancer who had just then secured a foothold on the stage of a current white musical comedy, to other shows, to a new book touching on Negroes. Thence to costumes for a coming masquerade dance, to a new jazz song, to Yvette Dawson's engagement to a Boston lawyer who had seen her one night at a party and proposed to her the next day at noon. Then back again to racial discrimination.

Why, Helga wondered, with unreasoning exasperation, didn't they find something else to talk of? Why must the race problem always creep in? She refused to go on to another gathering. It would, she thought, be simply the same old thing.

On her arrival home she was more disappointed than she cared to admit to find the house in darkness and even Anne gone off somewhere. She would have liked that night to have talked with Anne. Get her opinion of Dr. Anderson.

Anne it was who the next day told her that he had given up his work in Naxos; or rather that Naxos had given him up. He had been too liberal, too lenient, for education as it was inflicted in Naxos. Now he was permanently in New York, employed as welfare worker by some big manufacturing concern, which gave employment to hundreds of Negro men.

"Uplift," sniffed Helga contemptuously, and fled before the onslaught of Anne's harangue on the needs and ills of the race.

TEN

WITH THE WANING SUMMER the acute sensitiveness of Helga Crane's frayed nerves grew keener. There were days when the mere sight of the serene tan and brown faces about her stung her like a personal insult. The care-free quality of their laughter roused in her the desire to scream at them: "Fools, fools! Stupid fools!" This passionate and unreasoning protest gained in intensity, swallowing up all else like some dense fog. Life became for her only a hateful place where one lived in intimacy with people one would not have chosen had one been given choice. It was, too, an excruciating agony. She was continually out of temper: Anne, thank the gods! was away, but her nearing return filled Helga with dismay.

Arriving at work one sultry day, hot and dispirited, she found waiting a letter, a letter from Uncle Peter. It had originally been sent to Naxos, and from there it had made the journey back to Chicago to the Young Women's Christian Association, and then to Mrs. Hayes-Rore. That busy woman had at last found time between conventions and lectures to readdress it and had sent it on to New York. Four months, at least, it had been on its travels. Helga felt no curiosity as to its contents, only annoyance at the long delay, as she ripped open the thin edge of the envelope, and for a space sat staring at the peculiar foreign script of her uncle.

715 Sheridan Road[1]
Chicago, Ill.

Dear Helga:

It is now over a year since you made your unfortunate call here. It was unfortunate for us all, you, Mrs. Nilssen, and myself. But of course you couldn't know. I blame myself. I should have written you of my marriage.

I have looked for a letter, or some word from you; evidently, with your usual penetration, you understood thoroughly that I must terminate my outward relation with you. You were always a keen one.

Of course I am sorry, but it can't be helped. My wife must be considered, and she feels very strongly about this.

You know, of course, that I wish you the best of luck. But take an old man's advice and don't do as your mother did. Why don't you run over and visit your Aunt Katrina? She always wanted you. Maria Kirkeplads, No. 2,[2] will find her.

I enclose what I intended to leave you at my death. It is better and more convenient that you get it now. I wish it were more, but even this little may come in handy for a rainy day.

Best wishes for your luck.

Peter Nilssen

Beside the brief, friendly, but none the less final, letter there was a check for five thousand dollars. Helga Crane's first feeling was one of unreality. This changed almost immediately into one of relief, of liberation. It was stronger than the mere security from present financial worry which the check promised. Money as money was still not very important to Helga. But later, while on an errand in the big general office of the society, her puzzled bewilderment fled. Here the inscrutability of the dozen or more brown faces, all cast from the same indefinite mold, and so like her own, seemed pressing forward against her. Abruptly it flashed upon her that the harrowing irritation of the past weeks was a smoldering hatred. Then, she was overcome by another, so actual, so sharp, so horribly painful, that forever afterwards she preferred to forget it. It was as if she were shut up, boxed up, with hundreds of her race, closed up with that something in the racial character which had always been, to her, inexplicable, alien. Why, she demanded in fierce rebellion, should she be yoked to these despised black folk?

Back in the privacy of her own cubicle, self-loathing came upon her. "They're my own people, my own people," she kept repeating over and over to herself. It was no good. The feeling would not be routed. "I can't go on like this," she said to herself. "I simply can't."

There were footsteps. Panic seized her. She'd have to get out. She terribly needed to. Snatching hat and purse, she hurried to the narrow door, saying in a forced, steady voice, as it opened to reveal her employer: "Mr. Darling, I'm sorry, but I've got to go out. Please, may I be excused?"

At his courteous "Certainly, certainly. And don't hurry. It's much too hot," Helga Crane had the grace to feel ashamed, but there was no softening of her determination. The necessity for being alone was too urgent. She hated him and all the others too much.

Outside, rain had begun to fall. She walked bare-headed, bitter with self-reproach. But she rejoiced too. She didn't, in spite of her racial markings, belong to these dark segregated people. She was different. She felt it. It wasn't merely a matter of color. It was something broader, deeper, that made folk kin.

And now she was free. She would take Uncle Peter's money and advice and revisit her aunt in Copenhagen. Fleeting pleasant memories of her childhood visit there flew through her excited mind. She had been only eight, yet she had enjoyed the interest and the admiration which her unfamiliar color and dark curly hair, strange to those pink, white, and gold people, had evoked. Quite clearly now she recalled that her Aunt Katrina had begged for her to be allowed to remain. Why, she wondered, hadn't her mother consented? To Helga it seemed that it would have been the solution to all their problems, her mother's her stepfather's, her own.

At home in the cool dimness of the big chintz-hung living-room, clad only in a fluttering thing of green chiffon,[3] she gave herself up to day-dreams of a happy future in Copenhagen, where there were no Negroes, no problems, no prejudice, until she remembered with perturbation that this was the day of Anne's return from her vacation at the sea-shore. Worse. There was a dinner-party in her honor that very night. Helga sighed. She'd have to go. She couldn't possibly get out of a dinner-party for Anne, even though she felt that such an event on a hot night was little short of an outrage. Nothing but a sense of obligation to Anne kept her from pleading a splitting headache as an excuse for remaining quietly at home.

Her mind trailed off to the highly important matter of clothes. What should she wear? White? No, everybody would, because it was hot. Green? She shook her head, Anne would be sure to. The blue thing. Reluctantly she decided against it; she loved it, but she had worn it too often. There was that cobwebby black net touched with orange, which she had bought last spring in a fit of extravagance and never worn, because on getting it home both she and Anne had considered it too *décolleté*, and too *outré*.[4] Anne's words: "There's not enough of it, and what there is gives you the air of something about to fly," came back to her, and she smiled as she decided that she would certainly wear the black net. For her it would be a symbol. She was about to fly.

She busied herself with some absurdly expensive roses which she had ordered sent in, spending an interminable time in their arrangement. At last she was satisfied with their appropriateness in some blue Chinese jars of great age. Anne *did* have such lovely things, she thought, as she began conscientiously to prepare for her return, although there was really little to do; Lillie seemed to have done everything. But Helga dusted the tops of the books, placed the magazines in ordered carelessness, redressed Anne's bed in fresh-smelling sheets of cool linen, and laid out her best pale-yellow pajamas of *crêpe de Chine*.[5] Finally she set out two tall green glasses and made a great pitcher of lemonade, leaving only the ginger-ale and claret to be added on Anne's arrival. She was a little conscience-stricken, so she wanted to be particularly nice to Anne, who had been so kind to her when first she came to New York, a forlorn friendless creature. Yes, she was grateful to Anne; but, just the same, she meant to go. At once.

Her preparations over, she went back to the carved chair from which the thought of Anne's home-coming had drawn her. Characteristically she writhed at the idea of telling Anne of her impending departure and shirked the problem of evolving a plausible and inoffensive excuse for its suddenness. "That," she decided lazily, "will have to look out for itself; I can't be bothered just now. It's too hot."

She began to make plans and to dream delightful dreams of change, of life somewhere else. Some place where at last she would be permanently satisfied. Her anticipatory thoughts waltzed and eddied about to the sweet silent music of change. With rapture almost, she let herself drop into the blissful sensation of visualizing herself in different, strange places, among approving and admiring people, where she would be appreciated, and understood.

IT WAS NIGHT. The dinner-party was over, but no one wanted to go home. Half-past eleven was, it seemed, much too early to tumble into bed on a Saturday night. It was a sulky, humid night, a thick furry night, through which the electric torches shone like silver fuzz—an atrocious night for cabareting,[1] Helga insisted, but the others wanted to go, so she went with them, though half unwillingly. After much consultation and chatter they decided upon a place and climbed into two patiently waiting taxis, rattling things which jerked, wiggled, and groaned, and threatened every minute to collide with others of their kind, or with inattentive pedestrians. Soon they pulled up before a tawdry doorway in a narrow crosstown street and stepped out. The night was far from quiet, the streets far from empty. Clanging trolley bells, quarreling cats, cackling phonographs, raucous laughter, complaining motorhorns, low singing, mingled in the familiar medley that is Harlem. Black figures, white figures, little forms, big forms, small groups, large groups, sauntered, or hurried by. It was gay, grotesque, and a little weird. Helga Crane felt singularly apart from it all. Entering the waiting doorway, they descended through a furtive, narrow passage, into a vast subterranean room.[2] Helga smiled, thinking that this was one of those places characterized by the righteous as a hell.

A glare of light struck her eyes, a blare of jazz split her ears. For a moment everything seemed to be spinning round; even she felt that she was circling aimlessly, as she followed with the others the black giant who led them to a small table, where, when they were seated, their knees and elbows touched. Helga wondered that the waiter, indefinitely carved out of ebony, did not smile as he wrote their order—"four bottles of White Rock,[3] four bottles of ginger-ale." Bah! Anne giggled, the others smiled and openly exchanged knowing glances, and under the tables flat glass bottles were ex-

tracted from the women's evening scarfs and small silver flasks
drawn from the men's hip pockets. In a little moment she grew accustomed to the smoke and din.

They danced, ambling lazily to a crooning melody, or violently
twisting their bodies, like whirling leaves, to a sudden streaming
rhythm, or shaking themselves ecstatically to a thumping of un-
seen tomtoms. For the while, Helga was oblivious of the reek of
flesh, smoke, and alcohol, oblivious of the oblivion of other gyrat-
ing pairs, oblivious of the color, the noise, and the grand distorted
childishness of it all. She was drugged, lifted, sustained, by the ex-
traordinary music, blown out, ripped out, beaten out, by the joyous, wild, murky orchestra. The essence of life seemed bodily
motion. And when suddenly the music died, she dragged herself
back to the present with a conscious effort; and a shameful certainty that not only had she been in the jungle, but that she had
enjoyed it, began to taunt her. She hardened her determination to
get away. She wasn't, she told herself, a jungle creature.[4] She
cloaked herself in a faint disgust as she watched the entertainers
throw themselves about to the bursts of syncopated jangle, and
when the time came again for the patrons to dance, she declined.
Her rejected partner excused himself and sought an acquaintance a
few tables removed. Helga sat looking curiously about her as the
buzz of conversation ceased, strangled by the savage strains of
music, and the crowd became a swirling mass. For the hundredth
time she marveled at the gradations within this oppressed race of
hers. A dozen shades slid by. There was sooty black, shiny black,
taupe, mahogany, bronze, copper, gold, orange, yellow, peach,
ivory, pinky white, pastry white. There was yellow hair, brown
hair, black hair; straight hair, straightened hair, curly hair, crinkly
hair, woolly hair. She saw black eyes in white faces, brown eyes in
yellow faces, gray eyes in brown faces, blue eyes in tan faces.
Africa, Europe, perhaps with a pinch of Asia, in a fantastic motley
of ugliness and beauty, semi-barbaric, sophisticated, exotic, were
here. But she was blind to its charm, purposely aloof and a little
contemptuous, and soon her interest in the moving mosaic waned.

She had discovered Dr. Anderson sitting at a table on the far
side of the room, with a girl in a shivering apricot frock. Seriously
he returned her tiny bow. She met his eyes, gravely smiling, then
blushed, furiously, and averted her own. But they went back im-

mediately to the girl beside him, who sat indifferently sipping a colorless liquid from a high glass, or puffing a precariously hanging cigarette. Across dozens of tables, littered with corks, with ashes, with shriveled sandwiches, through slits in the swaying mob, Helga Crane studied her.

She was pale, with a peculiar, almost deathlike pallor. The brilliantly red, softly curving mouth was somehow sorrowful. Her pitch-black eyes, a little aslant, were veiled by long, drooping lashes and surmounted by broad brows, which seemed like black smears. The short dark hair was brushed severely back from the wide forehead. The extreme *décolleté* of her simple apricot dress showed a skin of unusual color, a delicate, creamy hue, with golden tones. "Almost like an alabaster," thought Helga.

Bang! Again the music died. The moving mass broke, separated. The others returned. Anne had rage in her eyes. Her voice trembled as she took Helga aside to whisper: "There's your Dr. Anderson over there, with Audrey Denney."

"Yes, I saw him. She's lovely. Who is she?"

"She's Audrey Denney, as I said, and she lives downtown.[5] West Twenty-second Street. Hasn't much use for Harlem any more. It's a wonder she hasn't some white man hanging about. The disgusting creature! I wonder how she inveigled Anderson? But that's Audrey! If there is any desirable man about, trust her to attach him. She ought to be ostracized."

"Why?" asked Helga curiously, noting at the same time that three of the men in their own party had deserted and were now congregated about the offending Miss Denney.

"Because she goes about with white people," came Anne's indignant answer, "and they know she's colored."

"I'm afraid I don't quite see, Anne. Would it be all right if they didn't know she was colored?"

"Now, don't be nasty, Helga. You know very well what I mean." Anne's voice was shaking. Helga didn't see, and she was greatly interested, but she decided to let it go. She didn't want to quarrel with Anne, not now, when she had that guilty feeling about leaving her. But Anne was off on her favorite subject, race. And it seemed, too, that Audrey Denney was to her particularly obnoxious.

"Why, she gives parties for white and colored people together.

And she goes to white people's parties. It's worse than disgusting, it's positively obscene."

"Oh, come, Anne, you haven't been to any of the parties, I know, so how can you be so positive about the matter?"

"No, but I've heard about them. I know people who've been."

"Friends of yours, Anne?"

Anne admitted that they were, some of them.

"Well, then, they can't be so bad. I mean, if your friends sometimes go, can they? Just what goes on that's so terrible?"

"Why, they drink, for one thing. Quantities, they say."

"So do we, at the parties here in Harlem," Helga responded. An idiotic impulse seized her to leave the place, Anne's presence, then, forever. But of course she couldn't. It would be foolish, and so ugly.

"And the white men dance with the colored women. Now you know, Helga Crane, that can mean only one thing." Anne's voice was trembling with cold hatred. As she ended, she made a little clicking noise with her tongue, indicating an abhorrence too great for words.

"Don't the colored men dance with the white women, or do they sit about, impolitely, while the other men dance with their women?" inquired Helga very softly, and with a slowness approaching almost to insolence. Anne's insinuations were too revolting. She had a slightly sickish feeling, and a flash of anger touched her. She mastered it and ignored Anne's inadequate answer.

"It's the principle of the thing that I object to. You can't get round the fact that her behavior is outrageous, treacherous, in fact. That's what's the matter with the Negro race. They won't stick together. She certainly ought to be ostracized. I've nothing but contempt for her, as has every other self-respecting Negro."

The other women and the lone man left to them—Helga's own escort—all seemingly agreed with Anne. At any rate, they didn't protest. Helga gave it up. She felt that it would be useless to tell them that what she felt for the beautiful, calm, cool girl who had the assurance, the courage, so placidly to ignore racial barriers and give her attention to people, was not contempt, but envious admiration. So she remained silent, watching the girl.

At the next first sound of music Dr. Anderson rose. Languidly the girl followed his movement, a faint smile parting her sorrowful lips at some remark he made. Her long, slender body swayed with an eager pulsing motion. She danced with grace and abandon, gravely, yet with obvious pleasure, her legs, her hips, her back, all swaying gently, swung by that wild music from the heart of the jungle. Helga turned her glance to Dr. Anderson. Her disinterested curiosity passed. While she still felt for the girl envious admiration, that feeling was now augmented by another, a more primitive emotion. She forgot the garish crowded room. She forgot her friends. She saw only two figures, closely clinging. She felt her heart throbbing. She felt the room receding. She went out the door. She climbed endless stairs. At last, panting, confused, but thankful to have escaped, she found herself again out in the dark night alone, a small crumpled thing in a fragile, flying black and gold dress. A taxi drifted toward her, stopped. She stepped into it, feeling cold, unhappy, misunderstood, and forlorn.

TWELVE

Helga Crane felt no regret as the cliff-like towers[1] faded. The sight thrilled her as beauty, grandeur, of any kind always did, but that was all.

The liner drew out from churning slate-colored waters of the river into the open sea. The small seething ripples on the water's surface became little waves. It was evening. In the western sky was a pink and mauve light, which faded gradually into a soft gray-blue obscurity. Leaning against the railing, Helga stared into the approaching night, glad to be at last alone, free of that great super-fluity of human beings, yellow, brown, and black, which, as the torrid summer burnt to its close, had so oppressed her. No, she hadn't belonged there. Of her attempt to emerge from that inherent aloneness which was part of her very being, only dullness had come, dullness and a great aversion.

Almost at once it was time for dinner. Somewhere a bell sounded. She turned and with buoyant steps went down. Already she had begun to feel happier. Just for a moment, outside the dining-salon, she hesitated, assailed with a tiny uneasiness which passed as quickly as it had come. She entered softly, unobtrusively. And, after all, she had had her little fear for nothing. The purser, a man grown old in the service of the Scandinavian-American Line,[2] remembered her as the little dark girl who had crossed with her mother years ago, and so she must sit at his table. Helga liked that. It put her at her ease and made her feel important.

Everyone was kind in the delightful days which followed, and her first shyness under the politely curious glances of turquoise eyes of her fellow travelers soon slid from her. The old forgotten Danish of her childhood began to come, awkwardly at first, from her lips, under their agreeable tutelage. Evidently they were interested, curious, and perhaps a little amused about this Negro girl on her way to Denmark alone.

Helga was a good sailor, and mostly the weather was lovely with the serene calm of the lingering September summer, under whose sky the sea was smooth, like a length of watered silk, unruffled by the stir of any wind. But even the two rough days found her on deck, reveling like a released bird in her returned feeling of happiness and freedom, that blessed sense of belonging to herself alone and not to a race. Again, she had put the past behind her with an ease which astonished even herself. Only the figure of Dr. Anderson obtruded itself with surprising vividness to irk her because she could get no meaning from that keen sensation of covetous exasperation that had so surprisingly risen within her on the night of the cabaret party. This question Helga Crane recognized as not entirely new; it was but a revival of the puzzlement experienced when she had fled so abruptly from Naxos more than a year before. With the recollection of that previous flight and subsequent half-questioning a dim disturbing notion came to her. She wasn't, she couldn't be, in love with the man. It was a thought too humiliating, and so quickly dismissed. Nonsense! Sheer nonsense! When one is in love, one strives to please. Never, she decided, had she made an effort to be pleasing to Dr. Anderson. On the contrary, she had always tried, deliberately, to irritate him. She was, she told herself, a sentimental fool.

Nevertheless, the thought of love stayed with her, not prominent, definite; but shadowy, incoherent. And in a remote corner of her consciousness lurked the memory of Dr. Anderson's serious smile and gravely musical voice.

On the last morning Helga rose at dawn, a dawn outside old Copenhagen. She lay lazily in her long chair watching the feeble sun creeping over the ship's great green funnels with sickly light; watching the purply gray sky change to opal, to gold, to pale blue. A few other passengers, also early risen, excited by the prospect of renewing old attachments, of glad home-comings after long years, paced nervously back and forth. Now, at the last moment, they were impatient, but apprehensive fear, too, had its place in their rushing emotions. Impatient Helga Crane was not. But she *was* apprehensive. Gradually, as the ship drew into the lazier waters of the dock, she became prey to sinister fears and memories. A deep pang of misgiving nauseated her at the thought of her aunt's husband, acquired since Helga's childhood visit. Painfully, vividly, she remembered the frightened anger of Uncle Peter's new wife, and looking back at her precipitate departure from America, she was amazed at her own stupidity. She had not even considered the remote possibility that her aunt's husband might be like Mrs. Nilssen. For the first time in nine days she wished herself back in New York, in America.

The little gulf of water between the ship and the wharf lessened. The engines had long ago ceased their whirring, and now the buzz of conversation, too, died down. There was a sort of silence. Soon the welcoming crowd on the wharf stood under the shadow of the great sea-monster, their faces turned up to the anxious ones of the passengers who hung over the railing. Hats were taken off, hand-kerchiefs were shaken out and frantically waved. Chatter. Deaf-ening shouts. A little quiet weeping. Sailors and laborers were yelling and rushing about. Cables were thrown. The gangplank was laid.

Silent, unmoving, Helga Crane stood looking intently down into the gesticulating crowd. Was anyone waving to her? She couldn't tell. She didn't in the least remember her aunt, save as a hazy pretty lady. She smiled a little at the thought that her aunt, or anyone waiting there in the crowd below, would have no diffi-culty in singling her out. But—had she been met? When she de-scended the gangplank she was still uncertain and was trying to decide on a plan of procedure in the event that she had not. A telegram before she went through the customs? Telephone? A taxi?

But, again, she had all her fears and questionings for nothing. A smart woman in olive-green came toward her at once. And, even in the fervent gladness of her relief, Helga took in the carelessly trailing purple scarf and correct black hat that completed the per-fection of her aunt's costume, and had time to feel herself a little shabbily dressed. For it was her aunt; Helga saw that at once, the resemblance to her own mother was unmistakable. There was the same long nose, the same beaming blue eyes, the same straying pale-brown hair so like sparkling beer. And the tall man with the fierce mustache who followed carrying hat and stick must be Herr Dahl,[3] Aunt Katrina's husband. How gracious he was in his wel-

come, and how anxious to air his faulty English, now that her aunt
had finished kissing her and exclaimed in Danish: "Little Helga!
Little Helga! Goodness! But how you have grown!"

Laughter from all three.

"Welcome to Denmark, to Copenhagen, to our home," said
the new uncle in queer, proud, oratorical English. And to Helga's
smiling, grateful "Thank you," he returned: "Your trunks? Your
checks?" also in English, and then lapsed into Danish.

"Where in the world are the Fishers? We must hurry the customs."

Almost immediately they were joined by a breathless couple, a
young gray-haired man and a fair, tiny, doll-like woman. It devel-
oped that they had lived in England for some years and so spoke
English, real English, well. They were both breathless, all apolo-
gies and explanations.

"So early!" sputtered the man, Herr Fisher, "We inquired last
night and they said nine. It was only by accident that we called
again this morning to be sure. Well, you can imagine the rush we
were in when they said eight! And of course we had trouble in
finding a cab. One always does if one is late." All this in Danish.
Then to Helga in English: "You see, I was especially asked to
come because Fru Dahl didn't know if you remembered your
Danish, and your uncle's English—well—"

More laughter.

At last, the customs having been hurried and a cab secured,
they were off, with much chatter, through the toy-like streets,
weaving perilously in and out among the swarms of bicycles.

It had begun, a new life for Helga Crane.

THIRTEEN

SHE LIKED IT, this new life. For a time it blotted from her mind
all else. She took to luxury as the proverbial duck to water. And
she took to admiration and attention even more eagerly.

It was pleasant to wake on that first afternoon, after the
insisted-upon nap, with that sensation of lavish contentment and
well-being enjoyed only by impecunious sybarites[1] waking in the
houses of the rich. But there was something more than mere contentment and well-being. To Helga Crane it was the realization of
a dream that she had dreamed persistently ever since she was old
enough to remember such vague things as day-dreams and longings. Always she had wanted, not money, but the things which
money could give, leisure, attention, beautiful surroundings.
Things. Things. Things.

So it was more than pleasant, it was important, this awakening
in the great high room which held the great high bed on which she
lay, small but exalted. It was important because to Helga Crane it
was the day, so she decided, to which all the sad forlorn past had
led, and from which the whole future was to depend. This, then,
was where she belonged. This was her proper setting. She felt con-
soled at last for the spiritual wounds of the past.

A discreet knocking on the tall paneled door sounded. In response to Helga's "Come in" a respectful rosy-faced maid entered
and Helga lay for a long minute watching her adjust the shutters.
She was conscious, too, of the girl's sly curious glances at her, although her general attitude was quite correct, willing and disinterested. In New York, America, Helga would have resented this sly
watching. Now, here, she was only amused. Marie, she reflected,
had probably never seen a Negro outside the pictured pages of her
geography book.[2]

Another knocking. Aunt Katrina entered, smiling at Helga's
quick, lithe spring from the bed. They were going out to tea, she

informed Helga. What, the girl inquired, did one wear to tea in
Copenhagen, meanwhile glancing at her aunt's dark purple dress
and bringing forth a severely plain blue *crêpe* frock. But no! It
seemed that that wouldn't at all do.

"Too sober," pronounced Fru Dahl. "Haven't you something
lively, something bright?" And, noting Helga's puzzled glance at
her own subdued costume, she explained laughingly: "Oh, I'm an
old married lady, and a Dane. But you, you're young. And you're
a foreigner, and different. You must have bright things to set off
the color of your lovely brown skin. Striking things, exotic things.
You must make an impression."

"I've only these," said Helga Crane, timidly displaying her
wardrobe on couch and chairs. "Of course I intend to buy here. I
didn't want to bring over too much that might be useless."

"And you were quite right too. Umm. Let's see. That black
there, the one with the cerise and purple trimmings. Wear that."

Helga was shocked. "But for tea, Aunt! Isn't it too gay? Too—
too—*outré?*"

"Oh dear, no. Not at all, not for you. Just right." Then after a
little pause she added: "And we're having people in to dinner
tonight, quite a lot. Perhaps we'd better decide on our frocks
now." For she was, in spite of all her gentle kindness, a woman
who left nothing to chance. In her own mind she had determined
the role that Helga was to play in advancing the social fortunes of
the Dahls of Copenhagen, and she meant to begin at once.

At last, after much trying on and scrutinizing, it was decided
that Marie should cut a favorite emerald-green velvet dress a little
lower in the back and add some gold and mauve flowers, "to liven
it up a bit," as Fru Dahl put it.

"Now that," she said, pointing to the Chinese red dressing-
gown in which Helga had wrapped herself when at last the fitting
was over, "suits you. Tomorrow we'll shop. Maybe we can get
something that color. That black and orange thing there is good
too, but too high. What a prim American maiden you are, Helga,
to hide such a fine back and shoulders. Your feet are nice too, but
you ought to have higher heels—and buckles."

Left alone, Helga began to wonder. She was dubious, too, and
not a little resentful. Certainly she loved color with a passion that
perhaps only Negroes and Gypsies know. But she had a deep faith

in the perfection of her own taste, and no mind to be bedecked in flaunting flashy things. Still—she had to admit that Fru Dahl was right about the dressing-gown. It did suit her. Perhaps an evening dress. And she knew that she had lovely shoulders, and her feet *were* nice.

When she was dressed in the shining black taffeta with its bizarre trimmings of purple and cerise, Fru Dahl approved her and so did Herr Dahl. Everything in her responded to his "She's beautiful; beautiful!" Helga Crane knew she wasn't that, but it pleased her that he could think so, and say so. Aunt Katrina smiled in her quiet, assured way, taking to herself her husband's compliment to her niece. But a little frown appeared over the fierce mustache, as he said, in his precise, faintly feminine voice: "She ought to have earrings, long ones. Is it too late for Garborg's? We could call up."

And call up they did. And Garborg, the jeweler, in Fredericksgaarde³ waited for them. Not only were earrings bought, long ones brightly enameled, but glittering shoe-buckles and two great bracelets. Helga's sleeves being long, she escaped the bracelets for the moment. They were wrapped to be worn that night. The earrings, however, and the buckles came into immediate use and Helga felt like a veritable savage as they made their leisurely way across the pavement from the shop to the waiting motor. This feeling was intensified by the many pedestrians who stopped to stare at the queer dark creature, strange to their city. Her cheeks reddened, but both Herr and Fru Dahl seemed oblivious of the stares or the audible whispers in which Helga made out the one frequently recurring word "*sorte*," which she recognized as the Danish word for "black."

Her Aunt Katrina merely remarked: "A high color becomes you, Helga. Perhaps tonight a little rouge—" To which her husband nodded in agreement and stroked his mustache meditatively. Helga Crane said nothing.

They were pleased with the success she was at the tea, or rather the coffee—for no tea was served—and later at dinner. Helga herself felt like nothing so much as some new and strange species of pet dog being proudly exhibited. Everyone was very polite and very friendly, but she felt the massed curiosity and interest, so discreetly hidden under the polite greetings. The very atmosphere was tense with it. "As if I had horns, or three legs," she thought. She was really nervous and a little terrified, but managed to present an outward smiling composure. This was assisted by the fact that it was taken for granted that she knew nothing or very little of the language. So she had only to bow and look pleasant. Herr and Fru Dahl did the talking, answered the questions. She came away from the coffee feeling that she had acquitted herself well in the first skirmish. And, in spite of the mental strain, she had enjoyed her prominence.

If the afternoon had been a strain, the evening was something more. It was more exciting too. Marie had indeed "cut down" the prized green velvet, until, as Helga put it, it was "practically nothing but a skirt." She was thankful for the barbaric bracelets, for the dangling earrings, for the beads about her neck. She was even thankful for the rouge on her burning cheeks and for the very powder on her back. No other woman in the stately pale-blue room was so greatly exposed. But she liked the small murmur of wonder and admiration which rose when Uncle Poul brought her in. She liked the compliments in the men's eyes as they bent over her hand. She liked the subtle half-understood flattery of her dinner partners. The women too were kind, feeling no need for jealousy. To them this girl, this Helga Crane, this mysterious niece of the Dahls, was not to be reckoned seriously in their scheme of things. True, she was attractive, unusual, in an exotic, almost savage way, but she wasn't one of them. She didn't at all count.

Near the end of the evening, as Helga sat effectively posed on a red satin sofa, the center of an admiring group, replying to questions about America and her trip over, in halting, inadequate Danish, there came a shifting of the curious interest away from herself. Following the others' eyes, she saw that there had entered the room a tallish man with a flying mane of reddish blond hair. He was wearing a great black cape, which swung gracefully from his huge shoulders, and in his long, nervous hand he held a wide soft hat. An artist, Helga decided at once, taking in the broad streaming tie. But how affected! How theatrical!

With Fru Dahl he came forward and was presented. "Herr Olsen, Herr Axel Olsen." To Helga Crane that meant nothing. The man, however, interested her. For an imperceptible second he bent over her hand. After that he looked intently at her for what seemed to her an incredibly rude length of time from under his heavy drooping lids. At last, removing his stare of startled satisfaction, he wagged his leonine head approvingly.

"Yes, you're right. She's amazing. Marvelous," he muttered.

Everyone else in the room was deliberately not staring. About Helga there sputtered a little staccato murmur of manufactured conversation. Meanwhile she could think of no proper word of greeting to the outrageous man before her. She wanted, very badly, to laugh. But the man was as unaware of her omission as of her desire. His words flowed on and on, rising and rising. She tried to follow, but his rapid Danish eluded her. She caught only words, phrases, here and there. "Superb eyes . . . color . . . neck column . . . yellow . . . hair . . . alive . . . wonderful. . . ." His speech was for Fru Dahl. For a bit longer he lingered before the silent girl, whose smile had become a fixed aching mask, still gazing appraisingly, but saying no word to her, and then moved away with Fru Dahl, talking rapidly and excitedly to her and her husband, who joined them for a moment at the far side of the room. Then he was gone as suddenly as he had come.

"Who is he?" Helga put the question timidly to a hovering young army officer, a very smart captain just back from Sweden. Plainly he was surprised.

"Herr Olsen, Herr Axel Olsen, the painter. Portraits, you know."

"Oh," said Helga, still mystified.

"I guess he's going to paint you. You're lucky. He's queer. Won't do everybody."

"Oh, no. I mean, I'm sure you're mistaken. He didn't ask, didn't say anything about it."

The young man laughed. "Ha ha! That's good! He'll arrange that with Herr Dahl. He evidently came just to see you, and it was plain that he was pleased." He smiled, approvingly.

"Oh," said Helga again. Then at last she laughed. It was too funny. The great man hadn't addressed a word to her. Here she was, a curiosity, a stunt, at which people came and gazed. And was she to be treated like a secluded young miss, a Danish *frøkken*,[4] not to be consulted personally even on matters affecting her per-

sonally? She, Helga Crane, who almost all her life had looked after
herself, was she now to be looked after by Aunt Katrina and her
husband? It didn't seem real.

It was late, very late, when finally she climbed into the great
bed after having received an auntly kiss. She lay long awake reviewing the events of the crowded day. She was happy again. Happiness covered her like the lovely quilts under which she rested.
She was mystified too. Her aunt's words came back to her.
"You're young and a foreigner and—and different." Just what did
that mean, she wondered. Did it mean that the difference was
to be stressed, accented? Helga wasn't so sure that she liked
that. Hitherto all her efforts had been toward similarity to those
about her.

"How odd," she thought sleepily, "and how different from
America!"

FOURTEEN

THE YOUNG OFFICER had been right in his surmise. Axel Olsen was going to paint Helga Crane. Not only was he going to paint her, but he was to accompany her and her aunt on their shopping expedition. Aunt Katrina was frankly elated. Uncle Poul was also visibly pleased. Evidently they were not above kotowing to a lion. Helga's own feelings were mixed; she was amused, grateful, and vexed. It had all been decided and arranged without her, and, also, she was a little afraid of Olsen. His stupendous arrogance awed her.

The day was an exciting, not easily to be forgotten one. Definitely, too, it conveyed to Helga her exact status in her new environment. A decoration. A curio. A peacock. Their progress through the shops was an event; an event for Copenhagen as well as for Helga Crane. Her dark, alien appearance was to most people an astonishment. Some stared surreptitiously, some openly, and some stopped dead in front of her in order more fully to profit by their stares. *"Den Sorte"* dropped freely, audibly, from many lips.[1]

The time came when she grew used to the stares of the population. And the time came when the population of Copenhagen grew used to her outlandish presence and ceased to stare. But at the end of that first day it was with thankfulness that she returned to the sheltering walls of the house on Maria Kirkeplads.

They were followed by numerous packages, whose contents all had been selected or suggested by Olsen and paid for by Aunt Katrina. Helga had only to wear them. When they were opened and the things spread out upon the sedate furnishings of her chamber, they made a rather startling array. It was almost in a mood of rebellion that Helga faced the fantastic collection of garments incongruously laid out in the quaint, stiff, pale old room. There were batik dresses[2] in which mingled indigo, orange, green, vermilion, and black; dresses of velvet and chiffon in screaming colors, blood-red, sulphur-yellow, sea-green; and one black and white thing in striking combination. There was a black Manila shawl[3] strewn with great scarlet and lemon flowers, a leopard-skin coat, a glittering opera-cape. There were turban-like hats of metallic silks, feathers and furs, strange jewelry, enameled or set with odd semi-precious stones, a nauseous Eastern perfume, shoes with danger-ously high heels. Gradually Helga's perturbation subsided in the unusual pleasure of having so many new and expensive clothes at one time. She began to feel a little excited, incited.

Incited. That was it, the guiding principle of her life in Copen-hagen. She was incited to make an impression, a voluptuous im-pression. She was incited to inflame attention and admiration. She was dressed for it, subtly schooled for it. And after a little while she gave herself up wholly to the fascinating business of being seen, gaped at, desired. Against the solid background of Herr Dahl's wealth and generosity she submitted to her aunt's arrange-ment of her life to one end, the amusing one of being noticed and flattered. Intentionally she kept to the slow, faltering Danish. It was, she decided, more attractive than a nearer perfection. She grew used to the extravagant things with which Aunt Katrina chose to dress her. She managed, too, to retain that air of remote-ness which had been in America so disastrous to her friendships. Here in Copenhagen it was merely a little mysterious and added another clinging wisp of charm.

Helga Crane's new existence was intensely pleasant to her; it gratified her augmented sense of self-importance. And it suited her. She had to admit that the Danes had the right idea. To each his own milieu. Enhance what was already in one's possession. In America Negroes sometimes talked loudly of this, but in their hearts they repudiated it. In their lives too. They didn't want to be like themselves. What they wanted, asked for, begged for, was to be like their white overloads. They were ashamed to be Negroes, but not ashamed to beg to be something else. Something inferior. Not quite genuine. Too bad!

Helga Crane didn't, however, think often of America, excepting in unfavorable contrast to Denmark. For she had resolved never to return to the existence of ignominy which the New World of op-portunity and promise forced upon Negroes. How stupid she had

been ever to have thought that she could marry and perhaps have
children in a land where every dark child was handicapped at the
start by the shroud of color! She saw, suddenly, the giving birth to
little, helpless, unprotesting Negro children as a sin, an unforgiv-
able outrage. More black folk to suffer indignities. More dark
bodies for mobs to lynch. No, Helga Crane didn't think often of
America. It was too humiliating, too disturbing. And she wanted
to be left to the peace which had come to her. Her mental difficulties and questionings had become simplified. She now believed
sincerely that there was a law of compensation, and that sometimes it worked. For all those early desolate years she now felt
recompensed. She recalled a line that had impressed her in her
lonely school-days, "The far-off interest of tears."

To her, Helga Crane, it had come at last, and she meant to cling
to it. So she turned her back on painful America, resolutely shutting out the griefs, the humiliations, the frustrations, which she
had endured there.

Her mind was occupied with other and nearer things.

The charm of the old city itself, with its odd architectural mixture of medievalism and modernity, and the general air of well-
being which pervaded it, impressed her. Even in the so-called poor
sections there was none of that untidiness and squalor which she
remembered as the accompaniment of poverty in Chicago, New
York, and the Southern cities of America. Here the door-steps
were always white from constant scrubbings, the women neat, and
the children washed and provided with whole clothing. Here were
no tatters and rags, no beggars. But, then, begging, she learned,
was an offense punishable by law. Indeed, it was unnecessary in a
country where everyone considered it a duty somehow to support
himself and his family by honest work; or, if misfortune and ill-
ness came upon one, everyone else, including the State, felt bound
to give assistance, a lift on the road to the regaining of independence.

After the initial shyness and consternation at the sensation
caused by her strange presence had worn off, Helga spent hours
driving or walking about the city, at first in the protecting company of Uncle Poul or Aunt Katrina or both, or sometimes Axel
Olsen. But later, when she had become a little familiar with the
city, and its inhabitants a little used to her, and when she had

learned to cross the streets in safety, dodging successfully the in-numerable bicycles like a true Copenhagener, she went often alone, loitering on the long bridge which spanned the placid lakes, or watching the pageant of the blue-clad, sprucely tailored soldiers in the daily parade at Amalienborg Palace,[4] or in the historic vicin-ity of the long, low-lying Exchange,[5] a picturesque structure in picturesque surroundings, skirting as it did the great canal, which always was alive with many small boats, flying broad white sails and pressing close on the huge ruined pile of the Palace of Chris-tiansborg.[6] There was also the Gammelstrand,[7] the congregating-place of the venders of fish, where daily was enacted a spirited and interesting scene between sellers and buyers, and where Helga's appearance always roused lively and audible, but friendly, interest, long after she became in other parts of the city an accepted curios-ity. Here it was that one day an old countrywoman asked her to what manner of mankind she belonged and at Helga's replying: "I'm a Negro," had become indignant, retorting angrily that, just because she was old and a countrywoman she could not be so eas-ily fooled, for she knew as well as everyone else that Negroes were black and had woolly hair.

Against all this walking the Dahls had at first uttered mild protest. "But, Aunt dear, I have to walk, or I'll get fat," Helga as-serted. "I've never, never in all my life, eaten so much." For the accepted style of entertainment in Copenhagen seemed to be a round of dinner-parties, at which it was customary for the hostess to tax the full capacity not only of her dining-room, but of her guests as well. Helga enjoyed these dinner-parties, as they were usually spirited affairs, the conversation brilliant and witty, often in several languages. And always she came in for a goodly measure of flattering attention and admiration.

There were, too, those popular afternoon gatherings for the ex-press purpose of drinking coffee together, where between much talk, interesting talk, one sipped the strong and steaming beverage from exquisite cups fashioned of Royal Danish porcelain[8] and par-took of an infinite variety of rich cakes and smørrebrød.[9] This smørrebrød, dainty sandwiches of an endless and tempting ar-ray, was distinctly a Danish institution. Often Helga wondered just how many of these delicious sandwiches she had consumed since setting foot on Denmark's soil. Always, wherever food was served, appeared the inevitable *smørrebrød*, in the home of the Dahls, in every other home that she visited, in hotels, in restaurants.

At first she had missed, a little, dancing, for, though excellent dancers, the Danes seemed not to care a great deal for that pastime, which so delightfully combines exercise and pleasure. But in the winter there was skating, solitary, or in gay groups. Helga liked this sport, though she was not very good at it. There were, however, always plenty of efficient and willing men to instruct and to guide her over the glittering ice. One could, too, wear such attractive skating-things.

But mostly it was with Axel Olsen that her thoughts were occupied. Brilliant, bored, elegant, urbane, cynical, worldly, he was a type entirely new to Helga Crane, familiar only, and that but little, with the restricted society of American Negroes. She was aware, too, that this amusing, if conceited, man was interested in her. They were, because he was painting her, much together. Helga spent long mornings in the eccentric studio opposite the Folkemuseum,[10] and Olsen came often to the Dahl home, where, as Helga and the man himself knew, he was something more than welcome. But in spite of his expressed interest and even delight in her exotic appearance, in spite of his constant attendance upon her, he gave no sign of the more personal kind of concern which—encouraged by Aunt Katrina's mild insinuations and Uncle Poul's subtle questionings—she had tried to secure. Was it, she wondered, race that kept him silent, held him back. Helga Crane frowned on this thought, putting it furiously from her, because it disturbed her sense of security and permanence in her new life, pricked her self-assurance.

Nevertheless she was startled when on a pleasant afternoon while drinking coffee in the Hotel Vivili,[11] Aunt Katrina mentioned, almost casually, the desirability of Helga's making a good marriage.

"Marriage, Aunt dear!"

"Marriage," firmly repeated her aunt, helping herself to another anchovy and olive sandwich. "You are," she pointed out, "twenty-five."

"Oh, Aunt, I couldn't! I mean, there's nobody here for me to marry." In spite of herself and her desire not to be, Helga was shocked.

"Nobody?" There was, Fru Dahl asserted, Captain Frederick Skaargaard—and very handsome he was too—and he would have money. And there was Herr Hans Tietgen, not so handsome, of course, but clever and a good business man; he too would be rich, very rich, some day. And there was Herr Karl Pedersen, who had a good berth with the Landmands-bank and considerable shares in a prosperous cement-factory at Aalborg.[12] There was, too, Christian Lende, the young owner of the new Odin Theater.[13] Any of these Helga might marry, was Aunt Katrina's opinion. "And," she added, "others." Or maybe Helga herself had some ideas.

Helga had. She didn't, she responded, believe in mixed marriages, "between races, you know." They brought only trouble—to the children—as she herself knew but too well from bitter experience.

Fru Dahl thoughtfully lit a cigarette. Eventually, after a satisfactory glow had manifested itself, she announced: "Because your mother was a fool. Yes, she was! If she'd come home after she married, or after you were born, or even after your father—er—went off like that, it would have been different. If even she'd left you when she was here. But why in the world she should have married again, and a person like that, I can't see. She wanted to keep you, she insisted on it, even over his protest, I think. She loved you so much, she said.—And so she made you unhappy. Mothers, I suppose, are like that. Selfish. And Karen was always stupid. If you've got any brains at all they came from your father."

Into this Helga would not enter. Because of its obvious partial truths she felt the need for disguising caution. With a detachment that amazed herself she asked if Aunt Katrina didn't think, really, that miscegenation was wrong, in fact as well as principle.

"Don't," was her aunt's reply, "be a fool too, Helga. We don't think of those things here. Not in connection with individuals, at least." And almost immediately she inquired: "Did you give Herr Olsen my message about dinner tonight?"

"Yes, Aunt." Helga was cross, and trying not to show it.

"He's coming?"

"Yes, Aunt," with precise politeness.

"What about him?"

"I don't know. *What* about him?"

"He likes you?"

"I don't know. How can I tell that?" Helga asked with irritating reserve, her concentrated attention on the selection of a sandwich. She had a feeling of nakedness. Outrage.

Now Fru Dahl was annoyed and showed it. "What nonsense! Of course you know. Any girl does," and her satin-covered foot tapped, a little impatiently, the old tiled floor.

"Really, I don't know, Aunt," Helga responded in a strange voice, a strange manner, coldly formal, levelly courteous. Then suddenly contrite, she added: "Honestly, I don't. I can't tell a thing about him," and fell into a little silence. "Not a thing," she repeated. But the phrase, though audible, was addressed to no one. To herself.

She looked out into the amazing orderliness of the street. Instinctively she wanted to combat this searching into the one thing which, here, surrounded by all other things which for so long she had so positively wanted, made her a little afraid. Started vague premonitions.

Fru Dahl regarded her intently. It would be, she remarked with a return of her outward casualness, by far the best of all possibilities. Particularly desirable. She touched Helga's hand with her fingers in a little affectionate gesture. Very lightly.

Helga Crane didn't immediately reply. There was, she knew, so much reason—from one viewpoint—in her aunt's statement. She could only acknowledge it. "I know that," she told her finally. Inwardly she was admiring the cool, easy way in which Aunt Katrina had brushed aside the momentary acid note of the conversation and resumed her customary pitch. It took, Helga thought, a great deal of security. Balance.

"Yes," she was saying, while leisurely lighting another of those long, thin, brown cigarettes which Helga knew from distressing experience to be incredibly nasty tasting, "it would be the ideal thing for you, Helga." She gazed penetratingly into the masked face of her niece and nodded, as though satisfied with what she saw there. "And you of course realize that you are a very charming and beautiful girl. Intelligent too. If you put your mind to it, there's no reason in the world why you shouldn't—" Abruptly she stopped, leaving her implication at once suspended and clear. Behind her there were footsteps. A small gloved hand appeared on her shoulder. In the short moment before turning to greet Fru Fischer she said quietly, meaningly: "Or else stop wasting your time, Helga."

Helga Crane said: "Ah, Fru Fischer. It's good to see you." She meant it. Her whole body was tense with suppressed indignation. Burning inside like the confined fire of a hot furnace. She was so harassed that she smiled in self-protection. And suddenly she was oddly cold. An intimation of things distant, but none the less disturbing, oppressed her with a faintly sick feeling. Like a heavy weight, a stone weight, just where, she knew, was her stomach.

Fru Fischer was late. As usual. She apologized profusely. Also as usual. And, yes, she would have some coffee. And some *smørrebrød*. Though she must say that the coffee here at the Vivili was atrocious. Simply atrocious. "I don't see how you stand it." And the place was getting so common, always so many Bolsheviks and Japs and things.[14] And she didn't—"begging your pardon, Helga"—like that hideous American music[15] they were forever playing, even if it was considered very smart. "Give me," she said, "the good old-fashioned Danish melodies of Gade and Heise.[16] Which reminds me, Herr Olsen says that Nielsen's "Helios" is being performed with great success just now in England.[17] But I suppose you know all about it, Helga. He's already told you. What?" This last was accompanied with an arch and insinuating smile.

A shrug moved Helga Crane's shoulders. Strange she'd never before noticed what a positively disagreeable woman Fru Fischer was. Stupid, too.

FIFTEEN

WELL INTO HELGA'S SECOND YEAR in Denmark, came an indefinite discontent. Not clear, but vague, like a storm gathering far on the horizon. It was long before she would admit that she was less happy than she had been during her first year in Copenhagen, but she knew that it was so. And this subconscious knowledge added to her growing restlessness and little mental insecurity. She desired ardently to combat this wearing down of her satisfaction with her life, with herself. But she didn't know how.

Frankly the question came to this: what was the matter with her? Was there, without her knowing it, some peculiar lack in her? Absurd. But she began to have a feeling of discouragement and hopelessness. Why couldn't she be happy, content, somewhere? Other people managed, somehow, to be. To put it plainly, didn't she know how? Was she incapable of it?

And then on a warm spring day came Anne's letter telling of her coming marriage to Anderson, who retained still his shadowy place in Helga Crane's memory. It added, somehow, to her discontent, and to her growing dissatisfaction with her peacock's life. This, too, annoyed her.

What, she asked herself, was there about that man which had the power always to upset her? She began to think back to her first encounter with him. Perhaps if she hadn't come away— She laughed. Derisively. "Yes, if I hadn't come away, I'd be stuck in Harlem. Working every day of my life. Chattering about the race problem."

Anne, it seemed, wanted her to come back for the wedding. This, Helga had no intention of doing. True, she had liked and admired Anne better than anyone she had ever known, but even for her she wouldn't cross the ocean.

Go back to America, where they hated Negroes! To America, where Negroes were not people. To America, where Negroes

83

were allowed to be beggars only, of life, of happiness, of security. To America, where everything had been taken from those dark ones, liberty, respect, even the labor of their hands. To America, where if one had Negro blood, one mustn't expect money, education, or, sometimes, even work whereby one might earn bread. Perhaps she was wrong to bother about it now that she was so far away. Helga couldn't, however, help it. Never could she recall the shames and often the absolute horrors of the black man's existence in America without the quickening of her heart's beating and a sensation of disturbing nausea. It was too awful. The sense of dread of it was almost a tangible thing in her throat.

And certainly she wouldn't go back for any such idiotic reason as Anne's getting married to that offensive Robert Anderson. Anne was really too amusing. Just why, she wondered, and how had it come about that he was being married to Anne? And why did Anne, who had so much more than so many others—more than enough—want Anderson too? Why couldn't she—"I think," she told herself, "I'd better stop. It's none of my business. I don't care in the least. Besides," she added irrelevantly, "I hate such nonsensical soul-searching."

One night not long after the arrival of Anne's letter with its curious news, Helga went with Olsen and some other young folk to the great Circus,¹ a vaudeville house, in search of amusement on a rare off night. After sitting through several numbers they reluctantly arrived at the conclusion that the whole entertainment was dull, unutterably dull, and apparently without alleviation, and so not to be borne. They were reaching for their wraps when out upon the stage pranced two black men, American Negroes undoubtedly, for as they danced and cavorted, they sang in the English of America an old rag-time song that Helga remembered hearing as a child, "Everybody Gives Me Good Advice."² At its conclusion the audience applauded with delight. Only Helga Crane was silent, motionless.

More songs, old, all of them old, but new and strange to that audience. And how the singers danced, pounding their thighs, slapping their hands together, twisting their legs, waving their abnormally long arms, throwing their bodies about with a loose ease! And how the enchanted spectators clapped and howled and shouted for more!

Helga Crane was not amused. Instead she was filled with a fierce hatred for the cavorting Negroes on the stage. She felt shamed, betrayed, as if these pale pink and white people among whom she lived had suddenly been invited to look upon something in her which she had hidden away and wanted to forget. And she was shocked at the avidity at which Olsen beside her drank it in.

But later, when she was alone, it became quite clear to her that all along they had divined its presence, had known that in her was something, some characteristic, different from any that they themselves possessed. Else why had they decked her out as they had? Why subtly indicated that she was different? And they hadn't despised it. No, they had admired it, rated it as a precious thing, a thing to be enhanced, preserved. Why? She, Helga Crane, didn't admire it. She suspected that no Negroes, no Americans, did. Else why their constant slavish imitation of traits not their own? Why their constant begging to be considered as exact copies of other people? Even the enlightened, the intelligent ones demanded nothing more. They were all beggars like the motley crowd in the old nursery-rhyme:

> Hark! Hark!
> The dogs do bark.
> The beggars are coming to town.
> Some in rags,
> Some in tags,
> And some in velvet gowns.[3]

The incident left her profoundly disquieted. Her old unhappy questioning mood came again upon her, insidiously stealing away more of the contentment from her transformed existence.

But she returned again and again to the Circus, always alone, gazing intently and solemnly at the gesticulating black figures, an ironical and silently speculative spectator. For she knew that into her plan for her life had thrust itself a suspensive conflict in which were fused doubts, rebellion, expediency, and urgent longings.

It was at this time that Axel Olsen asked her to marry him. And now Helga Crane was surprised. It was a thing that at one time she had much wanted, had tried to bring about, and had at last relinquished as impossible of achievement. Not so much because of its apparent hopelessness as because of a feeling, intangible almost, that, excited and pleased as he was with her, her origin a little repelled him, and that, prompted by some impulse of racial antagonism, he had retreated into the fastness of a protecting habit of self-ridicule. A mordantly personal pride and sensitiveness deterred Helga from further efforts at incitation.

True, he had made, one morning, while holding his brush poised for a last, a very last stroke on the portrait, one admirably draped suggestion, speaking seemingly to the pictured face. Had he insinuated marriage, or something less—and easier? Or had he paid her only a rather florid compliment, in somewhat dubious taste? Helga, who had not at the time been quite sure, had remained silent, striving to appear unhearing.

Later, having thought it over, she flayed herself for a fool. It wasn't, she should have known, in the manner of Axel Olsen to pay florid compliments in questionable taste. And had it been marriage that he had meant, he would, of course, have done the proper thing. He wouldn't have stopped—or, rather, have begun—by making his wishes known to her when there was Uncle Poul to be formally consulted. She had been, she told herself, insulted. And a goodly measure of contempt and wariness was added to her interest in the man. She was able, however, to feel a gratifying sense of elation in the remembrance that she had been silent, ostensibly unaware of his utterance, and therefore, as far as he knew, not affronted.

This simplified things. It did away with the quandary in which the confession to the Dahls of such a happening would have involved her, for she couldn't be sure that they, too, might not put it down to the difference of her ancestry. And she could still go attended by him, and envied by others, to openings in Kongen's Nytorv,[4] to showings at the Royal Academy or Charlottenborg's Palace.[5] He could still call for her and Aunt Katrina of an afternoon or go with her to Magasin du Nord[6] to select a scarf or a length of silk, of which Uncle Poul could say casually in the presence of interested acquaintances: "Um, pretty scarf"—or "frock"—"you're wearing, Helga. Is that the new one Olsen helped you with?"

Her outward manner toward him changed not at all, save

that gradually she became, perhaps, a little more detached and indifferent. But definitely Helga Crane had ceased, even remotely,
to consider him other than as someone amusing, desirable, and
convenient to have about—if one was careful. She intended,
presently, to turn her attention to one of the others. The decorative Captain of the Hussars,[7] perhaps. But in the ache of her growing nostalgia, which, try as she might, she could not curb, she no
longer thought with any seriousness on either Olsen or Captain
Skaargaard. She must, she felt, see America again first. When she
returned—

Therefore, where before she would have been pleased and
proud at Olsen's proposal, she was now truly surprised. Strangely,
she was aware also of a curious feeling of repugnance, as her eyes
slid over his face, as smiling, assured, with just the right note of
fervor, he made his declaration and request. She was astonished.
Was it possible? Was it really this man that she had thought, even
wished, she could marry?

He was, it was plain, certain of being accepted, as he was always
certain of acceptance, of adulation, in any and every place that he
deigned to honor with his presence. Well, Helga was thinking, that
wasn't as much his fault as her own, her aunt's, everyone's. He was
spoiled, childish almost.

To his words, once she had caught their content and recovered
from her surprise, Helga paid not much attention. They would,
she knew, be absolutely appropriate ones, and they didn't at all
matter. They meant nothing to her—now. She was too amazed to
discover suddenly how intensely she disliked him, disliked the
shape of his head, the mop of his hair, the line of his nose, the
tones of his voice, the nervous grace of his long fingers; disliked
even the very look of his irreproachable clothes. And for some inexplicable reason, she was a little frightened and embarrassed, so
that when he had finished speaking, for a short space there was
only stillness in the small room, into which Aunt Katrina had tactfully had him shown. Even Thor, the enormous Persian, curled on
the window ledge in the feeble late afternoon sun, had rested
for the moment from his incessant purring under Helga's idly
stroking fingers.

Helga, her slight agitation vanished, told him that she was surprised. His offer was, she said, unexpected. Quite.

A little sardonically, Olsen interrupted her. He smiled too. "But of course I expected surprise. It is, is it not, the proper thing? And always you are proper, Frøkken Helga, always."

Helga, who had a stripped, naked feeling under his direct glance, drew herself up stiffly. Herr Olsen needn't, she told him, be sarcastic. She *was* surprised. He must understand that she was being quite sincere, quite truthful about that. Really, she hadn't expected him to do her so great an honor.

He made a little impatient gesture. Why, then, had she refused, ignored, his other, earlier suggestion?

At that Helga Crane took a deep indignant breath and was again, this time for an almost imperceptible second, silent. She had, then, been correct in her deduction. Her sensuous, petulant mouth hardened. That he should so frankly—so insolently, it seemed to her—admit his outrageous meaning was too much. She said, coldly: "Because, Herr Olsen, in my country the men, of my race, at least, don't make such suggestions to decent girls. And thinking that you were a gentleman, introduced to me by my aunt, I chose to think myself mistaken, to give you the benefit of the doubt."

"Very commendable, my Helga—and wise. Now you have your reward. Now I offer you marriage."

"Thanks," she answered, "thanks, awfully."

"Yes," and he reached for her slim cream hand, now lying quiet on Thor's broad orange and black back. Helga let it lie in his large pink one, noting their contrast. "Yes, because I, poor artist that I am, cannot hold out against the deliberate lure of you. You disturb me. The longing for you does harm to my work. You creep into my brain and madden me," and he kissed the small ivory hand. Quite decorously, Helga thought, for one so maddened that he was driven, against his inclination, to offer her marriage. But immediately, in extenuation, her mind leapt to the admirable casualness of Aunt Katrina's expressed desire for this very thing, and recalled the unruffled calm of Uncle Poul under any and all circumstances. It was, as she had long ago decided, security. Balance.

"But," the man before her was saying, "for me it will be an experience. It may be that with you, Helga, for wife, I will become great. Immortal. Who knows? I didn't want to love you, but I had

to. That is the truth. I make of myself a present to you. For love."
His voice held a theatrical note. At the same time he moved forward putting out his arms. His hands touched air. For Helga had moved back. Instantly he dropped his arms and took a step away, repelled by something suddenly wild in her face and manner. Sitting down, he passed a hand over his face with a quick, graceful gesture.

Tameness returned to Helga Crane. Her ironic gaze rested on the face of Axel Olsen, his leonine head, his broad nose—"broader than my own"—his bushy eyebrows, surmounting thick, drooping lids, which hid, she knew, sullen blue eyes. He stirred sharply, shaking off his momentary disconcertion.

In his assured, despotic way he went on: "You know, Helga, you are a contradiction. You have been, I suspect, corrupted by the good Fru Dahl, which is perhaps as well. Who knows? You have the warm impulsive nature of the women of Africa, but, my lovely, you have, I fear, the soul of a prostitute. You sell yourself to the highest buyer. I should of course be happy that it is I. And I am." He stopped, contemplating her, lost apparently, for the second, in pleasant thoughts of the future.

To Helga he seemed to be the most distant, the most unreal figure in the world. She suppressed a ridiculous impulse to laugh. The effort sobered her. Abruptly she was aware that in the end, in some way, she would pay for this hour. A quick brief fear ran through her, leaving in its wake a sense of impending calamity. She wondered if for this she would pay all that she'd had.

And, suddenly, she didn't at all care. She said, lightly, but firmly: "But you see, Herr Olsen, I'm not for sale. Not to you. Not to any white man. I don't at all care to be owned. Even by you."

The drooping lids lifted. The look in the blue eyes was, Helga thought, like the surprised stare of a puzzled baby. He hadn't at all grasped her meaning.

She proceeded, deliberately: "I think you don't understand me. What I'm trying to say is this, I don't want you. I wouldn't under any circumstances marry you," and since she was, as she put it, being brutally frank, she added: "Now."

He turned a little away from her, his face white but composed,

and looked down into the gathering shadows in the little park
before the house. At last he spoke, in a queer frozen voice: "You
refuse me?"

"Yes," Helga repeated with intentional carelessness. "I refuse you."

The man's full upper lip trembled. He wiped his forehead,
where the gold hair was now lying flat and pale and lusterless. His
eyes still avoided the girl in the high-backed chair before him.
Helga felt a shiver of compunction. For an instant she regretted
that she had not been a little kinder. But wasn't it after all the
greatest kindness to be cruel? But more gently, less indifferently, she said: "You see, I couldn't marry a white man. I simply
couldn't. It isn't just you, not just personal, you understand. It's
deeper, broader than that. It's racial. Some day maybe you'll be
glad. We can't tell, you know; if we were married, you might come
to be ashamed of me, to hate me, to hate all dark people. My
mother did that."

"I have offered you marriage, Helga Crane, and you answer me
with some strange talk of race and shame. What nonsense is this?"

Helga let that pass because she couldn't, she felt, explain. It
would be too difficult, too mortifying. She had no words which
could adequately, and without laceration to her pride, convey to
him the pitfalls into which very easily they might step. "I might,"
she said, "have considered it once—when I first came. But you,
hoping for a more informal arrangement, waited too long. You
missed the moment. I had time to think. Now I couldn't. Nothing
is worth the risk. We might come to hate each other. I've been
through it, or something like it. I know. I couldn't do it. And I'm
glad."

Rising, she held out her hand, relieved that he was still silent. "Good afternoon," she said formally. "It has been a great
honor—"

"A tragedy," he corrected, barely touching her hand with his
moist finger-tips.

"Why?" Helga countered, and for an instant felt as if something sinister and internecine flew back and forth between them
like poison.

"I mean," he said, and quite solemnly, "that though I don't entirely understand you, yet in a way I do too. And—" He hesitated.

Went on. "I think that my picture of you is, after all, the true Helga Crane. Therefore—a tragedy. For someone. For me? Perhaps."

"Oh, the picture!" Helga lifted her shoulders in a little impatient motion.

Ceremoniously Axel Olsen bowed himself out, leaving her grateful for the urbanity which permitted them to part without too much awkwardness. No other man, she thought, of her acquaintance could have managed it so well—except, perhaps, Robert Anderson.

"I'm glad," she declared to herself in another moment, "that I refused him. And," she added honestly, "I'm glad that I had the chance. He took it awfully well, though—for a tragedy." And she made a tiny frown.

The picture—she had never quite, in spite of her deep interest in him, and her desire for his admiration and approval, forgiven Olsen for that portrait. It wasn't, she contended, herself at all, but some disgusting sensual creature with her features. Herr and Fru Dahl had not exactly liked it either, although collectors, artists, and critics had been unanimous in their praise and it had been hung on the line at an annual exhibition, where it had attracted much flattering attention and many tempting offers.

Now Helga went in and stood for a long time before it, with its creator's parting words in mind: ". . . a tragedy . . . my picture is, after all, the true Helga Crane." Vehemently she shook her head. "It isn't, it isn't at all," she said aloud. Bosh! Pure artistic bosh and conceit. Nothing else. Anyone with half an eye could see that it wasn't, at all, like her.

"Marie," she called to the maid passing in the hall, "do you think this is a good picture of me?"

Marie blushed. Hesitated. "Of course, Frøkken, I know Herr Olsen is a great artist, but no, I don't like that picture. It looks bad, wicked. Begging your pardon, Frøkken."

"Thanks, Marie, I don't like it either."

Yes, anyone with half an eye could see that it wasn't she.

SIXTEEN

GLAD THOUGH the Dahls may have been that their niece had had the chance of refusing the hand of Axel Olsen, they were anything but glad that she had taken that chance. Very plainly they said so, and quite firmly they pointed out to her the advisability of retrieving the opportunity, if, indeed, such a thing were possible. But it wasn't, even had Helga been so inclined, for, they were to learn from the columns of *Politikken*,[1] Axel Olsen had gone off suddenly to some queer place in the Balkans.[2] To rest, the newspapers said. To get Frøkken Crane out of his mind, the gossips said.

Life in the Dahl ménage went on, smoothly as before, but not so pleasantly. The combined disappointment and sense of guilt of the Dahls and Helga colored everything. Though she had resolved not to think that they felt that she had, as it were, "let them down," Helga knew that they did. They had not so much expected as hoped that she would bring down Olsen, and so secure the link between the merely fashionable set to which they belonged and the artistic one after which they hankered. It was of course true that there were others, plenty of them. But there was only one Olsen. And Helga, for some idiotic reason connected with race, had refused him. Certainly there was no use in thinking, even, of the others. If she had refused him, she would refuse any and all for the same reason. It was, it seemed, all-embracing.

"It isn't," Uncle Poul had tried to point out to her, "as if there were hundreds of mulattoes here. That, I can understand, might make it a little different. But there's only you. You're unique here, don't you see? Besides, Olsen has money and enviable position. Nobody'd dare to say, or even to think anything odd or unkind of you or him. Come now, Helga, it isn't this foolishness about race. Not here in Denmark. You've never spoken of it before. It can't be just that. You're too sensible. It must be something else. I wish you'd try to explain. You don't perhaps like Olsen?"

Helga had been silent, thinking what a severe wrench to Herr Dahl's ideas of decency was this conversation. For he had an almost fanatic regard for reticence, and a peculiar shrinking from what he looked upon as indecent exposure of the emotions.

"Just what is it, Helga?" he asked again, because the pause had grown awkward, for him.

"I can't explain any better than I have," she had begun tremulously, "it's just something—something deep down inside of me," and had turned away to hide a face convulsed by threatening tears.

But that, Uncle Poul had remarked with a reasonableness that was wasted on the miserable girl before him, was nonsense, pure nonsense.

With a shaking sigh and a frantic dab at her eyes, in which had come a despairing look, she had agreed that perhaps it was foolish, but she couldn't help it. "Can't you, won't you understand, Uncle Poul?" she begged, with a pleading look at the kindly worldly man who at that moment had been thinking that this strange exotic niece of his wife's was indeed charming. He didn't blame Olsen for taking it rather hard.

The thought passed. She was weeping. With no effort at restraint. Charming, yes. But insufficiently civilized. Impulsive. Imprudent. Selfish.

"Try, Helga, to control yourself," he had urged gently. He detested tears. "If it distresses you so, we won't talk of it again. You, of course, must do as you yourself wish. Both your aunt and I want only that you should be happy." He had wanted to make an end of this fruitless wet conversation.

Helga had made another little dab at her face with the scrap of lace and raised shining eyes to his face. She had said, with sincere regret: "You've been marvelous to me, you and Aunt Katrina. Angelic. I don't want to seem ungrateful. I'd do anything for you, anything in the world but this."

Herr Dahl had shrugged. A little sardonically he had smiled. He had refrained from pointing out that this was the only thing she could do for them, the only thing that they had asked of her. He had been too glad to be through with the uncomfortable discussion.

So life went on. Dinners, coffees, theaters, pictures, music, clothes. More dinners, coffees, theaters, clothes, music. And that nagging aching for America increased. Augmented by the uncomfortableness of Aunt Katrina's and Uncle Poul's disappointment with her, that tormenting nostalgia grew to an unbearable weight. As spring came on with many gracious tokens of following summer, she found her thoughts straying with increasing frequency to Anne's letter and to Harlem, its dirty streets, swollen now, in the warmer weather, with dark, gay humanity.

Until recently she had had no faintest wish ever to see America again. Now she began to welcome the thought of a return. Only a visit, of course. Just to see, to prove to herself that there was nothing there for her. To demonstrate the absurdity of even thinking that there could be. And to relieve the slight tension here. Maybe when she came back—

Her definite decision to go was arrived at with almost bewildering suddenness. It was after a concert at which Dvořák's "New World Symphony" had been wonderfully rendered. Those wailing undertones of "Swing Low, Sweet Chariot"[3] were too poignantly familiar. They struck into her longing heart and cut away her weakening defenses. She knew at least what it was that had lurked formless and undesignated these many weeks in the back of her troubled mind. Incompleteness.

"I'm homesick, not for America, but for Negroes. That's the trouble."

For the first time Helga Crane felt sympathy rather than contempt and hatred for that father, who so often and so angrily she had blamed for his desertion of her mother. She understood, now, his rejection, his repudiation, of the formal calm her mother had represented. She understood his yearning, his intolerable need for the inexhaustible humor and the incessant hope of his own kind, his need for those things, not material, indigenous to all Negro environments. She understood and could sympathize with his facile surrender to the irresistible ties of race, now that they dragged at her own heart. And as she attended parties, the theater, the opera, and mingled with people on the streets, meeting only pale serious faces when she longed for brown laughing ones, she was able to forgive him. Also, it was as if in this understanding and forgiving she had come upon knowledge of almost sacred importance.

Without demur, opposition, or recrimination Herr and Fru Dahl accepted Helga's decision to go back to America. She had expected that they would be glad and relieved. It was agreeable to discover that she had done them less than justice. They were, in spite of their extreme worldliness, very fond of her, and would, as they declared, miss her greatly. And they did want her to come back to them, as they repeatedly insisted. Secretly they felt as she did, that perhaps when she returned— So it was agreed upon that it was only for a brief visit, "for your friend's wedding," and that she was to return in the early fall.

The last day came. The last good-byes were said. Helga began to regret that she was leaving. Why couldn't she have two lives, or why couldn't she be satisfied in one place? Now that she was actually off, she felt heavy at heart. Already she looked back with infinite regret at the two years in the country which had given her so much, of pride, of happiness, of wealth, and of beauty.

Bells rang. The gangplank was hoisted. The dark strip of water widened. The running figures of friends suddenly grown very dear grew smaller, blurred into a whole, and vanished. Tears rose in Helga Crane's eyes, fear in her heart.

Good-bye Denmark! Good-bye. Good-bye!

SEVENTEEN

A SUMMER HAD RIPENED and fall begun. Anne and Dr. Anderson had returned from their short Canadian wedding journey. Helga Crane, lingering still in America, had tactfully removed herself from the house in One Hundred and Thirty-ninth Street to a hotel. It was, as she could point out to curious acquaintances, much better for the newly-married Andersons not to be bothered with a guest, not even with such a close friend as she, Helga, had been to Anne.

Actually, though she herself had truly wanted to get out of the house when they came back, she had been a little surprised and a great deal hurt that Anne had consented so readily to her going. She might at least, thought Helga indignantly, have acted a little bit as if she had wanted her to stay. After writing for her to come, too.

Pleasantly unaware was Helga that Anne, more silently wise than herself, more determined, more selfish, and less inclined to leave anything to chance, understood perfectly that in a large measure it was the voice of Robert Anderson's inexorable conscience that had been the chief factor in bringing about her second marriage—his ascetic protest against the sensuous, the physical. Anne had perceived that the decorous surface of her new husband's mind regarded Helga Crane with that intellectual and æsthetic appreciation which attractive and intelligent women would always draw from him, but that underneath that well-managed section, in a more lawless place where she herself never hoped or desired to enter, was another, a vagrant primitive groping toward something shocking and frightening to the cold asceticism of his reason. Anne knew also that though she herself was lovely—more beautiful than Helga—and interesting, with her he had not to struggle against that nameless and to him shameful impulse, that sheer delight, which ran through his nerves at mere proximity to

Helga. And Anne intended that her marriage should be a success. She intended that her husband should be happy. She was sure that it could be managed by tact and a little cleverness on her own part. She was truly fond of Helga, but seeing how she had grown more charming, more aware of her power, Anne wasn't so sure that her sincere and urgent request to come over for her wedding hadn't been a mistake. She was, however, certain of herself. She could look out for her husband. She could carry out what she considered her obligation to him, keep him undisturbed, unhumiliated. It was impossible that she could fail. Unthinkable.

Helga, on her part, had been glad to get back to New York. How glad, or why, she did not truly realize. And though she sincerely meant to keep her promise to Aunt Katrina and Uncle Poul and return to Copenhagen, summer, September, October, slid by and she made no move to go. Her uttermost intention had been a six or eight weeks' visit, but the feverish rush of New York, the comic tragedy of Harlem, still held her. As time went on, she became a little bored, a little restless, but she stayed on. Something of that wild surge of gladness that had swept her on the day when with Anne and Anderson she had again found herself surrounded by hundreds, thousands, of dark-eyed brown folk remained with her. *These* were her people. Nothing, she had come to understand now, could ever change that. Strange that she had never truly valued this kinship until distance had shown her its worth. How absurd she had been to think that another country, other people, could liberate her from the ties which bound her forever to these mysterious, these terrible, these fascinating, these lovable, dark hordes. Ties that were of the spirit. Ties not only superficially entangled with mere outline of features or color of skin. Deeper. Much deeper than either of these.

Thankful for the appeasement of that loneliness which had again tormented her like a fury, she gave herself up to the miraculous joyousness of Harlem. The easement which its heedless abandon brought to her was a real, a very definite thing. She liked the sharp contrast to her pretentious stately life in Copenhagen. It was as if she had passed from the heavy solemnity of a church service to a gorgeous care-free revel.

Not that she intended to remain. No. Helga Crane couldn't, she told herself and others, live in America. In spite of its glamour, existence in America, even in Harlem, was for Negroes too cramped, too uncertain, too cruel; something not to be endured for a lifetime if one could escape; something demanding a courage greater than was in her. No. She couldn't stay. Nor, she saw now, could she remain away. Leaving, she would have to come back.

This knowledge, this certainty of the division of her life into two parts in two lands, into physical freedom in Europe and spiritual freedom in America,[1] was unfortunate, inconvenient, expensive. It was, too, as she was uncomfortably aware, even a trifle ridiculous, and mentally she caricatured herself moving shuttle-like from continent to continent. From the prejudiced restrictions of the New World to the easy formality of the Old, from the pale calm of Copenhagen to the colorful lure of Harlem.

Nevertheless she felt a slightly pitying superiority over those Negroes who were apparently so satisfied. And she had a fine contempt for the blatantly patriotic black Americans.[2] Always when she encountered one of those picturesque parades in the Harlem streets, the Stars and Stripes streaming ironically, insolently, at the head of the procession tempered for her, a little, her amusement at the childish seriousness of the spectacle. It was too pathetic.

But when mental doors were deliberately shut on those skeletons that stalked lively and in full health through the consciousness of every person of Negro ancestry in America—conspicuous black, obvious brown, or indistinguishable white—life was intensely amusing, interesting, absorbing, and enjoyable; singularly lacking in that tone of anxiety which the insecurities of existence seemed to ferment in other peoples.

Yet Helga herself had an acute feeling of insecurity, for which she could not account. Sometimes it amounted to fright almost. "I must," she would say then, "get back to Copenhagen." But the resolution gave her not much pleasure. And for this she now blamed Axel Olsen. It was, she insisted, he who had driven her back, made her unhappy in Denmark. Though she knew well that it wasn't. Misgivings, too, rose in her. Why hadn't she married him? Anne was married—she would not say Anderson—Why not she? It would serve Anne right if she married a white man. But she knew in her soul that she wouldn't. "Because I'm a fool," she said bitterly.

→ spiritual Freedom Of America vs. physical
freedom of denmark
→ does not feel happy abt returning to Denm
→ Helga thinks abt how Anne would rct?
if married a white man.

EIGHTEEN

ONE NOVEMBER EVENING, impregnated still with the kindly
warmth of the dead Indian summer, Helga Crane was leisurely
dressing in pleasant anticipation of the party to which she had
been asked for that night. It was always amusing at the Tavenors'.
Their house was large and comfortable, the food and music always
of the best, and the type of entertainment always unexpected and
brilliant. The drinks, too, were sure to be safe.

And Helga, since her return, was more than ever popular at
parties. Her courageous clothes attracted attention, and her deliberate lure—as Olsen had called it—held it. Her life in Copenhagen
had taught her to expect and accept admiration as her due. This attitude, she found, was as effective in New York as across the sea. It
was, in fact, even more so. And it was more amusing too. Perhaps
because it was somehow a bit more dangerous.

In the midst of curious speculation as to the possible identity of
the other guests, with an indefinite sense of annoyance she wondered if Anne would be there. There was of late something about
Anne that was to Helga distinctly disagreeable, a peculiar half-
patronizing attitude, mixed faintly with distrust. Helga couldn't
define it, couldn't account for it. She had tried. In the end she had
decided to dismiss it, to ignore it.

"I suppose," she said aloud, "it's because she's married again.
As if anybody couldn't get married. Anybody. That is, if mere
marriage is all one wants."

Smoothing away the tiny frown from between the broad black
brows, she got herself into a little shining, rose-colored slip of a
frock knotted with a silver cord. The gratifying result soothed her
ruffled feelings. It didn't really matter, this new manner of Anne's.
Nor did the fact that Helga knew that Anne disapproved of her.
Without words Anne had managed to make that evident. In her
opinion, Helga had lived too long among the enemy, the de-

99

testable pale faces. She understood them too well, was too tolerant
of their ignorant stupidities. If they had been Latins, Anne might
conceivably have forgiven the disloyalty. But Nordics! Lynchers!
It was too traitorous. Helga smiled a little, understanding Anne's
bitterness and hate, and a little of its cause. It was of a piece with
that of those she so virulently hated. Fear. And then she sighed a
little, for she regretted the waning of Anne's friendship. But, in
view of diverging courses of their lives, she felt that even its complete extinction would leave her undevastated. Not that she wasn't
still grateful to Anne for many things. It was only that she had
other things now. And there would, forever, be Robert Anderson
between them. A nuisance. Shutting them off from their previous
confident companionship and understanding. "And anyway," she
said again, aloud, "he's nobody much to have married. Anybody
could have married him. Anybody. If a person wanted only to be
married— If it had been somebody like Olsen— That would be
different—something to crow over, perhaps."

The party was even more interesting than Helga had expected.
Helen, Mrs. Tavenor, had given vent to a malicious glee, and had
invited representatives of several opposing Harlem political and
social factions, including the West Indian, and abandoned them
helplessly to each other. Helga's observing eyes picked out several
great and near-great sulking or obviously trying hard not to sulk
in widely separated places in the big rooms. There were present,
also, a few white people, to the open disapproval or discomfort of
Anne and several others. There too, poised, serene, certain, surrounded by masculine black and white, was Audrey Denney.

"Do you know, Helen," Helga confided, "I've never met Miss
Denney. I wish you'd introduce me. Not this minute. Later, when
you can manage it. Not so—er—apparently by request, you
know."

Helen Tavenor laughed. "No, you wouldn't have met her, living as you did with Anne Grey. Anderson, I mean. She's Anne's
particular pet aversion. The mere sight of Audrey is enough to
send her into a frenzy for a week. It's too bad, too, because Audrey's an awfully interesting person and Anne's said some pretty
awful things about her. _You'll_ like her, Helga."

Helga nodded. "Yes, I expect to. And I know about Anne. One

night—" She stopped, for across the room she saw, with a stab of surprise, James Vayle. "Where, Helen did you get him?"

"Oh, that? That's something the cat brought in. Don't ask which one. He came with somebody, I don't remember who. I think he's shocked to death. Isn't he lovely? The dear baby. I was going to introduce him to Audrey and tell her to do a good job of vamping on him[1] as soon as I could remember the darling's name, or when it got noisy enough so he wouldn't hear what I called him. But you'll do just as well. Don't tell me you know him!" Helga made a little nod. "Well! And I suppose you met him at some shockingly wicked place in Europe. That's always the way with those innocent-looking men."

"Not quite. I met him ages ago in Naxos. We were engaged to be married. Nice, isn't he? His name's Vayle. James Vayle."

"Nice," said Helen throwing out her hands in a characteristic dramatic gesture—she had beautiful hands and arms—"is exactly the word. Mind if I run off? I've got somebody here who's going to sing. *Not* spirituals. And I haven't the faintest notion where he's got to. The cellar, I'll bet."

James Vayle hadn't, Helga decided, changed at all. Someone claimed her for a dance and it was some time before she caught his eyes, half questioning, upon her. When she did, she smiled in a friendly way over her partner's shoulder and was rewarded by a dignified little bow. Inwardly she grinned, flattered. He hadn't forgotten. He was still hurt. The dance over, she deserted her partner and deliberately made her way across the room to James Vayle. He was for the moment embarrassed and uncertain. Helga Crane, however, took care of that, thinking meanwhile that Helen was right. Here he did seem frightfully young and delightfully unsophisticated. He must be, though, every bit of thirty-two or more.

"They say," was her bantering greeting, "that if one stands on the corner of One Hundred and Thirty-fifth Street and Seventh Avenue[2] long enough, one will eventually see all the people one has ever known or met. It's pretty true, I guess. Not literally of course." He was, she saw, getting himself together. "It's only another way of saying that everybody, almost, some time sooner or later comes to Harlem, even you."

He laughed. "Yes, I guess that is true enough. I didn't come to stay, though." And then he was grave, his earnest eyes searchingly upon her.

"Well, anyway, you're here now, so let's find a quiet corner if that's possible, where we can talk. I want to hear all about you."

For a moment he hung back and a glint of mischief shone in Helga's eyes. "I see," she said, "you're just the same. However, you needn't be anxious. This isn't Naxos, you know. Nobody's watching us, or if they are, they don't care a bit what we do."

At that he flushed a little, protested a little, and followed her. And when at last they had found seats in another room, not so crowded, he said: "I didn't expect to see you here. I thought you were still abroad."

"Oh, I've been back some time, ever since Dr. Anderson's marriage. Anne, you know, is a great friend of mine. I used to live with her. I came for the wedding. But, of course, I'm not staying. I didn't think I'd be here this long."

"You don't mean that you're going to live over there? Do you really like it so much better?"

"Yes and no, to both questions. I was awfully glad to get back, but I wouldn't live here always. I couldn't. I don't think that any of us who've lived abroad for any length of time would ever live here altogether again if they could help it."

"Lot of them do, though," James Vayle pointed out.

"Oh, I don't mean tourists who rush over to Europe and rush all over the continent and rush back to America thinking they know Europe. I mean people who've actually lived there, actually lived among the people."

"I still maintain that they nearly all come back here eventually to live."

"That's because they can't help it," Helga Crane said firmly. "Money, you know."

"Perhaps, I'm not so sure. I was in the war. Of course, that's not really living over there, but I saw the country and the difference in treatment. But, I can tell you, I was pretty darn glad to get back. All the fellows were." He shook his head solemnly. "I don't think anything, money or lack of money, keeps us here. If it was only that, if we really wanted to leave, we'd go all right. No, it's something else, something deeper than that."

"And just what do you think it is?"

"I'm afraid it's hard to explain, but I suppose it's just that we like to be together. I simply can't imagine living forever away from colored people."

A suspicion of a frown drew Helga's brows. She threw out rather tartly: "I'm a Negro too, you know."

"Well, Helga, you were always a little different, a little dissatisfied, though I don't pretend to understand you at all. I never did," he said a little wistfully.

And Helga, who was beginning to feel that the conversation had taken an impersonal and disappointing tone, was reassured and gave him her most sympathetic smile and said almost gently: "And now let's talk about you. You're still at Naxos?"

"Yes I'm still there. I'm assistant principal now."

Plainly it was a cause for enthusiastic congratulation, but Helga could only manage a tepid "How nice!" Naxos was to her too remote, too unimportant. She did not even hate it now.

How long, she asked, would James be in New York?

He couldn't say. Business, important business for the school, had brought him. It was, he said, another tone creeping into his voice, another look stealing over his face, awfully good to see her. She was looking tremendously well. He hoped he would have the opportunity of seeing her again.

But of course. He must come to see her. Any time, she was always in, or would be for him. And how did he like New York, Harlem?

He didn't, it seemed, like it. It was nice to visit, but not to live in. Oh, there were so many things he didn't like about it, the rush, the lack of home life, the crowds, the noisy meaninglessness of it all.

On Helga's face there had come that pityingly sneering look peculiar to imported New Yorkers when the city of their adoption is attacked by alien Americans. With polite contempt she inquired: "And is that all you don't like?"

At her tone the man's bronze face went purple. He answered coldly, slowly, with a faint gesture in the direction of Helen Tavenor, who stood conversing gayly with one of her white guests: "And I don't like that sort of thing. In fact I detest it."

"Why?" Helga was striving hard to be casual in her manner.

James Vayle, it was evident, was beginning to be angry. It was also evident that Helga Crane's question had embarrassed him. But he seized the bull by the horns and said: "You know as well as I do, Helga, that it's the colored girls these men come up here to see. They wouldn't think of bringing their wives." And he blushed furiously at his own implication. The blush restored Helga's good temper. James was really too funny.

"That," she said softly, "is Hugh Wentworth, the novelist,³ you know." And she indicated a tall olive-skinned girl being whirled about to the streaming music in the arms of a towering black man.⁴ "And that is his wife. She isn't colored, as you've probably been thinking. And now let's change the subject again."

"All right! And this time let's talk about you. You say you don't intend to live here. Don't you ever intend to marry, Helga?"

"Some day, perhaps. I don't know. Marriage—that means children, to me. And why add more suffering to the world? Why add any more unwanted, tortured Negroes to America? Why *do* Negroes have children? Surely it must be sinful. Think of the awfulness of being responsible for the giving of life to creatures doomed to endure such wounds to the flesh, such wounds to the spirit, as Negroes have to endure."

James was aghast. He forgot to be embarrassed. "But Helga! Good heavens! Don't you see that if we—I mean people like us—don't have children, the others will still have. That's one of the things that's the matter with us. The race is sterile at the top. Few, very few Negroes of the better class have children, and each generation has to wrestle again with the obstacles of the preceding ones, lack of money, education, and background. I feel very strongly about this. We're the ones who must have the children if the race is to get anywhere."

"Well, I for one don't intend to contribute any to the cause. But how serious we are! And I'm afraid that I've really got to leave you. I've already cut two dances for your sake. Do come to see me."

"Oh, I'll come to see you all right. I've got several things that I want to talk to you about and one thing especially."

"Don't," Helga mocked, "tell me you're going to ask me again to marry you."

"That," he said, "is just what I intend to do."

Helga Crane was suddenly deeply ashamed and very sorry for James Vayle, so she told him laughingly that it was shameful of him to joke with her like that, and before he could answer, she had gone tripping off with a handsome coffee-colored youth whom she had beckoned from across the room with a little smile.

Later she had to go upstairs to pin up a place in the hem of her dress which had caught on a sharp chair corner. She finished the temporary repair and stepped out into the hall, and somehow, she never quite knew exactly just how, into the arms of Robert Anderson. She drew back and looked up smiling to offer an apology.

And then it happened. He stooped and kissed her, a long kiss, holding her close. She fought against him with all her might. Then, strangely, all power seemed to ebb away, and a long-hidden, half-understood desire welled up in her with the suddenness of a dream. Helga Crane's own arms went up about the man's neck. When she drew away, consciously confused and embarrassed, everything seemed to have changed in a space of time which she knew to have been only seconds. Sudden anger seized her. She pushed him indignantly aside and with a little pat for her hair and dress went slowly down to the others.

→ Helga goes to a party

→ friendship w/ Anne = fading

→ Helga sees James Vayle @ party
   ↳ doesn't approve of blacks &
      whites mingling @ party

→ Helga can't imagine bringing more black
   children into racist world

→ James says he's going to ask Helga to marry

→ Helga goes to fix her dress & runs into Dr.
   Anderson; he embraces & kisses her

→ she struggles @ first but then kisses him back

→ she becomes angry and pushes him away
   & returns to the party

NINETEEN

THAT NIGHT riotous and colorful dreams invaded Helga Crane's prim hotel bed. She woke in the morning weary and a bit shocked at the uncontrolled fancies which had visited her. Catching up a filmy scarf, she paced back and forth across the narrow room and tried to think. She recalled her flirtations and her mild engagement with James Vayle. She was used to kisses. But none had been like that of last night. She lived over those brief seconds, thinking not so much of the man whose arms had held her as of the ecstasy which had flooded her. Even recollection brought a little onrush of emotion that made her sway a little. She pulled herself together and began to fasten on the solid fact of Anne and experienced a pleasant sense of shock in the realization that Anne was to her exactly what she had been before the incomprehensible experience of last night. She still liked her in the same degree and in the same manner. She still felt slightly annoyed with her. She still did not envy her marriage with Anderson. By some mysterious process the emotional upheaval which had racked her had left all the rocks of her existence unmoved. Outwardly nothing had changed.

Days, weeks, passed; outwardly serene; inwardly tumultous. Helga met Dr. Anderson at the social affairs to which often they were both asked. Sometimes she danced with him, always in perfect silence. She couldn't, she absolutely couldn't, speak a word to him when they were thus alone together, for at such times lassitude encompassed her; the emotion which had gripped her retreated, leaving a strange tranquillity, troubled only by a soft stir of desire. And shamed by his silence, his apparent forgetting, always after these dances she tried desperately to persuade herself to believe what she wanted to believe: that it had not happened, that she had never had that irrepressible longing. It was of no use.

As the weeks multiplied, she became aware that she must get herself out of the mental quagmire into which that kiss had thrown her. And she should be getting herself back to Copenhagen, but she had now no desire to go.

Abruptly one Sunday in a crowded room, in the midst of teacups and chatter, she knew that she couldn't go, that she hadn't since that kiss intended to go without exploring to the end that unfamiliar path into which she had strayed. Well, it was of no use lagging behind or pulling back. It was of no use trying to persuade herself that she didn't want to go on. A species of fatalism fastened on her. She felt that, ever since that last day in Naxos long ago, somehow she had known that this thing would happen. With this conviction came an odd sense of elation. While making a pleasant assent to some remark of a fellow guest she put down her cup and walked without haste, smiling and nodding to friends and acquaintances on her way to that part of the room where he stood looking at some examples of African carving. Helga Crane faced him squarely. As he took the hand which she held out with elaborate casualness, she noted that his trembled slightly. She was secretly congratulating herself on her own calm when it failed her. Physical weariness descended on her. Her knees wobbled. Gratefully she slid into the chair which he hastily placed for her. Timidity came over her. She was silent. He talked. She did not listen. He came at last to the end of his long dissertation on African sculpture, and Helga Crane felt the intentness of his gaze upon her.

"Well?" she questioned.

"I want very much to see you, Helga. Alone."

She held herself tensely on the edge of her chair, and suggested: "Tomorrow?"

He hesitated a second and then said quickly: "Why, yes, that's all right."

"Eight o'clock?"

"Eight o'clock," he agreed.

Eight o'clock tomorrow came. Helga Crane never forgot it. She had carried away from yesterday's meeting a feeling of increasing elation. It had seemed to her that she hadn't been so happy, so exalted, in years, if ever. All night, all day, she had mentally prepared herself for the coming consummation; physically too, spending hours before the mirror.

Eight o'clock had come at last and with it Dr. Anderson. Only then had uneasiness come upon her and a feeling of fear for possible exposure. For Helga Crane wasn't, after all, a rebel from society, Negro society. It did mean something to her. She had no wish to stand alone. But these late fears were overwhelmed by the hardiness of insistent desire; and she had got herself down to the hotel's small reception room.

It was, he had said, awfully good of her to see him. She instantly protested. No, she had wanted to see him. He looked at her surprised. "You know, Helga," he had begun with an air of desperation, "I can't forgive myself for acting such a swine at the Tavenor's party. I don't at all blame you for being angry and not speaking to me except when you had to."

But that, she exclaimed, was simply too ridiculous. "I wasn't angry a bit." And it had seemed to her that things were not exactly going forward as they should. It seemed that he had been very sincere, and very formal. Deliberately. She had looked down at her hands and inspected her bracelets, for she had felt that to look at him would be, under the circumstances, too exposing.

"I was afraid," he went on, "that you might have misunderstood; might have been unhappy about it. I could kick myself. It was, it must have been, Tavenor's rotten cocktails."

Helga Crane's sense of elation had abruptly left her. At the same time she had felt the need to answer carefully. No, she replied, she hadn't thought of it at all. It had meant nothing to her. She had been kissed before. It was really too silly of him to have been at all bothered about it. "For what," she had asked, "is one kiss more or less, these days, between friends?" She had even laughed a little.

Dr. Anderson was relieved. He had been, he told her, no end upset. Rising, he said: "I see you're going out. I won't keep you."

Helga Crane too had risen. Quickly. A sort of madness had swept over her. She felt that he had belittled and ridiculed her. And thinking this, she had suddenly savagely slapped Robert Anderson with all her might, in the face.

For a short moment they had both stood stunned, in the deep silence which had followed that resounding slap. Then, without a word of contrition or apology, Helga Crane had gone out of the room and upstairs.

She had, she told herself, been perfectly justified in slapping Dr. Anderson, but she was not convinced. So she had tried hard to make herself very drunk in order that sleep might come to her, but had managed only to make herself very sick.

Not even the memory of how all living had left his face, which had gone a taupe gray hue, or the despairing way in which he had lifted his head and let it drop, or the trembling hands which he had pressed into his pockets, brought her any scrap of comfort. She had ruined everything. Ruined it because she had been so silly as to close her eyes to all indications that pointed to the fact that no matter what the intensity of his feelings or desires might be, he was not the sort of man who would for any reason give up one particle of his own good opinion of himself. Not even for her. Not even though he knew that she had wanted so terribly something special from him.

Something special. And now she had forfeited it forever. Forever. Helga had an instantaneous shocking perception of what forever meant. And then, like a flash, it was gone, leaving an endless stretch of dreary years before her appalled vision.

→ Helga can't forget kiss w/ Dr.
→ She still respects Anne but can't convince herself the kiss didn't matter
→ they decide to meet next day @ 8:00
→ Helga's so excited but then Anderson apologizes 3 said kiss was "between friends"
→ she slaps him 3 feels regret

TWENTY

THE DAY WAS A RAINY ONE. Helga Crane, stretched out on her bed, felt herself so broken physically, mentally, that she had given up thinking. But back and forth in her staggered brain wavering, incoherent thoughts shot shuttle-like. Her pride would have shut out these humiliating thoughts and painful visions of herself. The effort was too great. She felt alone, isolated from all other human beings, separated even from her own anterior existence by the disaster of yesterday. Over and over, she repeated: "There's nothing left but to go now." Her anguish seemed unbearable.

For days, for weeks, voluptuous visions had haunted her. Desire had burned in her flesh with uncontrollable violence. The wish to give herself had been so intense that Dr. Anderson's surprising, trivial apology loomed as a direct refusal of the offering. Whatever outcome she had expected, it had been something else than this, this mortification, this feeling of ridicule and self-loathing, this knowledge that she had deluded herself. It was all, she told herself, as unpleasant as possible.

Almost she wished she could die. Not quite. It wasn't that she was afraid of death, which had, she thought, its picturesque aspects. It was rather that she knew she would not die. And death, after the debacle, would but intensify its absurdity. Also, it would reduce her, Helga Crane, to unimportance, to nothingness. Even in her unhappy present state, that did not appeal to her. Gradually, reluctantly, she began to know that the blow to her self-esteem, the certainty of having proved herself a silly fool, was perhaps the severest hurt which she had suffered.

It was her self-assurance that had gone down in the crash. After all, what Dr. Anderson thought didn't matter. She could escape from the discomfort of his knowing gray eyes. But she couldn't escape from sure knowledge that she had made a fool of herself. This angered her further and she struck the wall with her hands and jumped up and began hastily to dress herself. She couldn't go on with the analysis. It was too hard. Why bother, when she could add nothing to the obvious fact that she had been a fool?

"I can't stay in this room any longer. I must get out or I'll choke." Her self-knowledge had increased her anguish. Distracted, agitated, incapable of containing herself, she tore open drawers and closets trying desperately to take some interest in the selection of her apparel.

It was evening and still raining. In the streets, unusually deserted, the electric lights cast dull glows. Helga Crane, walking rapidly, aimlessly, could decide on no definite destination. She had not thought to take umbrella or even rubbers. Rain and wind whipped cruelly about her, drenching her garments and chilling her body. Soon the foolish little satin shoes which she wore were sopping wet. Unheeding these physical discomforts, she went on, but at the open corner of One Hundred and Thirty-eighth Street a sudden more ruthless gust of wind ripped the small hat from her head. In the next minute the black clouds opened wider and spilled their water with unusual fury. The streets became swirling rivers. Helga Crane, forgetting her mental torment, looked about anxiously for a sheltering taxi. A few taxis sped by, but inhabited, so she began desperately to struggle through wind and rain toward one of the buildings, where she could take shelter in a store or a doorway. But another whirl of wind lashed her and, scornful of her slight strength, tossed her into the swollen gutter.

Now she knew beyond all doubt that she had no desire to die, and certainly not there nor then. Not in such a messy wet manner. Death had lost all of its picturesque aspects to the girl lying soaked and soiled in the flooded gutter. So, though she was very tired and very weak, she dragged herself up and succeeded finally in making her way to the store whose blurred light she had marked for her destination.[1]

She had opened the door and had entered before she was aware that, inside, people were singing a song which she was conscious of having heard years ago—hundreds of years it seemed. Repeated over and over, she made out the words:

. . . Showers of blessings,
Showers of blessings . . .[2]

She was conscious too of a hundred pairs of eyes upon her as she stood there, drenched and disheveled, at the door of this improvised meeting-house.

. . . Showers of blessings . . .

The appropriateness of the song, with its constant reference to showers, the ridiculousness of herself in such surroundings, was too much for Helga Crane's frayed nerves. She sat down on the floor, a dripping heap, and laughed and laughed and laughed.

It was into a shocked silence that she laughed. For at the first hysterical peal the words of the song had died in the singers' throats, and the wheezy organ had lapsed into stillness. But in a moment there were hushed solicitous voices; she was assisted to her feet and led haltingly to a chair near the low platform at the far end of the room. On one side of her a tall angular black woman under a queer hat sat down, on the other a fattish yellow man with huge outstanding ears and long, nervous hands.

The singing began again, this time a low wailing thing:

Oh, the bitter shame and sorrow
That a time could ever be,
When I let the Savior's pity
Plead in vain, and proudly answered:
"All of self and none of Thee,
All of self and none of Thee."

Yet He found me, I beheld Him,
Bleeding on the cursed tree;
Heard Him pray: "Forgive them, Father."
And my wistful heart said faintly,
"Some of self and some of Thee,
Some of self and some of Thee."

There were, it appeared, endless moaning verses. Behind Helga a woman had begun to cry audibly, and soon, somewhere else, another. Outside, the wind still bellowed. The wailing singing went on:

... Less of self and more of Thee,
Less of self and more of Thee.

Helga too began to weep, at first silently, softly; then with great racking sobs. Her nerves were so torn, so aching, her body so wet, so cold! It was a relief to cry unrestrainedly, and she gave herself freely to soothing tears, not noticing that the groaning and sobbing of those about her had increased, unaware that the grotesque ebony figure at her side had begun gently to pat her arm to the rhythm of the singing and to croon softly: "Yes, chile, yes, chile." Nor did she notice the furtive glances that the man on her other side cast at her between his fervent shouts of "Amen!" and "Praise God for a sinner!"

She did notice, though, that the tempo, that atmosphere of the place, had changed, and gradually she ceased to weep and gave her attention to what was happening about her. Now they were singing:

... Jesus knows all about my troubles ...

Men and women were swaying and clapping their hands, shouting and stamping their feet to the frankly irreverent melody of the song. Without warning the woman at her side threw off her hat, leaped to her feet, waved her long arms, and shouted shrilly: "Glory! Hallelujah!" and then, in wild, ecstatic fury jumped up and down before Helga clutching at the girl's soaked coat, and screamed: "Come to Jesus, you pore los' sinner!" Alarmed for the fraction of a second, involuntarily Helga had shrunk from her grasp, wriggling out of the wet coat when she could not loosen the crazed creature's hold. At the sight of the bare arms and neck growing out of the clinging red dress, a shudder shook the swaying man at her right. On the face of the dancing woman before her a disapproving frown gathered. She shrieked: "A scarlet 'oman. Come to Jesus, you pore los' Jezebel!"[3]

At this the short brown man on the platform raised a placating hand and sanctimoniously delivered himself of the words: "Remembah de words of our Mastah: 'Let him that is without sin cast de first stone.' Let us pray for our errin' sistah."

Helga Crane was amused, angry, disdainful, as she sat there, lis-

tening to the preacher praying for her soul. But though she was
contemptuous, she was being too well entertained to leave. And it
was, at least, warm and dry. So she stayed, listening to the fervent
exhortation to God to save her and to the zealous shoutings and
groanings of the congregation. Particularly she was interested in
the writhings and weepings of the feminine portion, which seemed
to predominate. Little by little the performance took on an almost
Bacchic vehemence. Behind her, before her, beside her, frenzied
women gesticulated, screamed, wept, and tottered to the praying
of the preacher, which had gradually become a cadenced chant.
When at last he ended, another took up the plea in the same moaning chant, and then another. It went on and on without pause with
the persistence of some unconquerable faith exalted beyond time
and reality.

Fascinated, Helga Crane watched until there crept upon her an
indistinct horror of an unknown world. She felt herself in the
presence of a nameless people, observing rites of a remote obscure
origin. The faces of the men and women took on the aspect of a
dim vision. "This," she whispered to herself, "is terrible. I must
get out of here." But the horror held her. She remained motionless, watching, as if she lacked the strength to leave the place—
foul, vile, and terrible, with its mixture of breaths, its contact of
bodies, its concerted convulsions, all in wild appeal for a single
soul. Her soul.

And as Helga watched and listened, gradually a curious influence penetrated her; she felt an echo of the weird orgy resound in
her own heart; she felt herself possessed by the same madness; she
too felt a brutal desire to shout and to sling herself about. Frightened at the strength of the obsession, she gathered herself for one
last effort to escape, but vainly. In rising, weakness and nausea
from last night's unsuccessful attempt to make herself drunk overcame her. She had eaten nothing since yesterday. She fell forward
against the crude railing which enclosed the little platform. For a
single moment she remained there in silent stillness, because she
was afraid she was going to be sick. And in that moment she was
lost—or saved. The yelling figures about her pressed forward,
closing her in on all sides. Maddened, she grasped at the railing,
and with no previous intention began to yell like one insane,
drowning every other clamor, while torrents of tears streamed

down her face. She was unconscious of the words she uttered, or their meaning: "Oh God, mercy, mercy. Have mercy on me!" but she repeated them over and over.

From those about her came a thunder-clap of joy. Arms were stretched toward her with savage frenzy. The women dragged themselves upon their knees or crawled over the floor like reptiles, sobbing and pulling their hair and tearing off their clothing. Those who succeeded in getting near to her leaned forward to encourage the unfortunate sister, dropping hot tears and beads of sweat upon her bare arms and neck.

The thing became real. A miraculous calm came upon her. Life seemed to expand, and to become very easy. Helga Crane felt within her a supreme aspiration toward the regaining of simple happiness, a happiness unburdened by the complexities of the lives she had known. About her the tumult and the shouting continued, but in a lesser degree. Some of the more exuberant worshipers had fainted into inert masses, the voices of others were almost spent. Gradually the room grew quiet and almost solemn, and to the kneeling girl time seemed to sink back into the mysterious grandeur and holiness of far-off simpler centuries.

TWENTY-ONE

ON LEAVING THE MISSION Helga Crane had started straight back to her room at the hotel. With her had gone the fattish yellow man who had sat beside her. He had introduced himself as the Reverend Mr. Pleasant Green[1] in proffering his escort for which Helga had been grateful because she had still felt a little dizzy and much exhausted. So great had been this physical weariness that as she had walked beside him, without attention to his verbose information about his own "field," as he called it, she had been seized with a hateful feeling of vertigo and obliged to lay firm hold on his arm to keep herself from falling. The weakness had passed as suddenly as it had come. Silently they had walked on. And gradually Helga had recalled that the man beside her had himself swayed slightly at their close encounter, and that frantically for a fleeting moment he had gripped at a protruding fence railing. That man! Was it possible? As easy as that?

Instantly across her still half-hypnotized consciousness little burning darts of fancy had shot themselves. No. She couldn't. It would be too awful. Just the same, what or who was there to hold her back? Nothing. Simply nothing. Nobody. Nobody at all.

Her searching mind had become in a moment quite clear. She cast at the man a speculative glance, aware that for a tiny space she had looked into his mind, a mind striving to be calm. A mind that was certain that it was secure because it was concerned only with things of the soul, spiritual things, which to him meant religious things. But actually a mind by habit at home amongst the mere material aspect of things, and at that moment consumed by some longing for the ecstasy that might lurk behind the gleam of her cheek, the flying wave of her hair, the pressure of her slim fingers on his heavy arm. An instant's flashing vision it had been and it was gone at once. Escaped in the aching of her own senses and the sudden disturbing fear that she herself had perhaps missed the supreme secret of life.

After all, there was nothing to hold her back. Nobody to care. She stopped sharply, shocked at what she was on the verge of considering. Appalled at where it might lead her.

The man—what was his name?—thinking that she was almost about to fall again, had reached out his arms to her. Helga Crane had deliberately stopped thinking. She had only smiled, a faint provocative smile, and pressed her fingers deep into his arms until a wild look had come into his slightly bloodshot eyes.

The next morning she lay for a long while, scarcely breathing, while she reviewed the happenings of the night before. Curious. She couldn't be sure that it wasn't religion that had made her feel so utterly different from dreadful yesterday. And gradually she became a little sad, because she realized that with every hour she would get a little farther away from this soothing haziness, this rest from her long trouble of body and of spirit; back into the clear bareness of her own small life and being, from which happiness and serenity always faded just as they had shaped themselves. And slowly bitterness crept into her soul. Because, she thought, all I've ever had in life has been things—except just this one time. At that she closed her eyes, for even remembrance caused her to shiver a little.

Things, she realized, hadn't been, weren't, enough for her. She'd have to have something else besides. It all came back to that old question of happiness. Surely this was it. Just for a fleeting moment Helga Crane, her eyes watching the wind scattering the gray-white clouds and so clearing a speck of blue sky, questioned her ability to retain, to bear, this happiness at such cost as she must pay for it. There was, she knew, no getting round that. The man's agitation and sincere conviction of sin had been too evident, too illuminating. The question returned in a slightly new form. Was it worth the risk? Could she take it? Was she able? Though what did it matter—now?

And all the while she knew in one small corner of her mind that such thinking was useless. She had made her decision. Her resolution. It was a chance at stability, at permanent happiness, that she meant to take. She had let so many other things, other chances, escape her. And anyway there was God, He would perhaps make it come out all right. Still confused and not so sure that it wasn't the fact that she was "saved" that had contributed to this after feeling of well-being, she clutched the hope, the desire to believe that now at last she had found some One, some Power, who was interested in her. Would help her.

She meant, however, for once in her life to be practical. So she would make sure of both things, God and man.

Her glance caught the calendar over the little white desk. The tenth of November. The steamer *Oscar II*[2] sailed today. Yesterday she had half thought of sailing with it. Yesterday. How far away!

With the thought of yesterday came the thought of Robert Anderson and a feeling of elation, revenge. She had put herself beyond the need of help from him. She had made it impossible for herself ever again to appeal to him. Instinctively she had the knowledge that he would be shocked. Grieved. Horribly hurt even. Well, let him!

The need to hurry suddenly obsessed her. She must. The morning was almost gone. And she meant, if she could manage it, to be married today. Rising, she was seized with a fear so acute that she had to lie down again. For the thought came to her that she might fail. Might not be able to confront the situation. That would be too dreadful. But she became calm again. How could he, a naïve creature like that, hold out against her? If she pretended to distress? To fear? To remorse? He couldn't. It would be useless for him even to try. She screwed up her face into a little grin, remembering that even if protestations were to fail, there were other ways.

And, too, there was God.

TWENTY-TWO

AND SO IN THE CONFUSION of seductive repentance Helga Crane was married to the grandiloquent Reverend Mr. Pleasant Green, that rattish yellow man, who had so kindly, so unctuously, proffered his escort to her hotel on the memorable night of her conversion. With him she willingly, even eagerly, left the sins and temptations of New York behind her to, as he put it, "labor in the vineyard of the Lord" in the tiny Alabama town where he was pastor to a scattered and primitive flock. And where, as the wife of the preacher, she was a person of relative importance. Only relative.

Helga did not hate him, the town, or the people. No. Not for a long time.

As always, at first the novelty of the thing, the change, fascinated her. There was a recurrence of the feeling that now, at last, she had found a place for herself, that she was really living. And she had her religion, which in her new status as a preacher's wife had of necessity become real to her. She believed in it. Because in its coming it had brought this other thing, this anæsthetic satisfaction for her senses. Hers was, she declared to herself, a truly spiritual union. This one time in her life, she was convinced, she had not clutched a shadow and missed the actuality. She felt compensated for all previous humiliations and disappointments and was glad. If she remembered that she had had something like this feeling before, she put the unwelcome memory from her with the thought: "This time I know I'm right. This time it will last."

Eagerly she accepted everything, even that bleak air of poverty which, in some curious way, regards itself as virtuous, for no other reason than that it is poor. And in her first hectic enthusiasm she intended and planned to do much good to her husband's parishioners. Her young joy and zest for the uplifting of her fellow men came back to her. She meant to subdue the cleanly scrubbed ugliness of her own surroundings to soft inoffensive beauty, and to help the other women to do likewise. Too, she would help them with their clothes, tactfully point out that sunbonnets, no matter how gay, and aprons, no matter how frilly, were not quite the proper things for Sunday church wear. There would be a sewing circle. She visualized herself instructing the children, who seemed most of the time to run wild, in ways of gentler deportment. She was anxious to be a true helpmate, for in her heart was a feeling of obligation, of humble gratitude.

In her ardor and sincerity Helga even made some small beginnings. True, she was not very successful in this matter of innovations. When she went about to try to interest the women in what she considered more appropriate clothing and in inexpensive ways of improving their homes according to her ideas of beauty, she was met, always, with smiling agreement and good-natured promises. "Yuh all is right, Mis' Green," and "Ah suttinly will, Mis' Green," fell courteously on her ear at each visit.

She was unaware that afterwards they would shake their heads sullenly over their wash-tubs and ironing-boards. And that among themselves they talked with amusement, or with anger, of "dat uppity, meddlin' No'the'nah," and "pore Reve'end," who in their opinion "would 'a done bettah to a ma'ied Clementine Richards." Knowing, as she did, nothing of this, Helga was unperturbed. But even had she known, she would not have been disheartened. The fact that it was difficult but increased her eagerness, and made the doing of it seem only the more worth while. Sometimes she would smile to think how changed she was.

And she was humble too. Even with Clementine Richards, a strapping black beauty of magnificent Amazon proportions and bold shining eyes of jet-like hardness. A person of awesome appearance. All chains, strings of beads, jingling bracelets, flying ribbons, feathery neck-pieces, and flowery hats. Clementine was inclined to treat Helga with an only partially concealed contemptuousness, considering her a poor thing without style, and without proper understanding of the worth and greatness of the man, Clementine's own adored pastor, whom Helga had somehow had the astounding good luck to marry. Clementine's admiration of the Reverend Mr. Pleasant Green was open. Helga was at first astonished. Until she learned that there was really no reason why it should be concealed. Everybody was aware of it. Besides, open adoration was the prerogative, the almost religious duty, of the female portion of the flock. If this unhidden and exaggerated approval contributed to his already oversized pomposity, so much the better. It was what they expected, liked, wanted. The greater his own sense of superiority became, the more flattered they were by his notice and small attentions, the more they cast at him killing glances, the more they hung enraptured on his words.

In the days before her conversion, with its subsequent blurring of her sense of humor, Helga might have amused herself by tracing the relation of this constant ogling and flattering on the proverbially large families of preachers; the often disastrous effect on their wives of this constant stirring of the senses by extraneous women. Now, however, she did not even think of it.

She was too busy. Every minute of the day was full. Necessarily. And to Helga this was a new experience. She was charmed by it. To be mistress in one's own house, to have a garden, and chickens, and a pig; to have a husband—and to be "right with God"— what pleasure did that other world which she had left contain that could surpass these? Here, she had found, she was sure, the intangible thing for which, indefinitely, always she had craved. It had received embodiment.

Everything contributed to her gladness in living. And so for a time she loved everything and everyone. Or thought she did. Even the weather. And it was truly lovely. By day a glittering gold sun was set in an unbelievably bright sky. In the evening silver buds sprouted in a Chinese blue sky, and the warm day was softly soothed by a slight, cool breeze. And night! Night, when a languid moon peeped through the wide-opened windows of her little house, a little mockingly, it may be. Always at night's approach Helga was bewildered by a disturbing medley of feelings. Challenge. Anticipation. And a small fear.

In the morning she was serene again. Peace had returned. And she could go happily, inexpertly, about the humble tasks of her household, cooking, dish-washing, sweeping, dusting, mending, and darning. And there was the garden. When she worked there, she felt that life was utterly filled with the glory and the marvel of God.

Helga did not reason about this feeling, as she did not at that time reason about anything. It was enough that it was there, coloring all her thoughts and acts. It endowed the four rooms of her ugly brown house with a kindly radiance, obliterating the stark bareness of its white plaster walls and the nakedness of its uncovered painted floors. It even softened the choppy lines of the shiny oak furniture and subdued the awesome horribleness of the religious pictures.

And all the other houses and cabins shared in this illumination. And the people. The dark undecorated women unceasingly concerned with the actual business of life, its rounds of births and christenings, of loves and marriages, of deaths and funerals, were to Helga miraculously beautiful. The smallest, dirtiest, brown child, barefooted in the fields or muddy roads, was to her an emblem of the wonder of life, of love, and of God's goodness.

For the preacher, her husband, she had a feeling of gratitude, amounting almost to sin. Beyond that, she thought of him not at all. But she was not conscious that she had shut him out from her mind. Besides, what need to think of him? He was there. She was at peace, and secure. Surely their two lives were one, and the companionship in the Lord's grace so perfect that to think about it would be tempting providence. She had done with soul-searching.

What did it matter that he consumed his food, even the softest varieties, audibly? What did it matter that, though he did no work with his hands, not even in the garden, his fingernails were always rimmed with black? What did it matter that he failed to wash his fat body, or to shift his clothing, as often as Helga herself did? There were things that more than outweighed these. In the certainty of his goodness, his righteousness, his holiness, Helga somehow overcame her first disgust at the odor of sweat and stale garments. She was even able to be unaware of it. Herself, Helga had come to look upon as a finicky, showy thing of unnecessary prejudices and fripperies. And when she sat in the dreary structure, which had once been a stable belonging to the estate of a wealthy horse-racing man and about which the odor of manure still clung, now the church and social center of the Negroes of the town, and heard him expound with verbal extravagance the gospel of blood and love, of hell and heaven, of fire and gold streets, pounding with clenched fists the frail table before him or shaking those fists in the faces of the congregation like direct personal

threats, or pacing wildly back and forth and even sometimes
shedding great tears as he besought them to repent, she was, she
told herself, proud and gratified that he belonged to her. In some
strange way she was able to ignore the atmosphere of self-
satisfaction which poured from him like gas from a leaking pipe.

And night came at the end of every day. Emotional, palpitating,
amorous, all that was living in her sprang like rank weeds at the
tingling thought of night, with a vitality so strong that it devoured
all shoots of reason.

→ Helga marries Reverand Green

→ live in small town in Alabama
  Reverand = pastor

→ Helgas pleased she's important as
  preachers wife

→ Helga works in church, women refer
  to her as "uppity, meddling northerners"

→ She's truly fulfilled

TWENTY-THREE

AFTER THE FIRST EXCITING MONTHS Helga was too driven, too occupied, and too sick to carry out any of the things for which she had made such enthusiastic plans, or even to care that she had made only slight progress toward their accomplishment. For she, who had never thought of her body save as something on which to hang lovely fabrics, had now constantly to think of it. It had persistently to be pampered to secure from it even a little service. Always she felt extraordinarily and annoyingly ill, having forever to be sinking into chairs. Or, if she was out, to be pausing by the roadside, clinging desperately to some convenient fence or tree, waiting for the horrible nausea and hateful faintness to pass. The light, care-free days of the past, when she had not felt heavy and reluctant or weak and spent, receded more and more and with increasing vagueness, like a dream passing from a faulty memory.

The children used her up. There were already three of them, all born within the short space of twenty months. Two great healthy twin boys, whose lovely bodies were to Helga like rare figures carved out of amber, and in whose sleepy and mysterious black eyes all that was puzzling, evasive, and aloof in life seemed to find expression. No matter how often or how long she looked at these two small sons of hers, never did she lose a certain delicious feeling in which were mingled pride, tenderness, and exaltation. And there was a girl, sweet, delicate, and flower-like. Not so healthy or so loved as the boys, but still miraculously her own proud and cherished possession.

So there was no time for the pursuit of beauty, or for the uplifting of other harassed and teeming women, or for the instruction of their neglected children.

Her husband was still, as he had always been, deferentially kind and incredulously proud of her—and verbally encouraging. Helga tried not to see that he had rather lost any personal interest in her, except for the short spaces between the times when she was preparing for or recovering from childbirth. She shut her eyes to the fact that his encouragement had become a little platitudinous, limited mostly to "The Lord will look out for you," "We must accept what God sends," or "My mother had nine children and was thankful for every one." If she was inclined to wonder a little just how they were to manage with another child on the way, he would point out to her that her doubt and uncertainty were a stupendous ingratitude. Had not the good God saved her soul from hell-fire and eternal damnation? Had He not in His great kindness given her three small lives to raise up for His glory? Had He not showered her with numerous other mercies (evidently too numerous to be named separately)?

"You must," the Reverend Mr. Pleasant Green would say unctuously, "trust the Lord more fully, Helga."

This pabulum did not irritate her. Perhaps it was the fact that the preacher was, now, not so much at home that even lent to it a measure of real comfort. For the adoring women of his flock, noting how with increasing frequency their pastor's house went unswept and undusted, his children unwashed, and his wife untidy, took pleasant pity on him and invited him often to tasty orderly meals, specially prepared for him, in their own clean houses.

Helga, looking about in helpless dismay and sick disgust at the disorder around her, the permanent assembly of partly emptied medicine bottles on the clock-shelf, the perpetual array of drying baby-clothes on the chair-backs, the constant debris of broken toys on the floor, the unceasing litter of half-dead flowers on the table, dragged in by the toddling twins from the forlorn garden, failed to blame him for the thoughtless selfishness of these absences. And, she was thankful, whenever possible, to be relieved from the ordeal of cooking. There were times when, having had to retreat from the kitchen in lumbering haste with her sensitive nose gripped between tightly squeezing fingers, she had been sure that the greatest kindness that God could ever show to her would be to free her forever from the sight and smell of food.

How, she wondered, did other women, other mothers, manage? Could it be possible that, while presenting such smiling and contented faces, they were all always on the edge of health? All always worn out and apprehensive? Or was it only she, a poor weak

city-bred thing, who felt that the strain of what the Reverend Mr.
Pleasant Green had so often gently and patiently reminded her
was a natural thing, an act of God, was almost unendurable?

One day on her round of visiting—a church duty, to be done
no matter how miserable one was—she summoned up sufficient
boldness to ask several women how they felt, how they managed.
The answers were a resigned shrug, or an amused snort, or an up-
ward rolling of eyeballs with a mention of "de Lawd" looking after us all.

" 'Tain't nothin', nothin' at all, chile," said one, Sary Jones,
who, as Helga knew, had had six children in about as many years.
"Yuh all takes it too ha'd. Jes' remembah et's natu'al fo' a 'oman to
hab chilluns an' don' fret so."

"But," protested Helga, "I'm always so tired and half sick. That
can't be natural."

"Laws, chile, we's all ti'ed. An' Ah reckons we's all gwine a be
ti'ed till kingdom come. Jes' make de bes' of et, honey. Jes' make
de bes' yuh can."

Helga sighed, turning her nose away from the steaming coffee
which her hostess had placed for her and against which her
squeamish stomach was about to revolt. At the moment the com-
pensations of immortality seemed very shadowy and very far
away.

"Jes' remembah," Sary went on, staring sternly into Helga's
thin face, "we all gits ouah res' by an' by. In de nex' worl' we's all
recompense'. Jes' put yo' trus' in de Sabioah."

Looking at the confident face of the little bronze figure on the
opposite side of the immaculately spread table, Helga had a sensation of shame that she should be less than content. Why couldn't
she be as trusting and as certain that her troubles would not overwhelm her as Sary Jones was? Sary, who in all likelihood had
toiled every day of her life since early childhood except on those
days, totalling perhaps sixty, following the birth of her six children. And who by dint of superhuman saving had somehow succeeded in feeding and clothing them and sending them all to
school. Before her Helga felt humbled and oppressed by the sense
of her own unworthiness and lack of sufficient faith.

"Thanks, Sary," she said, rising in retreat from the coffee, "you've done me a world of good. I'm really going to try to be more patient."

So, though with growing yearning she longed for the great ordinary things of life, hunger, sleep, freedom from pain, she resigned herself to the doing without them. The possibility of alleviating her burdens by a greater faith became lodged in her mind. She gave herself up to it. It *did* help. And the beauty of leaning on the wisdom of God, of trusting, gave to her a queer sort of satisfaction. Faith was really quite easy. One had only to yield. To ask no questions. The more weary, the more weak, she became, the easier it was. Her religion was to her a kind of protective coloring, shielding her from the cruel light of an unbearable reality.

This utter yielding in faith to what had been sent her found her favor, too, in the eyes of her neighbors. Her husband's flock began to approve and commend this submission and humility to a superior wisdom. The womenfolk spoke more kindly and more affectionately of the preacher's Northern wife. "Pore Mis' Green, wid all dem small chilluns at once. She suah do hab it ha'd. An' she don' nebah complains an' frets no mo'e. Jes' trus' in de Lawd lak de Good Book say. Mighty sweet lil' 'oman too."

Helga didn't bother much about the preparations for the coming child. Actually and metaphorically she bowed her head before God, trusting in Him to see her through. Secretly she was glad that she had not to worry about herself or anything. It was a relief to be able to put the entire responsibility on someone else.

> Helga has twin sons, daughter & pregnant
> constantly tired, sick, and house = dirty
> wonders how she can endure?
  ↳ talks to women in town (Sary Jones)

> She's successful in accepting spiritual submission, no longer worrying about herself or anything!!

TWENTY-FOUR

IT BEGAN, this next child-bearing, during the morning services of a breathless hot Sunday while the fervent choir soloist was singing: "Ah am freed of mah sorrow," and lasted far into the small hours of Tuesday morning. It seemed, for some reason, not to go off just right. And when, after that long frightfulness, the fourth little dab of amber humanity which Helga had contributed to a despised race was held before her for maternal approval, she failed entirely to respond properly to this sop of consolation for the suffering and horror through which she had passed. There was from her no pleased, proud smile, no loving, possessive gesture, no manifestation of interest in the important matters of sex and weight. Instead she deliberately closed her eyes, mutely shutting out the sickly infant, its smiling father, the soiled midwife, the curious neighbors, and the tousled room.

A week she lay so. Silent and listless. Ignoring food, the clamoring children, the comings and goings of solicitous, kind-hearted women, her hovering husband, and all of life about her. The neighbors were puzzled. The Reverend Mr. Pleasant Green was worried. The midwife was frightened.

On the floor, in and out among the furniture and under her bed, the twins played. Eager to help, the church-women crowded in and, meeting there others on the same laudable errand, stayed to gossip and to wonder. Anxiously the preacher sat, Bible in hand, beside his wife's bed, or in a nervous half-guilty manner invited the congregated parishioners to join him in prayer for the healing of their sister. Then, kneeling, they would beseech God to stretch out His all-powerful hand on behalf of the afflicted one, softly at first, but with rising vehemence, accompanied by moans and tears, until it seemed that the God to whom they prayed must in mercy to the sufferer grant relief. If only so that she might rise up and escape from the tumult, the heat, and the smell.

Helga, however, was unconcerned, undisturbed by the commotion about her. It was all part of the general unreality. Nothing reached her. Nothing penetrated the kind darkness into which her bruised spirit had retreated. Even that red-letter event, the coming to see her of the old white physician from downtown, who had for a long time stayed talking gravely to her husband, drew from her no interest. Nor for days was she aware that a stranger, a nurse from Mobile, had been added to her household, a brusquely efficient woman who produced order out of chaos and quiet out of bedlam. Neither did the absence of the children, removed by good neighbors at Miss Hartley's insistence, impress her. While she had gone down into that appalling blackness of pain, the ballast of her brain had got loose and she hovered for a long time somewhere in that delightful borderland on the edge of unconsciousness, an enchanted and blissful place where peace and incredible quiet encompassed her.

After weeks she grew better, returned to earth, set her reluctant feet to the hard path of life again.

"Well, here you are!" announced Miss Hartley in her slightly harsh voice one afternoon just before the fall of evening. She had for some time been standing at the bedside gazing down at Helga with an intent speculative look.

"Yes," Helga agreed in a thin little voice, "I'm back." The truth was that she had been back for some hours. Purposely she had lain silent and still, wanting to linger forever in that serene haven, that effortless calm where nothing was expected of her. There she could watch the figures of the past drift by. There was her mother, whom she had loved from a distance and finally so scornfully blamed, who appeared as she had always remembered her, unbelievably beautiful, young, and remote. Robert Anderson, questioning, purposely detached, affecting, as she realized now, her life in a remarkably cruel degree; for at last she understood clearly how deeply, how passionately, she must have loved him. Anne, lovely, secure, wise, selfish. Axel Olsen, conceited, worldly, spoiled. Audrey Denney, placid, taking quietly and without fuss the things which she wanted. James Vayle, snobbish, smug, servile. Mrs. Hayes-Rore, important, kind, determined. The Dahls, rich, correct, climbing. Flashingly, fragmentarily, other long-forgotten figures, women in gay fashionable frocks and men in formal black and white, glided by in bright rooms to distant, vaguely familiar music.

It was refreshingly delicious, this immersion in the past. But it was finished now. It was over. The words of her husband, the Reverend Mr. Pleasant Green, who had been standing at the window looking mournfully out at the scorched melon-patch, ruined because Helga had been ill so long and unable to tend it, were confirmation of that.

"The Lord be praised," he said, and came forward. It was distinctly disagreeable. It was even more disagreeable to feel his moist hand on hers. A cold shiver brushed over her. She closed her eyes. Obstinately and with all her small strength she drew her hand away from him. Hid it far down under the bed-covering, and turned her face away to hide a grimace of unconquerable aversion. She cared nothing, at that moment, for his hurt surprise. She knew only that, in the hideous agony that for interminable hours—no, centuries—she had borne, the luster of religion had vanished; that revulsion had come upon her; that she hated this man. Between them the vastness of the universe had come.

Miss Hartley, all-seeing and instantly aware of a situation, as she had been quite aware that her patient had been conscious for some time before she herself had announced the fact, intervened, saying firmly: "I think it might be better if you didn't try to talk to her now. She's terribly sick and weak yet. She's still got some fever and we mustn't excite her or she's liable to slip back. And we don't want that, do we?"

No, the man, her husband, responded, they didn't want that. Reluctantly he went from the room with a last look at Helga, who was lying on her back with one frail, pale hand under her small head, her curly black hair scattered loose on the pillow. She regarded him from behind dropped lids. The day was hot, her breasts were covered only by a nightgown of filmy *crêpe*, a relic of prematrimonial days, which had slipped from one carved shoulder. He flinched. Helga's petulant lip curled, for she well knew that this fresh reminder of her desirability was like the flick of a whip.

Miss Hartley carefully closed the door after the retreating husband. "It's time," she said, "for your evening treatment, and then you've got to try to sleep for a while. No more visitors tonight."

Helga nodded and tried unsuccessfully to make a little smile. She was glad of Miss Hartley's presence. It would, she felt, protect her from so much. She mustn't, she thought to herself, get well too fast. Since it seemed she was going to get well. In bed she could think, could have a certain amount of quiet. Of aloneness.

In that period of racking pain and calamitous fright Helga had learned what passion and credulity could do to one. In her was born angry bitterness and an enormous disgust. The cruel, unrelieved suffering had beaten down her protective wall of artificial faith in the infinite wisdom, in the mercy, of God. For had she not called in her agony on Him? And He had not heard. Why? Because, she knew now, He wasn't there. Didn't exist. Into that yawning gap of unspeakable brutality had gone, too, her belief in the miracle and wonder of life. Only scorn, resentment, and hate remained—and ridicule. Life wasn't a miracle, a wonder. It was, for Negroes at least, only a great disappointment. Something to be got through with as best one could. No one was interested in them or helped them. God! Bah! And they were only a nuisance to other people.

Everything in her mind was hot and cold, beating and swirling about. Within her emaciated body raged disillusion. Chaotic turmoil. With the obscuring curtain of religion rent, she was able to look about her and see with shocked eyes this thing that she had done to herself. She couldn't, she thought ironically, even blame God for it, now that she knew that He didn't exist. No. No more than she could pray to Him for the death of her husband, the Reverend Mr. Pleasant Green. The white man's God. And His great love for all people regardless of race! What idiotic nonsense she had allowed herself to believe. How could she, how could anyone, have been so deluded? How could ten million black folk credit it when daily before their eyes was enacted its contradiction? Not that she at all cared about the ten million. But herself. Her sons. Her daughter. These would grow to manhood, to womanhood, in this vicious, this hypocritical land. The dark eyes filled with tears.

"I wouldn't," the nurse advised, "do that. You've been dreadfully sick, you know. I can't have you worrying. Time enough for that when you're well. Now you must sleep all you possibly can."

Helga did sleep. She found it surprisingly easy to sleep. Aided by Miss Hartley's rather masterful discernment, she took advantage of the ease with which this blessed enchantment stole over her. From her husband's praisings, prayers, and caresses she sought refuge in sleep, and from the neighbors' gifts, advice, and sympathy.

There was that day on which they told her that the last sickly infant, born of such futile torture and lingering torment, had died after a short week of slight living. Just closed his eyes and died. No vitality. On hearing it Helga too had just closed her eyes. Not to die. She was convinced that before her there were years of living. Perhaps of happiness even. For a new idea had come to her. She had closed her eyes to shut in any telltale gleam of the relief which she felt. One less. And she had gone off into sleep.

And there was that Sunday morning on which the Reverend Mr. Pleasant Green had informed her that they were that day to hold a special thanksgiving service for her recovery. There would, he said, be prayers, special testimonies, and songs. Was there anything particular she would like to have said, to have prayed for, to have sung? Helga had smiled from sheer amusement as she replied that there was nothing. Nothing at all. She only hoped that they would enjoy themselves. And, closing her eyes that he might be discouraged from longer tarrying, she had gone off into sleep.

Waking later to the sound of joyous religious abandon floating in through the opened windows, she had asked a little diffidently that she be allowed to read. Miss Hartley's sketchy brows contracted into a dubious frown. After a judicious pause she had answered: "No, I don't think so." Then, seeing the rebellious tears which had sprung into her patient's eyes, she added kindly: "But I'll read to you a little if you like."

That, Helga replied, would be nice. In the next room on a high-up shelf was a book. She'd forgotten the name, but its author was Anatole France. There was a story, "The Procurator of Judea."[1] Would Miss Hartley read that? "Thanks. Thanks awfully."

" 'Lælius Lamia, born in Italy of illustrious parents,' "[2] began the nurse in her slightly harsh voice.

Helga drank it in.

" '. . . For to this day the women bring down doves to the altar as their victims. . . .' "

Helga closed her eyes.

" '. . . Africa and Asia have already enriched us with a considerable number of gods. . . .' "³

Miss Hartley looked up. Helga had slipped into slumber while the superbly ironic ending which she had so desired to hear was yet a long way off. A dull tale, was Miss Hartley's opinion, as she curiously turned the pages to see how it turned out.

" 'Jesus? . . . Jesus—of Nazareth? I cannot call him to mind.' "⁴

"Huh!" she muttered, puzzled. "Silly." And closed the book.

→ has 4th child but ignores people at bedside & becomes distant & unresponsive
→ prayers vigils needed & white doctor brought in
→ children = moved to neighbors care
→ In dream-state Helga recalls life & realizes she despises reverend.
→ begins to despise religion & no longer believes in god.
→ feels suffering of Blacks = proof "white man's god" doesn't exist
→ newborn dies c/d in week & Helga feels relief

DURING THE LONG PROCESS of getting well, between the dreamy intervals when she was beset by the insistent craving for sleep, Helga had had too much time to think. At first she had felt only an astonished anger at the quagmire in which she had engulfed herself. She had ruined her life. Made it impossible ever again to do the things that she wanted, have the things that she loved, mingle with the people she liked. She had, to put it as brutally as anyone could, been a fool. The damnedest kind of a fool. And she had paid for it. Enough. More than enough.

Her mind, swaying back to the protection that religion had afforded her, almost she wished that it had not failed her. An illusion. Yes. But better, far better, than this terrible reality. Religion had, after all, its uses. It blunted the perceptions. Robbed life of its crudest truths. Especially it had its uses for the poor—and the blacks.

For the blacks. The Negroes.

And this, Helga decided, was what ailed the whole Negro race in America, this fatuous belief in the white man's God, this childlike trust in full compensation for all woes and privations in "kingdom come." Sary Jones's absolute conviction, "In de nex' worl' we's all recompense'," came back to her. And ten million souls were as sure of it as was Sary. How the white man's God must laugh at the great joke he had played on them! Bound them to slavery, then to poverty and insult, and made them bear it unresistingly, uncomplainingly almost, by sweet promises of mansions in the sky by and by.

"Pie in the sky,"[1] Helga said aloud derisively, forgetting for the moment Miss Hartley's brisk presence, and so was a little startled at hearing her voice from the adjoining room saying severely: "My goodness! No! I should say you can't have pie. It's too indigestible. Maybe when you're better—"

"That," assented Helga, "is what I said. Pie—by and by. That's the trouble."

The nurse looked concerned. Was this an approaching relapse? Coming to the bedside, she felt at her patient's pulse while giving her a searching look. No. "You'd better," she admonished, a slight edge to her tone, "try to get a little nap. You haven't had any sleep today, and you can't get too much of it. You've got to get strong, you know."

With this Helga was in full agreement. It seemed hundreds of years since she had been strong. And she would need strength. For in some way she was determined to get herself out of this bog into which she had strayed. Or—she would have to die. She couldn't endure it. Her suffocation and shrinking loathing were too great. Not to be borne. Again. For she had to admit that it wasn't new, this feeling of dissatisfaction, of asphyxiation. Something like it she had experienced before. In Naxos. In New York. In Copenhagen. This differed only in degree. And it was of the present and therefore seemingly more reasonable. The other revulsions were of the past, and now less explainable.

The thought of her husband roused in her a deep and contemptuous hatred. At his every approach she had forcibly to subdue a furious inclination to scream out in protest. Shame, too, swept over her at every thought of her marriage. Marriage. This sacred thing of which parsons and other Christian folk ranted so sanctimoniously, how immoral—according to their own standards—it could be! But Helga felt also a modicum of pity for him, as for one already abandoned. She meant to leave him. And it was, she had to concede, all of her own doing, this marriage. Nevertheless, she hated him.

The neighbors and churchfolk came in for their share of her all-embracing hatred. She hated their raucous laughter, their stupid acceptance of all things, and their unfailing trust in "de Lawd." And more than all the rest she hated the jangling Clementine Richards, with her provocative smirkings, because she had not succeeded in marrying the preacher and thus saving her, Helga, from that crowning idiocy.

Of the children Helga tried not to think. She wanted not to leave them—if that were possible. The recollection of her own childhood, lonely, unloved, rose too poignantly before her for her to consider calmly such a solution. Though she forced herself to believe that this was different. There was not the element of race, of white and black. They were all black together. And they would have their father. But to leave them would be a tearing agony, a rending of deepest fibers. She felt that through all the rest of her lifetime she would be hearing their cry of "Mummy, Mummy, Mummy," through sleepless nights. No. She couldn't desert them.

How, then, was she to escape from the oppression, the degradation, that her life had become? It was so difficult. It was terribly difficult. It was almost hopeless. So for a while—for the immediate present, she told herself—she put aside the making of any plan for her going. "I'm still," she reasoned, "too weak, too sick. By and by, when I'm really strong—"

It was so easy and so pleasant to think about freedom and cities, about clothes and books, about the sweet mingled smell of Houbigant[2] and cigarettes in softly lighted rooms filled with inconsequential chatter and laughter and sophisticated tuneless music. It was so hard to think out a feasible way of retrieving all these agreeable, desired things. Just then. Later. When she got up. By and by. She must rest. Get strong. Sleep. Then, afterwards, she could work out some arrangement. So she dozed and dreamed in snatches of sleeping and waking, letting time run on. Away.

And hardly had she left her bed and become able to walk again without pain, hardly had the children returned from the homes of the neighbors, when she began to have her fifth child.

→ determined to leave reverand & wife
→ feels greatest failings is that Black society suffers w/ belief they'll be rewarded in "next world"
→ thinks abt leaving kids but too difficult
→ Helga begins w/ fifth child

EXPLANATORY NOTES

DEDICATION

1. *For E.S.I.:* Elmer Samuel Imes (1883–1941), Nella Larsen's husband, a member of a prominent African-American family, a research physicist (Ph.D., Michigan), and later a college professor at Fisk University, whom she married in 1919 and divorced in 1933.

EPIGRAPH

1. *"My old man died in a fine big house./ . . . /Being neither white nor black?"*: Lines from the poem "Cross," from *The Weary Blues* (Knopf, New York, 1926), the first book of poems by Langston Hughes. Themes of racial identity, racial inequity, paternal recognition, and social place, articulated by the mixed-race speaker of "Cross," reverberate throughout *Quicksand*.
2. *Langston Hughes:* (1902–1967), poet, novelist, playwright, and columnist, whose early poetry became emblematic of the confident new voices raised by African Americans during the 1920s, the period of the Harlem Renaissance and New Negro movement. One of the most prolific and admired modern writers, Hughes gained an international reputation for his awareness of the African diaspora and his use of material central to African-American cultural heritage in his writing.

CHAPTER ONE

1. *a pool of light on the blue Chinese carpet . . . oriental silk which covered the stool:* Interest in Asia, the Far East, the Near East, Africa, and Egypt involved a construction collapsing many distinct cultures, traditions, religions, politics, and goods into the Orient and an Orientalism focused on the objective destination of Columbus's voyage to discover a new route to the Orient and its fabled treasures and on the imperialist motives of American empire-building in the expansion of its capitalist marketplace, both receiving a boost just before the turn of the century from the 1893 Columbia Exposition of the New

World and in the early twentieth century from Egyptology and the archeological excavations of pyramids and tombs in Egypt.

2. *Naxos:* Fictionalized Tuskegee Institute in Alabama, where Larsen worked as a supervising nurse, with some hints of Fisk University, Nashville, Tennessee, where Larsen attended the Fisk Normal High School as a boarding student. The largest of the Greek Cycladic Islands, Naxos was the place where Theseus abandoned Ariadne in Greek mythology, so that the name "Naxos" became evocative of abandonment, exile, longing, and despair.

3. *Marmaduke Pickthall's* Saïd the Fisherman: Novel (1903) traces the life of an amoral, opportunistic, yet observant Muslim fisherman between 1860 to 1882 when he leaves his home on the Palestinian coast outside Haida, to seek his fortune in Damascus, and follows his roguelike adventures from Syria to Beirut, to London and finally to Alexandria, where he dies in the aftermath of a British attack on Alexandria, when Egyptian troops left the city to a plundering mob. The author, Marmaduke Pickthall (1875–1936), born in Britain and the son of an upper-middle-class Suffolk clergyman, became an orientalist and spiritualist after traveling to Egypt, Palestine, and Syria as a youth. Pickthall wrote his unsentimental portrait of Islamic life at the turn of the century, but not until the novel's appearance in Alfred A. Knopf's Blue Jade Series in 1925 did it gain an audience in the United States.

4. *hewers of wood and drawers of water:* (Genesis 9:20–27; Genesis 10:6–20) The descendants of Ham, one of the sons of Noah who survived the destruction of a wicked world by flooding, suffered for mocking Noah's drunkenness and nakedness. Ham's punishment for disrespecting his father fell upon his children, the Semitic-speaking people of Canaan, then belonging to Egypt, and the Hamitic-speaking people of Northern Africa, including Egypt, Ethiopia, and Nubia, who were cursed to become the servants of Ham's brothers' children. Slave holders in the nineteenth-century United States and racial supremacists in the twentieth century applied the Biblical account of Ham's punishment to blacks, using it as a justification for slavery and for consigning them to menial labor and subservient positions.

5. *this monument to one man's genius and vision:* Suggestive of Booker T. Washington's founding of Tuskegee Institute in Tuskegee, Alabama, in 1881 to provide industrial education for freed people of color. A racial accomodationist, Washington courted white patronage, especially northern industrialists and southern politicians, to build Tuskegee and in exchange promised African Americans' acquiescence to inequality and lack of civil rights. By the time of his death in 1915,

Washington had become the foremost black leader in the United States and his "Tuskegee Machine" exercised arbitrary and uncontrolled power over most of the decisions and activities regarding race relations in America.

6. *the black belt:* The area of the Deep South (Georgia, Alabama, and Mississippi) with large black populations historically connected to farming and agriculture.

7. *the Naxos policy of uplift:* An ethic of service, accommodation, racial self-help promoted by Booker T. Washington at Tuskegee Institute, where thrift, patience, and perseverance combined with high morals, good manners, and manual labor were considered the keys to improved conditions for black people. Racial self-help focused on the black masses generally permeated black middle-class ideology from emancipation through the first decades of the twentieth century, when social advancement was considered the distinguishing feature of racial progress. The work of racial uplift for middle-class blacks in the helping professions, such as teaching, medicine, social work, became more difficult after World War I when mass black migration from the rural South to northern urban areas, in particular New York and Chicago, threatened to overwhelm the resources for improving the material and moral condition of poor blacks.

8. *her former loneliness in Nashville:* The location of Fisk University, founded in 1865 under the auspices of the American Missionary Society of New York and the Western Freedman's Aid Commission of Cincinnati for the purpose of educating young people of color, and the now-defunct Fisk Normal School where Larsen matriculated as a high school sophomore in 1907–08.

9. *Negro society . . . if you were a Rankin, or a Leslie, or a Scoville; in other words, if you had a family:* In the years after emancipation, educated and better-off blacks, referred to as the black bourgeoisie, began to insulate themselves from identification with the vulnerable undereducated, poor black masses by forming exclusive clubs, fraternities, cotillions, and boules not merely to consolidate their social distinction but also to protect themselves from the discriminatory and prejudicial practices of racial segregation. Their own exclusionary strategies for self-preservation from racism often depended less upon phenotype and more upon the recognition of family names, school ties, and accumulated wealth.

CHAPTER TWO

1. *The goose-step began:* A stiff-legged march associated with military parades.

2. *the black list:* Names of individuals who were not to be accepted for teaching positions. Because of segregation, the few institutions employing black teachers were all well known to one another and could all be coerced into uniformly preventing an individual from obtaining a job based on the judgment or whim of an influential race leader or a well-placed white person.

CHAPTER THREE

1. *Dr. Anderson . . . He was a new man, this principal:* Based loosely on Booker T. Washington's successor, Robert Russa Moton (1867–1940), who became principal of Tuskegee Institute following Washington's death in 1915. Although Moton continued Washington's practice of accommodation to whites and industrial education for blacks, he added a college department to the Tuskegee curriculum, and he pushed for the training of black officers and combat units during World War I, and in the 1920s for reforms in the hiring of black doctors and supervisors at a veterans' hospital built in Tuskegee.

2. *a sudden attack of nerves . . . a disease:* Symptoms of discomfort linked to agoraphobia and perhaps also claustrophobia, as in a fear of being trapped in a crowd, causing both an aversion to strangers and new places but also a personality tendency toward shyness and introversion.

CHAPTER FOUR

1. *a school for Negroes:* Suggestive of Fisk University in Nashville, Tennessee, which had a boarding school for elementary and high school students.

2. *Ten hours to Chicago. Would she be lucky enough to prevail upon the conductor to let her occupy a berth:* In *Plessy v. Ferguson* (1896), the Supreme Court of the United States upheld racial segregation in public conveyances, and instituted the "separate but equal" approach to public facilities. Railway cars in the aftermath of *Plessy* were not required to provide berths, sleeping accomodations, or club cars, dining accomodations, for people of color, who as a result slept in their seats and brought their own food onboard trains.

CHAPTER FIVE

1. *Young Women's Christian Association:* The YWCA, founded in 1887 to promote the spiritual, intellectual, social, and physical welfare of young women. The YWCA for black women in Chicago operated a

dormitory, vocational classes, employment registry, recreational programs, summer camp, and a library, all for the purpose of elevating the spiritual and moral nature of the women.

2. *the North Side:* One of the wealthier areas of Chicago, bordering Lake Michigan and Lincoln Park.

CHAPTER SIX

1. *the Young Women's Christian Association maintained an employment agency:* The black Southside branch of the YWCA of Chicago, founded in 1914 and affiliated with the national organization in 1915, offered an employment bureau, housed on its premises and staffed by blacks, to assist young black women, most typically newcomers to Chicago from the South, seeking jobs as well as housing. The jobs were primarily domestic—housework, childcare, and cooking. In Chicago, the Negro Fellowship League, like its larger counterpart, the Chicago Urban League, also operated an employment office to help assist migrants new to the city in finding jobs.

2. *the hustling streets of the Loop district:* The main business district in downtown Chicago.

3. *A graduate of Devon:* Modeled on Fisk University in Nashville, Tennessee, which was held in high esteem for the quality of its liberal arts curriculum.

4. *an employment agency on State Street:* During the Great Migration, white employment agencies in downtown Chicago frequently misled black applicants regarding jobs in an effort to restrict them from better and less menial jobs.

5. *the very fashionable, very high services in the Negro Episcopal church on Michigan Avenue:* Reference to St. Thomas Episcopal Church, founded in the 1870s and, until well into the twentieth century, the only congregation of black Episcopalians in Chicago. Affiliated with a major white denomination, St. Thomas appealed to the black elite who preferred the reserved worship of high church services.

6. *the home of Mrs. Hayes-Rore on Grand Boulevard:* A fashionable residential area favored by upper middle-class and elite black bankers, doctors, merchants, attorneys, and politicians in Chicago. Mrs. Jeanette Hayes-Rore suggests Mrs. Eva Jenifer-Rice, a Chicago matron, widow of a minister and a leader among the black clubwomen and ministers' wives, who founded the Chicago South Side YWCA of 3424 Rhodes Avenue in 1914. Jenifer-Rice became the first president of the black South Side branch of the Y in 1915 after shepherding its affiliation with the national organization; thereafter as its first president, she spearheaded its move into more spacious quarters at

3451 Indiana Avenue in 1919, and remained the guiding spirit behind its 1927 move to a new building at 4555-59 South Parkway, one of the finest YWCA facilities in the West at that time. A primary mission of the South Side Y was the assistance of young girls arriving in Chicago seeking housing and employment.

7. *I'm on the Board of Managers:* The governing board of the YWCA.

CHAPTER SEVEN

1. *to attract the jade's notice:* Literally in this context "Fortune," but also slang for a flirtatious or disreputable woman.

2. *a dark thread in the fabric of Chicago's South Side politics:* The controlling of the political interests of the large black population living on the South Side by white ward bosses, politicians, and appointees through a few black leaders. Also precinct politics with ward bosses dispensing political favors for votes.

3. *Negro Women's League of Clubs:* The club movement among middle-class black women was especially active in volunteer social and political work during the early decades of the twentieth century. On the local level, the Chicago Federation of Colored Women's Clubs was an amalgamated group of all the women's clubs in the city of Chicago, organized to perform the work of racial uplift and self-help, particularly for girls and young women of color. On the national level, the National Association of Colored Women, formed in 1896 when the National Federation of Afro-American Women and the National League of Colored Women merged, also promoted racial uplift.

4. *previous orations and published works of Wendell Phillips, Frederick Douglass, Booker T. Washington, and other doctors of the race's ills:* Wendell Phillips (1811–1884), Frederick Douglass (1817–1895), and Booker T. Washington (1856–1915), all African-American race leaders who attempted to provide antidotes to American racism and remedies to the treatment of black people in America, and all of whom were known for their oratory as well as for their writings.

5. *a peppery dash of Du Bois:* Dr. W. E. B. Du Bois (1868–1963), race leader, intellectual, scholar, educator, activist, a founder of the National Association for the Advancement of Colored People, the editor of *Crisis* magazine during the 1920s and writer of fiery editorials condemning racism and colonialization of Africa. He supported the full rights of citizenship for African Americans, particularly enfranchisement, social equality, and higher education for blacks.

6. *running into the shadow of the tunnel:* Trains entered New York City via one of the Hudson Tunnels under the Hudson River, which con-

nected Jersey City to Manhattan and the Pennsylvania Terminal Station.

7. *"come uptown and stay"*: Harlem, the area across 110th Street and the upper portion of Manhattan, attracting African-American residents in record numbers throughout the 1920s.

8. *"The war, you know"*: World War I.

9. *Turning out of the park into the broad thoroughfare of Lenox Avenue:* The upper or northern end of Central Park at 110th Street opens out onto one of the two central north-south streets in Harlem, where businesses, restaurants, and especially clubs flourished in the 1920s.

CHAPTER EIGHT

1. *tables that might be by Duncan Phyfe:* Scottish born, early American cabinet maker (1768–1854), whose workshop in New York made fine quality furniture. Known for his designs and workmanship, he produced a large group of furniture for customers in New York and the East. In 1922, a major exhibition of his authenticated work at New York's Metropolitan Museum of Art popularized his name and his craftsmanship, so that Duncan Phyfe became a commanding presence in early American furniture.

2. *davenports:* Originally a term for a writing desk with a knee-hole opening, in the late nineteenth century, it came into use for sofas. Davenports were popularized in the United States in 1922 with the exhibition of Duncan Phyfe furniture at the Metropolitan Museum of Art in New York City, and resultantly coinages such "davenportbed" for sofa bed and "davenport table" for a long, low coffee table came into popular usage.

3. *lustrous Eastern rugs, ancient copper, Japanese prints:* Appointments and artifacts associated with the fashion for rare materials from the East and with the popularity of the fabrics and designs from the Orient during the 1920s.

4. *furs from Bendel's and Revillon Frères':* Henri Bendel, an exclusive fashion house in New York, began as a hat shop in the 1890s and transformed to include furs and designer dresses by 1896. Revillon Frères', furrier, began its operations in the Canadian fur trade in 1901 and leased space in upscale department stores for its fur salons.

5. *Her existence was bounded by Central Park, Fifth Avenue, St. Nicholas Park, and One Hundred and Forty-fifth Street:* The boundaries of Harlem, with the uptown end of Central Park at 110th Street forming the south border, Fifth Avenue forming the east border, St. Nicholas Park forming the west border, and 145th Street forming the north border leading to the Bronx.

CHAPTER NINE

1. *Negro yellow press:* Yellow journalism, muckraking, and expose reports about the social and economic mistreatment and exploitation of blacks, and in particular the more sensational stories.
2. *that made Lenox and Seventh Avenues the rich spectacles which they were:* Considered the bustling and vibrant center of Harlem life during the 1920s, when black people from all parts of the African diaspora strolled the avenues as a form of recreation; Lenox Avenue, technically a continuation of Sixth Avenue above the Central Park, was Harlem's principal boulevard, a station of the Bronx branch of the Interborough Subway and the location of the famous dance hall, the Savoy Ballroom, while Seventh Avenue, the widest street in Harlem, featured the Hotel Teresa, the Alhambra Theatre, the Lafayette Theatre, Connie's Inn, Small's Paradise, and restaurants, clubs, shops, and apartment houses.
3. *Negro prostitute that walks One Hundred and Thirty-fifth Street:* The area around 135th Street and Fifth Avenue, was home to prostitutes, pimps, gamblers, and crowded cabarets such as the Sugar Cane Club, which served a rough clientele. Ironically, west of that area, 135th Street was at the opposite end of the social scale with many of Harlem's leading institutions, the Harlem Branch of the Young Men's Christian Association (YMCA), the 135th Street Branch of the New York Public Library, the local offices of the Urban League and of the National Association for the Advancement of Colored People (N.A.A.C.P.), the New York *Age* newspaper, the offices of doctors and lawyers, and the street on which Larsen herself and her husband lived when they moved to New York from Jersey City, New Jersey, in 1927.
4. *not excepting Abraham Lincoln:* (1809–1865), Republican, sixteenth President of the United States (1861–1865) who, during the Civil War (1861–1865), issued the Emancipation Proclamation (1863), outlawing slavery in the nation.
5. *like the despised people of the white race, she preferred Pavlova to Florence Mills, John McCormack to Taylor Gordon, Walter Hampden to Paul Robeson:* Anna Pavlova (1881–1931), classical ballerina from Russia, ethereal, delicate, expressive, and passionate in style, and one of the great and most influential ballerinas of the twentieth century, famous for popularizing ballet throughout the world and especially in the U.S. by traveling over 350,000 miles in ten years to perform in small towns and rural areas. Florence Mills (1895–1927), popular singer and dancer, called "The Little Blackbird" and the first black international star, appeared in the musical comedies *Shuffle Along*

(1921), *Plantation Revue* (1922), and *Blackbirds of 1926*, which made her a star in New York, London, and Paris. Her untimely death from appendicitis caused an outpouring of feeling from the Harlem community. John McCormack (1884–1945), tenor, born in Ireland, and acclaimed for his operatic performances with the Boston and Chicago opera companies, as well as for his bel canto artistry and made famous by his recordings of simple, often sentimental songs. Taylor Gordon (1893–1971), black singer, whose tenor voice and engaging personality made him a major figure on the concert stage during the 1920s, when he teamed with J. Rosamund Johnson in a series of concerts of American Negro spirituals. His autobiography, *Born to Be* (1929), presents his origins in White Sulphur Springs, Montana, a mining town, his years as a chauffeur for John Ringling of the Ringling Brothers Circus, and his rise to prominence in New York vaudeville. Walter Hampden [Dougherty] (1879–1955), an actor born in Brooklyn, known best for his work in classical theatre, particularly, his performances in Ibsen's plays and in Shakespearean drama. He became a major and beloved figure in American theatre after he purchased New York's Colonial Theater in 1925, renamed it Hampden's, and appeared there with his own stage company. Paul Robeson (1898–1976), famous black actor and singer whose roles in Eugene O'Neill's plays *All God's Chillun Got Wings* (1924) and *The Emperor Jones* (1925) were major breakthroughs for blacks on the New York stage. A powerful and melodic bass singer, he was celebrated for his interpretation of spirituals, and for his performance in Jerome Kern's musical *Show Boat* (1928).

6. *Ibsen's remark about there being assuredly something very wrong with the drains, but after all there were other parts of the edifice:* Henrik Ibsen (1828–1906), Norwegian playwright and poet, who pioneered modern directions in social drama and broke with nineteenth-century conventions for theatre and whose *A Doll's House* (1879) and *Hedda Gabler* (1890) created unforgettable married women struggling against gender conventions. His artistic and commercial success is associated with Copenhagen, which first recognized and rewarded his genius when his play *Brand* (1865) appeared, and his play, *Peer Gynt* (1867), set not only in Scandinavia, but also on the coast of Morocco, in Cairo, Egypt, and the Sahara Desert, may have been Larsen's source for the name Helga.

7. *a health meeting, held in a large church:* Mother Zion AME Church on West 136 Street often hosted meetings on urban health care, such as meetings of the National Association of Colored Graduate Nurses, of which Nella Larsen was herself a member.

8. *the house on One Hundred and Thirty-ninth Street:* One of the ele-

gant, Italianate-styled brownstones on "Strivers' Row," West 138th and West 139th Streets, designed in 1891 by the famous architect Stanford White (1853–1906) and by the 1920s owned by prominent and mainly wealthy blacks.

9. *John Wellinger's lawsuit for discrimination because of race against a downtown restaurant:* Fictional lawsuit, composite of several suits filed in New York in the early 1920s under the provisions of the Civil Rights Act. In particular, a suit filed in 1921 by Victor R. Daly, his wife, and his mother-in-law may have been a model for Larsen's reference. Daly, the business manager of *The Messenger,* the official organ of the Brotherhood of Sleeping Car Porters and one of the important magazines of the Harlem Renaissance, and his family were refused service at the Pig and Whistle Restaurant on West Fourth; the Appellate Court found the owner in violation of the Civil Rights law and ordered her to pay $100 each to Daly, his wife, and mother-in-law.

10. *the advantages of living in Europe, especially in France:* After the heroics of black soldiers in Europe during World War I, Europeans and the French in particular, because of the remarkable valor of black regiments such as Harlem's Hell Fighters, the 369th Infantry Division, in liberating France, welcomed black Americans without the racism and segregation codes they faced in the United States.

11. *the Garvey movement:* Marcus Garvey (1887–1940), Jamaican-born black leader, founded the Universal Negro Improvement Association to promote what he first termed "the New Negro" and race pride, self-respect, and love. By means of his rousing soapbox oratory and his influential weekly, *Negro World* (founded in 1918), Garvey encouraged the black masses to claim their African heritage and to support Africa for Africans in his Back-to-Africa movement. With large numbers of devoted followers among the black population of New York and other urban centers, the movement was the first widespread, popular mobilization of black people in the United States. In 1927, Garvey was deported after having spent two years in a federal penitentiary in Atlanta for mail fraud, connected with his solicitation of funds through the U.S. mail for his Black Star Line shipping company in his efforts to resettle New World blacks in Africa.

CHAPTER TEN

1. *718 Sheridan Road/Chicago, Ill:* Fictitious number on a desirable residential street in the expensive Lake Shore area on Chicago's fashionable North Side.

2. *Maria Kirkeplads, No. 2:* A small street in the center of Copenhagen's Latin Quarter linked to the Cathedral, Vor Frue Kirke (Our Lady's

Church) named for Mary (also Maria and Marie in Danish), the mother of Jesus Christ, situated in University Square, and Frue Plads, the street running between the church and the university, in central Copenhagen. Frue Kirke is famous for the marble figures of the Twelve Apostles by Thorvaldsen, the famous Danish sculptor.

3. *chintz-hung living room, clad only in a fluttering of green chiffon:* Chintz, a printed calico fabric from India, became popularly reproduced in the U.S., and the name applied to any heavy glazed printed cotton fabrics, typically used for curtains and upholstery. Chiffon, a soft sheer fabric usually of a fine lightweight silk, was a favorite fabric for women's delicate ballgowns and elegant party dresses, as well as for negligees.

4. *too décolleté and too outré:* Exposure of the shoulders, neck, and cleavage in an exaggerated and suggestive way.

5. *her best pale-yellow pajamas of crêpe de Chine:* Sleepwear and also new lounging clothing for women, made of a finely crinkled silk fabric.

CHAPTER ELEVEN

1. *cabareting:* Going from one night club or cabaret to another for dancing and entertainment.

2. *they descended through a furtive, narrow passage into a vast subterranean room:* A speakeasy. A drinking and dancing room typically below ground or on a ground-floor level, popular during Prohibition.

3. *four bottles of White Rock:* The White Rock beverage company, founded in 1871, marketed an assortment of mixers for alcoholic beverages as well as bottled water.

4. *She wasn't . . . a jungle creature . . . . she watched the entertainers throw themselves about to the burst of syncopated jangle:* Description of the new music, jazz, and its hard-driving rhythms for dancing that were associated with Africa, the jungle, and primitivism, especially after 1923 when the Cotton Club opened in Harlem with a jungle decor and later in 1927 when its house band leader Duke Ellington was dubbed "the King of Jungle Music." During the 1920s, the area on 133rd Street between Seventh and Lenox Avenues was also called "Jungle Alley" or "The Jungle" for the wild clubs associated with so-called "primitive abandon": Dickie Wells, The Nest, Pod's and Jerry's, Mexico's, The Clam House, and Tillie's Chicken Shack.

5. *Audrey Denney . . . she lives downtown:* Based on Blanche Dunn, the exquisitely dressed, alabaster-skinned beauty known in the 1920s for her unique ability to do nothing and to do it better than anyone else. Admired for her languid beauty, social sophistication, and racial im-

partiality, Dunn was variously described as calm, serene, unflappable, elegant, and glamorous, and always remarked for her indifference to race, racial hierarchies, racial prejudice, or racial protocol. A widely recognizable, unique figure during Harlem's heyday, she went from elegant restaurants, to Broadway openings, exclusive speakeasies, to shopping trips in Paris, races at Saratoga, and the shore at Atlantic City, and was equally comfortable in the company of whites and blacks. Downtown refers to the lower part of Manhattan, where in the 1920s primarily whites resided.

CHAPTER TWELVE

1. *cliff-like towers:* The skyscraper buildings creating the famous Manhattan skyline.
2. *the Scandinavian-American line:* Steamship line traveling between New York and Denmark, Sweden, and Norway. The company's main Scandinavian port was Copenhagen, which had a free port. With no duties and no tide, it was considered the central point for all trade on the Baltic Sea and the key gateway to the Baltic and Northern Europe.
3. *Herr Dahl:* Name derived from H. C. Dahl's Succ., 5, Heibroplads, Kobenhavn, shoemaker to the Danish courts, who advertised the best hand-sewn footwear in Copenhagen.

CHAPTER THIRTEEN

1. *impecunious Sybarites:* The residents of the ancient Greek city Sybaris gave their name to lovers of luxury and to sensualists seeking pleasure.
2. *Marie . . . had probably never seen a Negro outside the pictured pages of her geography book:* The servant is given Larsen's own Danish mother's first name and occupation (seamstress).
3. *Garborg, the jeweler, in Fredericksgaarde:* A fashionable street in central Copenhagen opening onto Amalienborg, part of the Frederiksstaden laid out by Frederik V (1746–1766).
4. *a Danish frøkken:* an unmarried Danish girl.

CHAPTER FOURTEEN

1. *"Den Sorte" dropped freely, audibly, from many lips:* Danish for "black."
2. *batik dresses:* Hand-printed, usually bright colors in patterns produced by coating with wax the parts not to be dyed.

3. *a black Manila shawl:* Triangular wrapper covering the shoulders or head.

4. *blue-clad, sprucely tailored soldiers in the daily parade at Amalienborg Palace:* The royal residence in Copenhagen consisting of four identical Rococo palaces situated around a large courtyard, in the middle of which an equestrian statue of King Frederik V was placed in 1768. Named for a residence of Sofie Amalie that was formerly on the same site, the Amalienborg palaces are connected by a grand wooden colonnade, and there daily a military band plays as the palace royal guard is relieved at noon. The Vagtparade, or the parade of the Royal Danish Life Guard for the changing of the guard, led by their band in plain blue uniforms when the royals are away and in a spectacular blue and red full-dress uniform when the king is in Amalienborg, is one of the Copenhagen's major attractions.

5. *the long, low-lying Exchange:* The Stock Exchange, or Børsen, in Copenhagen built (1619–1640) between two harbors in the style of the Dutch Renaissance and surrounded by water on both sides, was intended as a marketplace for commodities brought to the city by ship.

6. *the huge ruined pile of the Palace of Christiansborg:* Built between 1733 and 1745 for Christian VI on the site of the original stronghold of Bishop Absalon, founder of Copenhagen, the royal residence was twice destroyed by fire (1794, 1886). During the period in which Larsen set *Quicksand,* the third Christianborg was being built as the seat of the Danish Parliament, Supreme Court, and the Ministry of Foreign Affairs.

7. *the Gammelstrand:* Fishmarket Square at the Gammel Strand's wharf was used daily by the fishwives from Skovshoved, north of Copenhagen, to sell their fish.

8. *exquisite cups fashioned of Royal Danish porcelain:* Hand-decorated porcelain ware made in the Royal Copenhagen Porcelain Factory, which was founded in 1779.

9. *smørrebrød:* Literally, bread and butter; typically, Danish appetizers, a variety of open-faced sandwiches, and hor d'oeuvres served buffet style and known as "smorgasbord" in English.

10. *the eccentric studio opposite the Folkemuseum:* Founded in 1885 by Bernard Olsen, a former director of Tivoli Garden, the famous and fanciful amusement park in Copenhagen, the Dansk Folkemuseum, located in Copenhagen's Vesterbrogarde, demonstrated in full-room settings with mannequins and wax figures showing how Danes lived in earlier times, particularly in rural areas. Farmhouses from different places in Denmark were moved to Frilandsmuseet, the open-air folk museum site founded by Olsen in 1901, and used as cultural exhibits

to further this form of educational entertainment. Larsen places Axel Olsen's painting studio across from the Folkenmuseum and makes use of Bernard Olsen's name in creating her artist figure.

11. *Hotel Vivili:* Based on the Grand Hotel National, Vesterbro Passage, opposite Tivoli Garden, the popular Pleasure Garden with a concert hall and variety of restaurants and amusements.

12. *Herr Karl Pedersen, who had a good berth with the Landmands-bank and considerable shares in a prosperous cement-factory at Aalborg:* The Danish Landmandsbank, founded in 1871, provided services in foreign exchanges, letters of credit. Aalborg [Alborg], a city of 35,000 in the 1920s.

13. *Christian Lende, the young owner of the new Odin Theater: Det Ny Teater,* or the New Theatre, opened in 1908 as a center for foreign art and not-too-high Danish art, including vaudeville and revue. Lende is also a play upon "Linde," the name of the deceased husband from the loveless marriage Kristine Linde describes to Nora in Ibsen's play, *A Doll's House.*

14. *Bolsheviks and Japs and things:* Reference to members of the Russian Social Democratic Party, who seized power in the Russian Revolution of November 1917, and to the Japanese in a disparaging short form to suggest Fru Fischer's aristocratic, nationalist sympathies and racial prejudices.

15. *that hideous American music:* Jazz, or what was termed "the new music," was introduced in Denmark in 1925 by the black musician and band leader, William Gooding, who initiated interest in jazz among the Danish people, particularly musicians. Along with France and Sweden, Denmark became one of the first European countries to herald jazz for its artistic creativity.

16. *"the good old-fashioned Danish melodies of Gade and Heise":* Neils Wilhelm Gade (1817–1890), Danish composer known for his waltzes and immortalized in a statue in the famous Tivoli Garden depicting him playing his violin. Peter Arnold Heise (1830–1879), Danish composer whose work included symphonies, organ music, choral music, chamber music, and cantos for the piano and string instruments, as well as melodies for traditional Danish stories.

17. *"Nielsen's 'Helios' is being performed with great success just now in England":* Overture (op. 17, 1903) composed during a trip to Athens by Carl August Nielsen (1865–1931), who during his long career earned a reputation as Denmark's greatest composer. "Helios" is an orchestral piece reflecting Nielsen's interest in musical characterization and thematic metamorphosis, but he is best known for making accessible popular Danish songs (*20 Popular Melodies*, 1917–21, *Ten Little Danish Songs*, 1923–24), folk melodies (*Folkenhøjskolens*

melodibog, 1922), and thus for a strong influence on twentieth-century Danish music.

CHAPTER FIFTEEN

1. *the great Circus:* Opposite the Hovedbanegaarden, the main railway station, the circus held equestrian and acrobatic performances during the summer and variety entertainments during the winter.
2. *an old rag-time song that Helga remembered hearing as a child, "Everybody Gives Me Good Advice.".:* Popular song written by Alfred Brian, James Kendiss, and Herman Paley at the turn of the century for traveling shows and published in the 1920s during the rise in popularity of musical shows and revues.
3. *"Hark! Hark!/ The dogs do bark./ The beggars are coming to town./ Some in rags,/ Some in tags,/ And some in velvet gowns.".:* Nursery rhyme from seventeenth-century England. This version using "tags," rather than "jags," appears to be from Kate Greenaway's *Mother Goose* (1881), which end with the lines "Some gave then white bread,/ And some gave them brown,/ And some gave them a good horsewhip,/ And sent them out of the town."
4. *openings in Kongen's Nytorv:* King's New Square (Kongens Nytorv), main square in central Copenhagen intended as a military post for the city's main guard, but famous for the Royal Theatre, Det Konelige Theater, the leading stage in Denmark for comedy, opera, and ballet.
5. *showings at the Royal Academy or Charlottenborg's Palace:* Built in 1672–1683 and named for the dowager queen Charlotte Amalie, the place in Kongens Nytorv has housed the Royal Academy of Fine Arts since 1753 and its annual Exhibition of Paintings.
6. *Magasin du Nord:* A department store in Kongens Nytorv, advertised as "The largest house for drygoods and novelties in Scandinavia."
7. *decorative Captain of the Hussars:* The Royal Hussars or Royal Hussar Regiment, the elite corp of the Danish Life Guards, whose duty is the protection of the Danish royal family and whose dress uniform of pale blue trousers and a red dolman trimmed with a silver stripe is a remnant of the link between the kings of Denmark and the Russian Imperial Court.

CHAPTER SIXTEEN

1. *from the columns of* Politikken: The newspaper of the Radical Party in Denmark.
2. *some queer place in the Balkans:* Countries called the Balkan States and occupying the Balkan peninsula, Yugoslavia, Romania, Bulgaria,

Albania, Greece, Turkey; also the Balkan Mountains in Bulgaria, extending from the border with Yugoslavia to the Black Sea.

3. *Dvorák's "New World Symphony". . . . Those wailing undertones of "Swing Low, Sweet Chariot":* The Fifth Symphony, in E minor, op.95 (1893), by Czech composer, Antonin Dvorák (1841–1904), is best known as "From the New World." Written with the assistance of the African-American musician and singer Harry T. Burleigh (1866–1949), and introduced in New York, it incorporated the African-American spiritual "Swing Low, Sweet Chariot" and African-American musical motifs as representative of the music of the United States.

CHAPTER SEVENTEEN

1. *physical freedom in Europe and spiritual freedom in America:* The tension between the freedom from racism and especially Jim Crow or segregation laws in Europe and the comfort of racial companionship with other blacks in America was the theme Larsen returned to in her second novel, *Passing* (1929), and in her successful application for a Guggenheim Fellowship in Creative Writing (1930).

2. *blatantly patriotic black Americans . . . the Stars and Stipes streaming:* Picturesque parades replete with American flags took place regularly in the streets of Harlem from the end of the First World War when the Fighting 369th Infantry Division, an all-black regiment with white officers, returned to a historic parade up Fifth Avenue to Harlem, through the 1920s and 1930s when black Harlemites continued to display their loyalty to the U.S. despite the government-sanctioned segregation laws and the culture of violence against blacks manifested most obviously in lynchings. Larsen's critique of these spectacles omits their also being venues for protests, including one of the most famous parades of all, the Silent Protest Parade in 1917 when 10,000 to 15,000 blacks marched down Fifth Avenue in silence, except for the muffled roll of drums, to protest lynchings in Waco, Texas, and Memphis, Tennessee, and the race riots in Houston and East St. Louis.

CHAPTER EIGHTEEN

1. *vamping on him:* Slang for a woman's seductive, sexually tempting behavior.

2. *the corner of One Hundred and Thirty-fifth Street and Seventh Avenue:* The intersection of Harlem's two main commercial thoroughfares in the 1920s.

3. *"Hugh Wentworth, the novelist":* Modeled on Carl Van Vechten

(1886–1984), music critic, drama critic, novelist, and photographer, who was one of the leading white New Yorkers actively encouraging the black cultural and literary movement known as the Harlem Renaissance or New Negro Movement and who was instrumental in the 1928 publication of Nella Larsen's *Quicksand*. Van Vechten's interracial parties and his excursions to Harlem combined with his novel *Nigger Heaven* (1926) made him controversial among blacks and whites during the 1920s.

4. *a tall olive-skinned girl being whirled about to the streaming music in the arms of a towering black man:* The interracial dancers suggest the pairing of Fania Marinoff (1887–1972), the Russian-born stage and film actress who was the wife of Carl Van Vechten (the novelist Wentworth in *Quicksand*), and Taylor Gordon (1893–1971), a tall black singer from Montana whose autobiography, *Born to Be* (1929) included a foreword by Van Vechten. Marinoff was comfortable both hosting interracial parties in her own home and attending public or private gatherings in Harlem.

CHAPTER TWENTY

1. *the store whose bright light she had marked for her destination:* Churches, especially of the Holiness denominations, opened in many of Harlem's first-floor or ground-floor spaces with large plate-glass windows originally intended for commercial businesses or stores, from which the name "storefront" churches derived.

2. *". . . Showers of blessings,/Showers of blessings":* Hymn composed by David Whittle (1840–1903) and James McGranaham (1840–1907) and based on Ezekiel 34:26.

3. *"A scarlet 'oman. Come to Jesus, you pore los' Jezebel!":* A Phoenician and the wife of Ahab (Kings I and II), Jezebel pressed the cult of Baal on the Israelites over the god Jehovah, and whose death for her brazen, shameless, impudent act was prophesied by Elijah. The name is also associated with an abandoned woman. The color scarlet symbolized a flagrantly, openly sinful woman.

CHAPTER TWENTY-ONE

1. *Reverend Mr. Pleasant Green:* Name adapted from the Pleasant Green Missionary Baptist Church, on Jefferson Street, in Nashville, Tennessee, near where Larsen attended the Fisk University Normal Department High School in 1907–08.

2. *The steamer Oscar II:* Scandinavian-American Line steamship on the route between New York and Copenhagen.

CHAPTER TWENTY-FOUR

1. *its author was Anatole France. There was a story, "The Procurator of Judea.":* Anatole France (1844–1924), French author whose given name was Jacques Anatole Francois Thibault, won the 1921 Nobel Prize in literature and was best known for his provocative and erudite short fiction. "The Procurator of Judea" appeared in his short-story collection *Mother of Pearl* (1908; reprinted 1923).

2. *" 'Laelius Lamia, born in Italy of illustrious parents,' " began the nurse in her slightly harsh voice:* Opening lines of "The Procurator of Judea," an historical story of early Christianity by Anatole France, from the perspective of Lamia who travels first to Athens to study philosophy, and then to Rome where he has an affair with the married Lepida, for which he is exiled by Tiberius Ceasar, and subsequently travels for eighteen years in Syria, Palestine, Cappadocia, and Armenia, as well as in the cities of Jerusalem, Antioch, and Caesarea, before being allowed to return to Rome. His later encounter with the aged Pontius Pilate, who now resides in Sicily and cultivates wheat, and who had befriended Lamia thirty years before in Syria and Jerusalem, prompts memories of that tumultuous time.

3. *" '... For to this day the women bring down doves to the altar as their victims...' " and " '... Africa and Asia have already enriched us with a considerable number of gods.":* Lines from "The Procurator of Judea," which point to the thematic concerns with sacrifice, victimization, worship, gods, exotic women, distant places, especially those associated with people of color. Larsen makes symbolic use of the women in the primitive rural church community in Alabama and by inference links them to the role of women in early religions depicted in Anatole France's story.

4. *" 'Jesus? ... Jesus—of Nazareth? I cannot call him to mind' ":* Concluding lines of "The Procurator of Judea," in which Pilate cannot remember Jesus, the Christ and the most important person to appear before him during his tenure as procurator.

CHAPTER TWENTY-FIVE

1. *"Pie in the sky":* Popular term for a nonrational faith in delayed compensation for earthly suffering, a theology of future vindication, rewards, and fulfillment in a time and space outside of natural empirical history.

2. *the sweet mingled smell of Houbigant:* Perfume fragrance by Coty popular in the 1920s.